THE WARLORD OF WILLOW RIDGE

Published by Kensington Publishing Corp.

Also by Gary Phillips

Bangers

Shooter's Point

High Hand

Published by Kensington Publishing Corp.

THE WARLORD OF WILLOW RIDGE

GARY PHILLIPS

Kensington Publishing Corp.

http://www.kensingtonbooks.com

DAFINA BOOKS are published by

Kensington Publishing Corp.
119 West 40th Street
New York, NY 10018

All Kensington Titles, Imprints, and Distributed Lines are available at special quantity discounts for bulk purchases for sales promotions, premiums, fund-raising, and educational or institutional use. Special book excerpts or customized printings can also be created to fit specific needs. For details, write or phone the office of the Kensington special sales manager: Kensington Publishing Corp., 119 West 40th Street, New York, NY 10018, attn: Special Sales Department, Phone: 1-800-221-2647.

Dafina and the Dafina logo Reg. U.S. Pat. & TM Off.

ISBN-13: 978-0-7582-0385-4
ISBN-10: 0-7582-0385-3

First Kensington mass market printing: October 2012

10 9 8 7 6 5 4 3 2 1

Printed in the United States of America

For Tom Murrin, the swingingest, grooviest cat there ever was.

Acknowledgments

My thanks to the various newspapers, cable and television networks, and radio programs, including the *L.A. Times*, *This American Life* on NPR, *60 Minutes*, *Current TV*, and MSNBC, for their reportage on the housing crisis and the financial meltdown, which helped inform this work.

Chapter One

The fourteen-year-old Kawasaki KZ 1000 motorcycle sputtered again as he came off the 215 Freeway. He could feel in his lower legs at least two of the four pistons slap, that is, knock against the sides of the engine's cylinders. This caused the frame to shudder.

A small eddy of gray smoke rose from the tailpipe. He'd bought the motorcycle at a police auction in Tempe, Arizona, for $545; that was the majority of the 750 in cash he'd had on him. O'Conner had hoped to make it one way to the Bay Area on the oil burner, with a few planned stops along the way to bulk up his war chest. The last time he'd been north, a job he'd run had gone wrong. But O'connor had managed to get out whole, and there were no immediate enemies left up there from back then.

The rider had been aware the piston rings were in need of replacement in the bike when he purchased the machine. Now he could barely get up a medium-grade hill, having to ride on the shoulder of the highway, lest he get run over. There was no getting farther on the bike.

The Kawasaki idling roughly, he put his left foot on the ground and looked down on the lights among some darkened structures. He frowned, realizing this wasn't an artificial oasis of gas stations and Stuckey's-style roadside restaurants for the weary traveler. Below, in the near distance, was a large oval-shaped area, which, he surmised, was a planned community, a subdivision housing tract out here in the Inland Empire.

O'Conner checked the luminescent face of his watch. It was past one in the morning, and he'd been going at it steadily since nine this morning. Only one stop for coffee and a microwaved machaca and egg burrito at three that afternoon. Shifting into second, he coaxed his failing machine a little farther along the road. Soon with his headlights he saw a sign indicating a turnoff for Rose Saffron Avenue. This would take him down to the housing tract, he hoped, as he took the veering ramp. He doubted he'd find a motel, as those types of facilities wouldn't be allowed within sight by the upright and up-tight taxpayers who populated these sorts of places.

The lawns would be cared for, and the backyards populated with propane-powered, shiny barbecue grills. Of course, the overhanging bougainvillea would be trimmed just so. There would also be a plentiful number of kidney-shaped swimming pools O'Conner assumed. He almost sneered at his imaginings of such banality.

Naturally, there wouldn't be a back room to rent for a night, but then, certain niceties of polite society made no never mind to him. He'd manage. He always did.

The Kawasaki putt-putted and stalled once, but he got it restarted and approached a guard booth on its little island, a gate beyond that. This was the main entrance to the development. In the moonlight he could read on a wall in sweeping three-dimensional script the words Willow Ridge. They were so cool, they didn't have Estates or

Acres in the title, he noted bemusedly. This area was in the flatlands, so why the ridge bit? But then, he wasn't in the real estate business.

O'Conner stopped, and from the angle he was at, he could discern no light, like, say, from a CCTV monitor, coming from inside the guard booth. He came closer slowly, straddling his bike and walking it, figuring he'd hear a radio or a TV on low, but there was no sound from within, no sudden flashlight beam washing across his form. He peered inside and could tell the booth had been empty for some time. There was a cobweb between the inactive monitor bank and the desk. He drifted closer to the massive wrought-iron gate.

Beyond was a wide street that curved to the right. A few late-model cars and family vans were parked at the curb or in driveways. He could see a light on in the upstairs of a house on one side of the street, and at the far end, a set of lights behind curtains. He counted three porch lights on, as well.

O'Conner cut the dying engine on the motorcycle and put the kickstand down. He swung his leg over, took off his helmet, and walked to the double gate. Though it was closed, he pushed on one half of the gate, and it opened silently on oiled hinges. He paused and listened. Stepping inside and walking forward, he could better see a FOR SALE sign hammered into a not-so-trim lawn. There was other such signage about, as well.

He stopped again at the sound of a scream. Rather, it was a squeal of delight, he determined, and now he could hear muffled voices. He followed the sounds to a two-story modified Cape Cod model with an overgrown lawn, the weeds up to his calves. He strode across the yellowed grass, past another FOR SALE sign posted in the ground, this one with a foreclosed plaque superimposed over the broker's name and logo.

At the side of the Cape Codder he could see in through a tear in a drawn window shade behind a cracked window. Shadowed figures moved about inside what had been the living room, candlelight giving off chiaroscuro-like illumination. Rock music was playing, and the familiar fragrance of marijuana was evident.

O'Conner smiled and withdrew, not worrying about being as quiet as he'd been on his approach. He went back out the gate. A tricked-out 1996 Impala Super Sport cruised along on the access road. The car slowed, its occupants taking in the motorcyclist. There was a nylon equipment bag held in place by bungee cords on a rack attached to its rear fender.

A back window rolled down partway in the Chevy, and a cloud of marijuana smoke billowed out. Spanish-flavored rap music bumped from inside the vehicle. Chronic and their tunes are the universal accoutrements of wayward youth, O'Conner reflected.

He waited, his face impassive. The car went on. O'Conner tried to start the Kawasaki, but the engine had cooled sufficiently that the pistons seemed frozen in the motor block's cylinders. Standing beside the motorcycle and holding on to the handlebars, he pushed the bike inside Willow Ridge.

Stumbling out of the house with the party going on was a solidly built, dark-haired woman in low-cut jeans and a top that exposed her muscled midriff. Giggling, she pushed part of her long hair out of her eyes, catching sight of O'Conner and his motorcycle.

In the diffused light, he couldn't nail down her age, but if he'd been pressed, he would have said she was no more than twenty-five. She put a beer to her lips as they exchanged a look, and he went on down the continuation of Saffron Rose Avenue. A younger man, no more than seventeen, came out of the house and coaxed her back inside. As O'Conner continued, he wondered what else he'd find in Willow Ridge.

Chapter Two

At the corner Steve Brill turned his car onto Larkspur Lane. He'd told his wife, Janey, he wouldn't get so worked up, but he couldn't help himself. Deliberately, he drove slowly along what was once the showcase street of Willow Ridge. This long stretch had been specifically designed by the builder to be a mix of the several styles of homes, and variations thereof, available in their community. From neo-Spanish-Mediterranean to American Gothic, you could take your pick.

He grunted as he sipped his coffee from his travel mug. You could take your pick now, too, he observed sourly. In the yard of one of the few remaining occupied homes on the block, he saw the single mother, Mary, Marci, something like that. She was in curlers, arguing with her teenage son, who was doing his best to ignore her. His backpack held in one hand of his lanky frame, he alternately said a few words to her, then resumed talking on his cell phone to one of his homeys, Brill noted.

Section Eighters they were. Subsidized renters. On the public dole, yet able to move into what was to have been an upscale village. That was how the broker had presented the tract to the husband and wife when they'd decided to move in six years ago.

The kid, looking down at his mother over the top of his sunglasses, yelled a reply to her, then walked off, half dragging his backpack by its straps. She fumed, hands on her hips. The mother pointed and blared her response at her son as he walked away, uncaring and unknowing. Finished for the moment, the woman returned to her house, a modified New England–style cottage model.

As the teen walked toward the end of the block, still talking on his cell, Brill was just behind him on the street. He shifted his focus from the surly high schooler to a man in Levi's and an athletic-type T-shirt, hacking away at the vegetation of an overgrown lawn. He was over six feet, but not by much, and was muscular in a middleweight boxer way. Given his athletic build and the rhythmic ease with which he swung the weed cutter, Brill at first assumed he was younger than he was. But closer now, he could see lines in his face and gray edging into his temples. Sweat made the yoke of his undershirt wet.

"Hello," Brill said as he stopped the car, his passenger window gliding down. "You doing work for the new owner?" he asked hopefully. The FOR SALE sign had been removed from the lawn and leaned on the porch of the 1930s-style Beaux Arts house. This model, he recalled, was said to be based on a home once owned by Lana Turner in the Hollywood Hills. Or so the previous occupant, a car salesman named Arthur Patterson, had boasted at a residents' mixer once.

He had been a fleet sales manager and used to wear his dress shirts, ostentatious cuff links glittering on his wrists, even to go bowling. It seemed like there was no end to the good times then.

"No," the man answered. He'd propped the handle of the weed cutter against his leg and wiped at the sweat on his brow with his palm. He regarded Brill, a hardness coming over his face, then evaporating, like an alligator assessing a distracted crane, then deciding to let it be.

Laying the weed cutter down, he stepped forward. He bent down to the passenger side, extended his hand, smiling. "O'Conner's my name. Call me Connie."

Brill told him his and shook the man's hand. "You just moved in, huh?"

"Something like that." He straightened up. "Well, I wish these weeds would cut themselves, but I better get back to my work . . . Steve." He said his name as if it were a foreign sound to him—like being familiar was a new concept.

"Okay, then. Don't work too hard."

"Have a good day."

The man returned to his tool and began executing short, precise strokes of the blade back and forth, back and forth across the lawn, clearing a swath as he went. Hesitating, Brill could see leaning or lying about here and there other gardening implements, such as a bow rake and a large pruning saw. Brill put the window up on his Prius and, clicking the floor shift out of neutral, drove off, eyeing the man in his undershirt as he got smaller in his rearview.

A little over an hour later, O'Conner was raking up his efforts. The harassed mom who had the curlers in her hair had taken them out and had put on her blue matching work pants and shirt. Her name tag read MARCI, and she wore clunky work shoes, too. She also drove past O'Conner but didn't stop, though she appreciated that a man his age was in the shape he was. Nice biceps. Marci

Vickers smiled, shaking her head slightly. Flirting with a new neighbor? Didn't she have enough trouble with her school-ditching lunkhead son, Cullen? What was it they taught the kids when Cullen was in preschool? Stranger danger?

She laughed to herself and turned up Bettye LaVette, who was singing "A Change Is Gonna Come" on the car's CD unit, and drove on to her job at the Pearson Plastics plant, sports bottle specialists, in Perris.

That evening back at home, after dinner and after helping their daughter, Millicent, with her history homework, Steve Brill and Jane Grainger-Brill loaded the plates and what have you into the dishwasher.

He said, "Someone moved into the house over on Larkspur. The one that used to belong to the slickster, Patterson, the car guy."

She chuckled as she had a sip of her wine. "Let me guess. This one sells gold on TV."

Brill smiled, rinsing out a pot. "Doesn't seem to me that's what this guy does. Connie, he calls himself. But I don't think that's what his mother named him."

She regarded her husband. "How do you mean?"

"I think he's squatting."

"What? He was in the front yard, sitting on his lawn chair and drinking beer from a cooler? A pickup truck with a gun rack and the Stars and Bars on the bumper?" She put the casserole dish and its top in the dishwasher.

"Oh no, he's not the Stars and Bars type. Just the opposite. He was cleaning up the yard. Working hard at it, too, 'cause when I drove back by this evening, it was neat and trim."

She put a hand to her mouth in mock horror. "Oh my

God. Next, he'll be clearing out the gutters. What a criminal mastermind he is."

"Smart-ass." He kissed her quickly. "But I drive that way every day."

"Yesterday was Sunday."

"Okay, I was jogging on Saturday morning and went by there and didn't see a moving truck. You telling me he could move in on Sunday, and today, Monday, there's no evidence of that?"

"You just said he was doing yard work." She poured more wine for both of them, and they traipsed into the living room, Brill talking.

"You know what I'm saying. There would be trash bags piled up in the driveway or empty boxes, some signs." He and his wife sat on the couch.

"That house has been empty for nearly a year and a half, Steve. Except for those crackheads camping out there for a few nights, till we at least ran them off. Like everything else around here, it's gotta be going for a god-damn song." She lowered her voice. When she swore, she didn't want Millie overhearing her. Their older child, Doug, a teenager, was out, supposedly studying, but they both doubted it given his middling grades.

"Don't remind me," he groused. Briefly looking at their exposed-beam ceiling, he tried to guess how much their home had depreciated this month. He didn't have the heart to look it up on Zillow, a real estate site with a zip code search function.

"So no car in the driveway?" his wife was saying.

"No." He paused. "But he had gardening tools. Though he could have gotten those from the Home Depot. Or they were left behind."

She trilled her fingers against the rim of her wineglass.

"Maybe he's just been sent ahead by someone else to prepare the house."

"Maybe," her husband said with little conviction.

"What?"

"There's something about him, is all. Doesn't seem like the suburban type—worried about the aphids attacking the azaleas and leaky kitchen faucets."

"Neither did we once upon a time."

He tipped his wineglass to her and had a sip.

"How old is he?"

He made a face. "'Bout my age, maybe a little less." He didn't mention he was envious of the guy for being in better condition than he was. *Fuck that.*

"Well, you want to call the substation?"

He didn't work up the energy to roll his eyes or sneer. "Right. Maybe a deputy will get out here by the end of next week to see what the Willow Whiners want yet again." As they were aware that's how the Sheriff's Department referred to the residents of the subdivision.

A county unemployment rate hovering several digits above the national average, bar brawls, robbery-assaults, gang activity, and domestic abuse calls—those took priority over squawks about squatters or loud music. Especially with a station that had seen a reduction in staffing due to several factors, the county's budget deficit among them.

"Hell"—he shrugged—"he's cleaning up the place. Maybe he is working for some speculator. Like what's-her-name over on Ridge Crest."

"Maybe," Jane Grainger-Brill said, doubting this was so, but not sure why.

Chapter Three

Three days later Steve Brill was leaving for work at a later time. He'd had a meeting on Skype with the Houston office, so he was able to do that from home. Now driving past the Beaux Arts house on Larkspur, he saw a SoCal Edison van parked at the curb in front. An orange cone had been placed at its rear bumper by the maintenance tech, who then went up the walkway to the front door. Various tools and testing equipment jangled on the tech's equipment belt as he walked.

Brill wasn't sure how he felt about this as he drove a few more blocks to the side exit of their walled-in community. Restoring electricity to a residence wasn't something a handyman in the employ of a speculator did, unless there were some eager potential buyers—and in this economic environment, that seemed fairly implausible.

It made sense to get the lawn in shape, as you wouldn't want it to be a distraction, even to lookie loos. But getting the juice back on was different. What about water? Was that getting turned on, too? And why, he admonished himself as he merged onto the road, was he so concerned with the house on Larkspur when there were more pressing issues to be concerned with in Willow Ridge?

Brill drove to work on the freeway, absently listening to an NPR *Morning Edition* report about a Supreme Court decision in a medical marijuana case. He realized why he'd become fixated on the Larkspur house. He hoped it was a signal that the corner had been turned and the real estate market was going back up. Hell, damn the market. He just wanted the property values in their section to be going up so he and Janey could get out from under.

He knew he was being a bad dad for admitting this, if only to himself, but maybe it was a good thing his son, Doug, wasn't such a sterling student. While state college fees were also climbing like kudzu, they were more manageable than the tuition and incidentals at an institution back East costing some forty to fifty thousand dollars a year. Brill shook his head, smiling thinly. The age of lesser expectations—what a legacy for his kids.

The man in the torn tank top, long basketball shorts, and shiny new signature tennis shoes stumbled into the backyard through the broken wooden gate. The gate was hanging on barely by a hinge. He walked across what was left of a patch of yellowed lawn and dirt to what was once the pool. Incongruously, a fig tree was still alive, and its splayed green leaves and thin branches, heavy with fruit, overhung part of the cement hole in the ground.

The twentysomething man stood, teetering, on the edge of the empty concrete cavity that had once been filled with water.

He pulled down the front of his shorts and started peeing into the concrete cavity, pleased with his bright idea. Suddenly a light came on behind him, and he turned his close-shaven head around, mouth slightly agape.

"I'd appreciate it if this was the last time you did that," a man said. His form was backlit, framed by light in the square of the sliding glass door he'd opened. Taped to the inside of the glass was thick cardboard, light haloing around its sides.

"Who the fuck are you?" Basketball Shorts turned back to shake himself and pull up his shorts.

"I live here now." The man had stepped closer.

Basketball Shorts faced him, reassessing this civilian, whom he figured he would intimidate. Hadn't this fool seen the tats up and down his arms and chest? His muscles swolled and shit?

"So, like, this is your place?" he asked, slurring. The strong fragrance of marijuana came off him. His high was sharpened by the vodka he'd been imbibing.

"As far as you're concerned."

Motherfucka didn't talk like a civilian. Talked like a stiff-dick cop. "Yeah, well . . . ," Basketball Shorts began, looking around. In the light, though there were shadows in it, he could see the graffiti thick on the walls of the empty pool. "Looks like you got a whole lot of cleaning up to do."

"That's my lookout. Don't be peeing in my yard. Okay?"

"Know you," the younger man replied, shaking a finger at O'Conner. "You was on the motorcycle a few nights ago." He frowned. "You renting this place in this shit hole?" He waved a hand listlessly in the air. "Man, you got took."

"Be that as it may," O'Conner said, "I'm asking you to respect my space."

"Respect?" Basketball Shorts blared. "You know who

the fuck we are, ese?" He was proudly tapping one of his tattoos on his chest, partially obscured by the material of his tank top.

"No," O'Conner answered blandly.

"Sheeet. Then maybe you should find out."

"I intend to."

"Fuck, what's that s'pose to mean?" He focused his pinpoint eyes on O'Conner.

"What I said." Down at his side he'd been holding a can of beer. He brought this up and took a pull, his gaze steady on the gang member's face.

Basketball Shorts considered several options. He could get all up in this chump's grill, but stomping on the home owners was off-limits unless necessary. There wasn't much of a law presence, and the homeys needed to keep it that way. But this dude was straight challenging him without directly sounding like he was challenging him. Like a motherfucka who'd done time, he concluded.

"You out the joint, man?"

"That where you earned your stripes?"

Basketball Shorts chuckled. "You old school, ain't you?"

"Old enough. Thanks for your time." With that he turned, went back inside, and slid the glass door closed. Basketball Shorts's view of the inside of the house was blocked by the cardboard.

The Mas Trece gang member stood there for a moment, considering busting out the door's glass just to see what this fool would do. But there was no patio furniture, and letting his impulse subside, he wasn't so sure this older dude wasn't carrying. He left the yard but promised himself this wasn't the last time he'd have words with this *puto*. Oh no, not at all.

Chapter Four

O'Conner could take a bus over to Perris or Moreno Valley. Or maybe there was a light rail that could take him, but he hadn't checked on that. He didn't know either area, though he knew there were a few people from his past living in both places—people who for one reason or another were indebted to him. But that was still unfamiliar territory, and he didn't want those individuals knowing he was around. That left getting to Los Angeles or San Diego to hustle up some money. L.A. had better bars and eats.

He decided not to steal a car and drive it into L.A. and then just wipe down and abandon the vehicle when he was done. But in the off chance some eager rookie was actually reading the bulletin board or an MDT, or however it was cops put out hot sheets these days, why take an unnecessary chance?

Beyond the northern end of Willow Ridge, across a wide boulevard beyond its outer wall, was the Willow Heights Shopping Center, which included a small knot of office buildings. Tenants in the large open-air mall included an Earth Harvest supermarket. This was the sort of high-end chain that carried grass-fed beef, cutlets from free-range chickens, and organic peaches. O'Conner imagined orchards where kindly grand-mothers were paid to whisper encouraging words to apples and pears as they grew to be plucked for sale in tony markets like Earth Harvest.

There was also the standard nail salon, dry cleaners, and chain sandwich and fried chicken outlets in the shop-ping center, as well as the storefront for Allen Real Estate. Among these retailers was a storefront with a closed glass door and a window to which reflective ma-terial had been tacked in place. This stuff bounced your image back but allowed those inside to see out. Small sans serif letters in a corner of the window stated ANSON SERVICES. Whatever services they offered, the door was currently locked. The shopping center included several vacant shops, as well. Above, in a clearing in the hills, O'Conner could partially see some sort of concrete am-phitheater.

O'Conner also found in the shopping center a photo-copy store called the Print Shack, which included the rental of computers. Any printouts were extra. O'Conner had several credit cards in several names and didn't want to use one if it wasn't necessary. He got to talking to a tall, sinewy kid with Che Guevara's iconic face on his T-shirt behind the counter. Che wore sunglasses. His messenger-style bike was in a corner.

"Look, I've got the cash, so was wondering if there was a way I could rent time on one of your computers without having to, you know, have a credit card."

The youngster looked at him appreciatively. "I hear you, man. I'm all about being off the grid as much as pos-sible. Nobody should be tracked by the NSA or whoever."

O'Conner nodded back. An arrangement was made

using a company override computer code the young man, Ian Childes, put in. O'Conner gave him a ten. Online he learned that Amtrak maintained a bus service in areas where it had no train station. You could take their bus to the train station, which in this case was in Corona. It took a little more doing, but he figured out how to buy his ticket with cash, rather than using a credit card over the Internet. At some point he'd have to finagle some new credit cards in several fake names, he concluded. This meant he had to go to the Garden Shores senior care facility, which was one of the two stops the special bus made in Hemet.

And so at 8:15 on a sunny morning, after helping two elderly sisters with their overhead bags, O'Conner rode the Amtrak Thruway bus over to Corona, to the train station. From there he took the train into Union Station in downtown Los Angeles. By this time it was past one in the afternoon. O'Conner was hungry, so he walked over to Philippe's, not too far to the north on Alameda and at the beginning of Chinatown. He hadn't been there in at least six years, he reflected. Maybe more.

Philippe's was a cavernous place with 1920s decor, where you stepped down onto a sawdust-covered floor and stood in line to order from the toughened women in their uniforms behind a long deli case. There were long tables and stools to sit on and eat on the ground level and doorless communal rooms on the second floor. There were even old-fashioned working phone booths, too.

The selections on the menu weren't diet-conscious chic. But if freshly sliced roasted meat was your thing, the sandwich roll the goods were served on dipped in au jus or not, then you could eat well with a side of home-made potato or macaroni salad.

Hungry, O'Conner got two sandwiches, one turkey,

the other lamb; coffee; and a side of macaroni salad. He would have had a beer but didn't want to be sleepy or slipping, given the possibilities of how the rest of his day and the evening might unfold.

Upstairs he slowly had his lunch, his sandwiches heavy with the tangy mustard that was the house specialty. Among the other diners in the room were two Latinas over forty, he decided. Making no effort at eavesdropping, from the snippets of their lively conversation, he gathered the two worked for the city. One of them—and he'd heard her name, Gabby—was divorced and was dating a younger man, who wanted to take her to a concert featuring a band she disliked.

The other one, in pants and a man's white shirt, attractive-looking with long dark hair and hoop earrings, occasionally glanced at O'Conner. He looked back. Given that the duo were on the clock and in the room before he was, they finished first.

"Hope the rest of your day goes well, ladies," O'Conner said as they stood, gathering up their purses and putting their trash away.

"Thank you," the one with the big earrings replied. "You have a good day, too." She smiled. Her friend gave her a questioning look.

"I hope you're successful in your day, too," big earrings added.

He smiled back and nodded. The two women talked low and laughed as they left. O'Conner had the rest of his lunch, then went back outside and returned to Union Station. Across from the train station was Olvera Street, a tourist and historic area where the city of Los Angeles was founded. O'Conner saw a large group of people with placards walking past Olvera Street south on Alameda. He gathered these were protestors on their way to City Hall for a rally, given their signs stated things like FORECLOSE ON WALL STREET, NOT MAIN STREET and PEOPLE BEFORE PROFITS. They seemed festive, and there were drummers drumming, as well.

O'Conner smiled at this and got a cab and had the driver take him to an office park with angular, squat green buildings and a drive-in courtyard on Wilshire Boulevard, across from the Los Angeles County Museum of Art, in what was called the Miracle Mile—an old term resurrected by the hipster crowd.

He took an elevator in a specific building and entered an office marked RED ZONE ENTERPRISES, a sports paraphernalia concern. The receptionist, a stocky, thirty-plus, auburn-haired woman with an iguana tattooed on her neck and upper shoulder, was talking pleasantly on a headset. When she glanced over at him, she began stammering.

"Ah . . . look . . . yeah, ah, sorry to cut you off, Mike, but I need to take this. I'll get right back with you. Five minutes." She severed the connection and took off her headset.

"The fuck are you doing here?" Lilly Nash seethed in a low tone. To the right of her desk and the counter, there was an open doorway. Through there he could hear the relaxed sales patter of the reps selling caps and water bottles festooned with team logos.

"Where can I find Voss, Lilly?"

"Get the fuck out of here before I get security up here."

O'Conner made a gesture. "Go ahead. Call them."

Nash glared at him for a moment, then came around her desk. The woman put her purple fingernails on his upper arm, tugging. "Come here, idiot, so you don't get me fired."

He followed her into an empty office through another doorway.

She addressed him, hands on her hips. "Can't you see I'm out of that life? Why you have to come around and bring me grief?"

"It's a simple request, Lil."

"Nothing's ever simple with you."

"It's not like he doesn't owe me."

"Only you don't have him on speed dial."

"There is that."

She looked beyond him to the outer reception area, as if gauging her chances of returning to normalcy. Nash then let out a breath. "You gotta go away. You know goddamn well what this means to me."

"Then don't mess it up."

"You're too chivalrous."

"Big word. Building your vocabulary is a good thing, Lilly. Particularly in this swell little job of yours, where I'm sure you're looking to move up."

She worried her bottom lip. "You're a bastard."

He lifted a shoulder and let it down again.

After he got an address from Nash, he was back on the street. O'Conner walked to Fairfax and found another copy place, part of an office-supply outlet. This time he didn't have to negotiate paying cash for the rental of a computer. In this place you could put your money into a machine and receive a card good for copies and the computer. On the Metropolitan Transit Authority site he looked up how to get to his destination.

He had far to go, and it would take time using public transportation, but he wasn't in a rush to get out to Wilmington. He knew Lilly Nash wouldn't call ahead to let Zev Voss know he was on his way. She couldn't take the chance he wouldn't be coming back. He printed out his directions.

The late afternoon turning cool, O'Conner walked along a residential street in Wilmington, a working-class community in the harbor area, with street names such as Gulf and Bay View, and union halls, such as the Masters, Mates and Pilots building. There was also a Harry Bridges Boulevard, named for the militant longshore organizer from the last century.

Turning a corner, he could see on a rectangular sign in faded letters CHANNEL MARINE MACHINING, a boat motor repair facility. A large pickup was leaving the place, two boat engines in its bed. O'Conner entered the yard, which had several small boat hulls about on unhitched trailers. He spotted a fresh-faced younger man in jeans and rolled-up sleeves pushing an engine on a dolly.

"Zev around?"

"In the shop." He pointed his chin toward the building with the sign on it.

"Thanks." O'Conner took in the rest of the compact work yard. As far as he could tell, there was only this single employee out here. How many inside? Only one way to find out, and he went into the shop. There was another man there, a compact older fellow with wiry white hair and broad shoulders. He was holding an engine part with wires sprouting from it in his hand, with a cloth partly wrapped around it. He was talking to Voss.

"Tellin' you, Zev, this fuel pump is done, and so is the other. I gotta rebuild these suckers."

"Okay, Pete," the other man said, noticing O'Conner for the first time. "Go ahead and I'll let Allard know."

O'Conner stepped closer, and Voss, a beefy man with

a receding hairline and a beer belly, said tersely, "Back here." He turned and led the way to a small office of old-fashioned sectioned glass panes, with paper and manuals stacked about.

Zev Voss perched crossways on a stool before a draft table, upon which were charts and rolled-up blueprints. There was a drawer built into the underside of this.

"You know I don't have it," he began.

"I doubt you—" O'Conner began but didn't finish. In a flash Voss had pulled out the drawer and was reaching for a revolver.

O'Conner grabbed a parts catalog, thick as a phone book, and flung it at Voss's head as he got the handgun clear. Reflexively, he squeezed the trigger, but the barrel was down and the bullet went into the floor. O'Conner came in low and tackled Voss, who'd been smacked with the catalog.

He was aware of the voices and footsteps of the other two men getting closer as he and Voss tussled. Their grappling bodies were twisted onto each other next to the wall, punching and grunting and straining. There was a framed, faded photo from a magazine of a nude and young Pam Grier, the actress who had gained fame in the Blaxploitation era. The picture was undisturbed as their bodies banged into the wall

"Zev, what's going on here?" said Pete, the older man, as he rushed to the doorway of the small office.

O'Conner jabbed his elbow into Voss's throat, and this got him untangled. The gun had been knocked to the floor, and he scooped it up as the younger mechanic also arrived.

"Tell them to back the fuck off, Zev." O'Conner was pressed against the wall, gulping air. "Go on back to straightening out propellers and what not."

Voss got to his feet, grasping the edge of the draft table to steady himself. He was also breathing hard, more than O'Conner, and sweating, as well. "It's okay, guys. I got this."

"But," Pete began.

Voss waved a hand. "It's okay. It's just how we negotiate."

The older man and the younger man exchanged a look but withdrew.

"We'll be right out here," the twentysomething added.

Voss put a hand on the knocked-over stool and righted it. O'Conner didn't move, didn't make any unnecessary gesture with the revolver. He didn't have to. Voss knew he was too out of shape to be quicker than him. He sat heavily on the stool.

O'Conner said, "Money and a car. Preferably five or six years old. Nothing flashy. The blend-in type."

Voss sat forward, rubbing his hands on his upper legs. "You're bleeding me."

"Like I haven't stood up."

"It's not like that."

"It's exactly like that, Voss." He pointed the barrel. "I'm owed."

Voss sighed. There was going to be no arguing with him. "What will satisfy you?"

O'Conner smiled crookedly. "All this and heaven, too."

Voss chuckled dryly. "Utopian."

O'Conner tossed the gun on top of the draft table. The two walked out of the office.

"Lock up, huh?" Voss said to Pete.

"Sure, Zev." He watched the two who'd been fighting walk out of the shop together. Pete and the younger man again exchanged questioning looks.

At a strip club on Aviation Boulevard called the Takeoff, beneath the glide path of the airport, Voss retrieved seventeen thousand in small and large bills from an old-fashioned standing safe. This he put in a gym bag he got from one of the dancers, a bleached blonde with green eyes and heavy hips. She stood watching them in the office they occupied, clad solely in her platform high heels and sequined thong, arms folded, chewing gum.

Whether she was a witness or a guard, O'Conner couldn't say. She gave him a disinterested glare as he walked over to her and stuck a five in her G-string.

"Thanks for the thrill," he said.

"Anytime, sport," she replied.

O'Conner left town in the evening with the money and a 2001 Sable station wagon. The car was older than he wanted, but work had been done on the engine and there were recaps on the rims. He drove back to Willow Ridge. There were no delays on the freeways, the traffic light and moving.

Chapter Five

Jane Grainger-Brill walked briskly through the Earth Harvest supermarket. She realized she was going to run late to meet with a client, and had already left her a message. But she wasn't going to dally and stopped only to get a prepackaged salad for her lunch. Passing through the vegetable section, she spotted Gwen Gardner bagging a bunch of green onions.

"Hey, now," Grainger-Brill said, touching her arm. "Rushing. Just stopped to pick up something to eat."

"Let's get the girls together for cards next week." Gardner placed her goods in her hand basket.

Automatically, Grainger-Brill removed her Black-Berry and checked her calendar. "Thursday instead of Wednesday? Millie has a softball game Wednesday. And I pinkie swore I wouldn't miss this one, like I did the last one."

Gardner was checking her smartphone, too. "Okay. I'll check with the others." She looked up and, lowering her voice, said to her friend, "The mystery man."

Grainger-Brill followed her gaze. O'Conner was on the other side of the grapefruit display, in a flannel shirt, tail out, and in work chinos. His arms folded, he was glaring at an assortment of lettuce like a NASA scientist examining photos beamed from the Martian landscape.

"He's taken over that house on Larkspur," Gardner continued. "And he's not paying a mortgage or rent."

"You know that for sure?"

Gardner said, "Blanche looked it up." Blanche Allen was a real estate broker among their card-playing friends. "There was no title change or any other legal action taken on the property."

O'Conner made his decision and plucked out a head of romaine and walked off.

"She report this to the bank?" Grainger-Brill turned her gaze from the departing man.

"What for? she figured," Gardner answered. "He's tidied up the lawn, fixed broken windows, and cleaned up the backyard."

"How you know all this? Blanche been over there?"

Gwen Gardner had a dazzling smile. Both her ex-husbands had said so. "She spied on him with those binoculars her and Marty used to take to the 'SC football games."

"What?"

"You know she's got a few of the houses in our development on her books. She was in the upstairs of one that just happens to overlook the backyard of the Larkspur house."

"And just happened to have the binoculars with her," Grainger-Brill intoned breathlessly.

"She is a nosy so-and-so," Gardner said appreciatively. "Good for us."

"Yeah." They both laughed.

"Okay," Grainger-Brill said, "I gotta go."

"All right, sweetie. Talk to you later," Gardner said as the other woman marched off, renewing her task.

At the self-checkout, with her braised ahi tuna salad and asparagus tips, Grainger-Brill glanced down the cereal and coffee aisle. At the far end she could see Gwen Gardner talking with the man occupying the Larkspur house. Putting her purchase in her reusable cloth shopping bag, she snickered. Lately Gardner, a Pilates and free weights enthusiast, had been frequenting a cougar bar. Could be she was tired of boy toys and was desirous of a more mature man. Or maybe it was just for variety's sake, Grainger-Brill surmised, walking out of the market.

"Hey, Jane," Kimberly Schmitz greeted her in the parking lot.

"Hey now, yourself, Kim. How's it going?"

"It's going," the other woman said.

"Yeah, yeah, I know. Sorry, but I'm running. You hang in there. Cards next week, okay? We can talk then."

"Sure. Let me know." Schmitz walked away.

Grainger-Brill watched her go. The woman had been through a bruising divorce last year and recently had lost her job. Schmitz entered the Earth Harvest market. As Grainger-Brill looked toward the store, she couldn't see Gardner or the man, O'Conner, now through the windows. A momentary pang of an emotion knifed through her, then was gone. Getting in her car, she frowned, unsure of what the feeling was and why she'd felt it.

Leaving the parking lot to enter traffic, a Swift Trans delivery truck rumbled past Granger-Brill's car. On its side was a large cardboard-colored poster, which had been inserted in a slotted frame for this purpose. The advert was for a new Stef Agar action film, *Blown to Hell*. Agar was atop a motorcycle flying through the air as he shot machine guns in each hand at various bad guys as a building was on fire behind him. The truck went on as she turned right to make her meeting.

O'Conner stepped out the front door. Idling at the curb was the '96 Impala SS. He noted the car's custom paint job and the expensive, gleaming rims, evident in the morning light. The windows were smoked, and the front one on the passenger side was down enough so he could see the man he'd confronted in his backyard.

"You all homesteading and shit, huh?" Basketball Shorts said.

"Where's yours?"

"Say what?"

"Where do you lay your head?"

Basketball Shorts's thick eyebrows rose above the top of his sunglasses. "Funny man, aren't you?"

"You seem entitled to come by here uninvited."

"The fuck's up with you, man? You don't belong around here."

"I'm bringing up the property values."

"And we're doing what?"

"I couldn't say."

Somebody else in the car said something in Spanglish to Basketball Shorts. He mumbled a response, then said, "Stay up, homey." The Impala slowly drove away and turned the corner, going farther into the housing tract.

O'Conner put on his own sunglasses. The way he figured it, Basketball Shorts's gang, the Mas Trece, must have taken over a house in the subdivision. Meth was big out here in the Inland Empire, so it didn't take Jim Rockford to figure out that was probably what they were using the house for, the manufacture of the drug.

Meth production gave off an odor and was volatile given chemicals such as ephedrine were involved. But there were any number of empty abodes, so it could be they'd picked an isolated block for their lab, or they might actually have been enterprising enough to put in the proper equipment for venting.

One more item on his survey checklist, he concluded as he began his walk, a small notepad in his hip pocket. Patiently, O'Conner had been reconnoitering the environs of Willow Ridge. He knew there was Wi-Fi, but not being a dues-paying member of the home owners' association and not knowing the pass code, there was little incentive for him to get a laptop to look up facts about the development.

Though maybe if more than afternoon flirting with that Gwen Gardner developed, he could use her computer, O'Conner briefly imagined. Too, there was always the helpful, conspiracy-wary college student Ian Childes at the copy place with its computers, but he didn't want to wear out his welcome there. Besides, he needed to see things for himself.

On the south side of the development was an artificial lake populated with ducks and, apparently, fish. As the lake came into view, he saw a few people either throwing bread crumbs to the quacking fowl or dangling their fishing poles. There was a pickup truck with a municipal seal on its door parked on a drive-up path near an oak tree. A city worker in a khaki uniform was changing the plastic liner of the trash container.

O'Conner walked down a small incline to the lake, which resided in a bowl dug out of the earth, bordered with greenery. Beyond the shrubbery on a far rise was a low-slung industrial-looking building with a tile roof. He came close to an older man, who, he estimated, was in his seventies. He was sitting in a lawn chair, one of those floppy fishing hats pushed down on his head. His nose was slightly bulbous and red-veined—from booze, the sun, or both O'Conner surmised.

"How're they biting today?" O'Conner asked, hands in his pockets, striking a casual pose. The other man was holding a fishing pole.

The AARPer chuckled. "I do this more to pass the time while I listen to the ball game. Gives me an excuse to be outside." He pointed the toe of his tennis shoe toward a small radio/CD player on the ground near him. A sports talk show was on. Warren Casey, the star forward of the L.A. Comets basketball team, was being interviewed. "Present from my grandson." The old man regarded O'Conner. "You're the newcomer, aren't you?"

"Talk gets around."

The oldster showed even teeth. "It surely does."

He put out his hand and said, "O'Conner. Call me Connie."

"Stan, Stan Yamashira," the other man said, turning in his chair and returning the offered handshake.

"Good to meet you."

"Same."

Yamashira, who wore thin, rimless glasses, and O'Conner looked out on the lake, at a knot of ducks that had gathered on the water, flapping their wings and making noise. Momentarily, their excitement subsided, and the group dispersed.

"I'm not pressuring you, Connie, but if you're going to be around, you might think about coming to an association meeting." He reeled out some more fishing line, more from habit than actual need. The lake had to be fairly shallow.

"Association?"

"The home owners' group," Yamashira added, glancing up at O'Conner from underneath his hat. "But these days belonging to it is a lot looser than when we first moved in here."

"You and your wife."

Yamashira nodded briefly. "Naomi died about two years ago. The kids come to see me on holidays, if that." He squinted up at O'Conner. "Don't get old. That's my sage advice."

"Or get caught," O'Conner amended.

Yamashira remarked flatly, "Little chance of that around here." He jutted his chin at the departing city pickup truck. "Parks and Rec service, not a problem. But try and get one of the streetlights that's been broken replaced. There's no personnel or budget for that."

"That bunch, the Mas Trece, they a particular problem?"

Two middle-aged women in designer sweat outfits power walked by on their way around the lake. The two talked about the benefits of solar panels.

"There's those brigands, for sure. But relatively speaking, we give them a wide berth, and they don't bother us noncombatants. Now, when it comes to those lads and the sheriff's department, should deputies show up on a rare occasion to do more than evict somebody for the bank, that's a different matter."

He regarded O'Conner, wondering if there was ever a time since his early teens when he fit the definition of a noncombatant. "But it's the ones who roam through here at night, the ones looking to rip off a CD player in a car or the car itself. The druggies who defecate on your lawn, the homeless squatters who, well . . ." He stopped himself.

"No worries, Stan. I'm not easily offended."

"Anyway, we've got the Section Eighters, plus the regular renters and what have you coming to the meetings. You know, people who care about the properties they're on, who want to live in a decent place and keep it that way. We're hardly in a position to impose class restrictions."

"I'll think about it . . . comrade."

Yamashira made a wave of his hand, either dismissing the loaded word or O'Conner's sarcasm. "Sure. Hey, I'll drop off a flyer, all right? We've got a barbecue coming up."

O'Conner was going to object but didn't. "Hope you catch your limit." He started to walk off.

"See you around, Connie."

"Absolutely, Stan."

Returning that evening from an errand, O'Conner drove up to the Larkspur address. He saw two men and a woman across the street, at a darkened house. There were also two silhouettes of chopper motorcycles leaning on their kickstands on the dried lawn. One of the men fell down laughing as O'Conner parked the station wagon in the driveway.

"Fuckin' uptight bitch," this one said loudly.

"Fuck you, Kenny," the woman said.

"Come on. Be cool, Inga. This is for the club," the other man said, laughing. He was thick in the middle and arms.

"Fuck that. No three way, no way, H."

Kenny, the one that had fallen down, was back on his feet and was tugging on the woman, Inga. "What? All of a sudden you're shy? Used to be you'd suck a dick at the rev of an engine," he said.

Both men chuckled.

Inga pulled free and started to walk off. "Why don't you two do each other? How about that?"

"Not hardly," said the thickset one, whom she'd called H. He got his hands on her shoulders, turning her around. "Now, come on and do right and give us your glorious snatch."

"And ass," Kenny merrily added.

She put her hands on H's chest and pushed him back to free herself again.

Kenny had come up and was crowding her now. "You ain't being friendly, Inga."

"I said no, assholes."

"What?" H put a hand to his ear, as if he was hard of hearing. He then brought up his left and slugged her.

Inga was tough; she staggered but didn't drop. She slugged him back.

"Hardheaded, ho," H hollered. He grabbed her hair as Kenny got his hands on her. They began forcing her toward the darkened house. Their feet kicked over a small sign posted in the yellowed grass for an alarm service long deactivated.

"I believe the lady said she didn't want your company."

H, the one with the large waist, looked over at O'Conner, huffing from effort. "Better get on back inside, pops, so you don't miss *American Idol*." O'Conner was dressed in chinos and a loose cotton shirt.

"This is club business," Kenny remarked.

Inga said, "I can handle these clowns, mister. You don't want no hurt."

"It's not my intention to be the one that's going to get hurt."

"This motherfucker," Kenny exclaimed. He stalked toward O'Conner, pointing. "Were you held back in school, shit wad? Slow class? That it? Get the fuck out of here."

"You like dick sucking so much, how about you suck mine? I'm sure you're all the boys' bottom, bitch," O'Conner growled.

As he hoped, the other man roared and rushed him. O'Conner timed his swing and brought up the cricket bat he'd been holding down at his side. It hadn't been noticed in the gloom. Pivoting batter fashion, he leveled it across the charging man's jaw, breaking it and the bat in half. He also knocked out two teeth.

"Oh, fuck me," Kenny moaned, back on the ground again, on his side.

H and Inga came over, openmouthed.

"Mister, I tried to tell you," Inga said, glaring at him.

"You got real pain coming for what you done," H warned the older man.

O'Conner used the end of the broken cricket bat to indicate the emblem on the back of the vest of the moaning man. "Didn't know the Vandal Vikings went in for treating their women like chattel. Now, what would Long Slim have to say about such a lack of discipline?"

Inga also had on such a vest, and she exchanged a look with H. "What do you know about him?" she challenged.

"I know he hears about shit like this," O'Conner said. The man on the ground stopped moaning. He cradled his jaw in his hand and blinked at the stranger. Marvin "Long Slim" Satterwaite was one of the founders of the Vandal Vikings motorcycle gang. He was eight years down on a twenty-year sentence at Corcoran, but his presence was still felt among the chosen ones, as they referred to themselves internally.

"So you read the papers," H said. He went to help his friend off the ground. "So you know our colors."

O'Conner leaned his torso forward, what remained of the bat held in front of him in a tight fist. "How about you ask Levon Wyler, and he can see what Long Slim thinks? How about that?" Wyler was the gang's buttoned-down attorney in San Francisco who operated behind the scenes. Such information wasn't found by Googling.

The three glared at O'Conner.

"Now, why don't you all ride out of here peaceful like and keep your psycho sex games to your side of town? It being near my bedtime and what not, I don't want to miss the finalists on *Idol*." O'Conner walked off to the house he was occupying on the other side of the street. The cricket bat had been among several items in the back of the Sable station wagon he'd obtained from Voss.

Witnessing this—the last part, where he turned from the three bikers, broken bat in hand—was Jane Grainger-Brill in her hybrid Civic. She was returning home with her daughter in the car after picking her up from her violin lesson.

She watched O'Conner cross the street in the rearview. Moonlight glinted briefly on the piece of polished wood he carried. Grainger-Brill depressed the accelerator and slowly went on, looking back at the subdued bikers, as well, in her side mirror.

"What do you think he said to them, Mom?" Millicent asked.

She felt the corners of her mouth turn up. "I'm sure he asked them nicely to keep the noise down, dear."

Her daughter made a face at her mother. She didn't believe that for a second.

Chapter Six

Two days later Stan Yamashira broke federal law. Nonchalantly, he put a flyer folded lengthwise in the mail slot of the house on Larkspur. Next, he drove to have lunch and retell worn stories with two other men he'd worked with at a restaurant in Moreno Valley.

When O'Conner got home that afternoon and read the flyer, his first reaction was to crumple it up and throw it away. Then he reconsidered. He'd go to the get-together the Willow Ridge residents, otherwise known as the home owners' association, were having at the community center. Why the hell not? It might be good for a laugh.

The community center was the one-story, industrial-looking building with the tile roof overlooking the lake. There was a park area attached to the facility, and that was where several large rectangular grills had been set up. Strips of squash and marinated strips of beef were being cooked over hot gray coals. There was a traditional separation of tasks, as the men did the grilling and the women prepared green and carbohydrate-rich salads.

On the table where the seltzer and wine were out was a medium-size stack of the local community paper, the *Inland Gazette*.

"We just moved in on Oaklawn," a youngish man with studs in an earlobe and a nostril said to an older couple as he offered to ladle punch into their cups. "Really, this was the best place we could find for the money. It was so affordable. We might even move our medical marijuana shop over to the shopping center here." The stud in his ear was a bright green cloisonné piece in the shape of a budding marijuana leaf.

The older couple gave wan smiles of resignation.

O'Conner moved past the three, holding a beer, though he wasn't much of a drinker. But he wanted to look like he fit in. He nodded slightly at a Rubenesque woman with black hair streaked with gray, in a dress too short for her age and size. There was a younger, shapely woman standing next to this one, and she zeroed in on O'Conner with a look. Her bloodred lips glowed seductively.

"To me, chlorine generators are overrated," a gray-bearded man in a Hawaiian shirt said to a lanky, balding man. He drank some of his white wine. "If you really want a beautiful pool, you have to use enzymes. Nothing beats 'em."

The lanky man murmured, concurring. O'Conner moved on once more.

"Shit, Blanche told me I'd be lucky to get a fourth of what I paid for my place," a middle-aged man in slacks and an open-collar dress shirt told a woman in pedal pushers. "And I'd be dang good at that," he added.

"I know," she replied, empathizing. "Jason and Sally are moving back in with us, and we're ecstatic about it, given they both still have their jobs—albeit at less hours."

Three pretty Vietnamese American women in their

thirties were standing together, looking about and talking to each other alternately in English and Vietnamese. Two of them held refreshments, and the third idly fingered a set of fake pearls around her neck. At various intervals one of them would break away and walk up to someone and hand out a postcard advertising their business.

O'Conner was handed one of these postcards. It depicted a woman wrapped in a towel, another towel around her head, floating on her back through a firmament of sparkling lights and multicolored mists. Cucumber slices were on her closed eyes; her face was beatific. The business the women had was a spa called the Bronze Bough, on a street he didn't know but assumed was in the area.

"I hear they massage men or women in their slinky underwear," Gwen Gardner said. She'd walked up, sipping chilled Campari and orange juice.

O'Conner flapped the postcard. "You've been?"

"I've indulged in various modes of relaxation, Connie."

"I'll try not to imagine that too much."

"Yeah?"

"Wouldn't want to overtax myself."

"I bet." She regarded him for a moment. "Does your presence here mean you intend to be staying awhile?"

"If I have a reason."

She inclined her head, her earrings tinkling. "Where'd you come from?"

He hooked a thumb in a direction behind his back.

"And going to before you stopped here?"

He pointed in a northerly direction.

"Smart-ass." She laughed briefly and had more of her drink, the stacked ice in her glass tumbling like a falling miniature cliff face.

"How about you? How'd you get here?"

"Husband number two, the podiatrist."

He looked down at her open-toed shoes and dark lavender–painted toenails—even half-moons properly proportioned.

"Nice." He fantasized about what those toes might look like flapping his ears. He returned his gaze to her face.

Maybe she was imagining it, too, as she gazed up at him with a quizzical, then settled expression. "Heard about your escapade the other day."

"Oh, that little thing," he remarked deadpan.

"Weren't you scared?"

"Only a fool or a movie cowboy says they aren't scared, Gwen. The one person you better never kid is yourself," he revealed, surprised he did so. "It's tapping that heightened sense, the quickening of the pulse, the breath short in your throat like lead shot. Your mouth dry like sandpaper, the smell of fear in your sweat. But you gotta push the anxiety back inside you, because it's the fuel you'll need to get your shit in gear."

He'd taken a hold of her wrist, but she didn't pull away. She wet her bottom lip with the tip of her tongue, aware he was watching her do it.

"Sounds like you've had a lot of experiences quickening your pulse, Mr. O'Conner. In the war? As a cop?"

He got a little closer to her. "I'm not much for uniforms."

Gardner grinned. "I bet you know a thing or two about discipline, though."

He showed blunt teeth, tightening his grip on her wrist.

"Did you guys try the bratwurst?" Stan Yamashira interjected. "They're great. You gotta try 'em." He had a half-eaten sausage with mustard tucked into a hot dog bun on his paper plate.

"You want something to eat?" Gardner asked O'Conner.

"I could stand one of those brats. Maybe two."

"Hungry, aren't you?" she asked.

"Indescribably."

Yamashira blithely munched on his hot dog as the two-time divorcée walked off in her white stretch jeans and breezy top. Swallowing, he pointed with the remains of his food at groupings of trees on an open field beyond a chain-link fence—which had several holes in it. On the far side was a structure.

"That was going to be the golf course, until the housing crash and the Great Recession." He chewed some more. "You golf, Connie?"

"I've swung a club a few times."

Yamashira chuckled. "I meant at a helpless ball."

The old man and O'Conner shared a grin. The man who'd opined about enzymes cleaning pools rapped a car key against the wine flute in his hand.

"Our fearless leader," Yamashira said sotto voce.

"Folks, I won't take up too much of your time," the bearded man began, raising his voice to be heard in the outdoors.

"That'll be a first," someone joked, and several people laughed.

"Be that as it may," he went on, "but I just wanted to say I'm very pleased, as I'm sure we all are, to see some faces here today we haven't seen in a while." He waved a hand overhead. "Now, I'm sure the great weather and free food have something to do with that, but I choose to interpret this as a sign. You all know I'm no Pollyanna, but in the past month we've had several newbies come to Willow Ridge."

He gestured again. "I also know it's economic reasons that have brought you here or, in some cases, have kept you here. These are hard times, for sure. We are all acutely aware of that." He paused, casting his gaze about the faces of his neighbors and acquaintances. "I'm saddened it's less about the amenities we want to have in our humble acreage as to why you're here. But we can turn things around. We can have our slice of the American pie. It's not too late. No, it is not."

The gray-bearded man turned a little, pointing. "Ramon there took it upon himself to stay on top of the desk jockeys in the county's street services bureau and got that sinkhole fixed on Grantha, which had been like that since the bad storm."

"And this was after we complained to Supervisor Robinson, who didn't do jack," a woman in large sunglasses added.

"Right," said the gray-bearded man, who was head of the home owners' association. He pointed again. "Mary here, with Barbara, and, oh, sorry . . . I'm forgetting his name."

"Victor," Mary said.

"Victor," the gray-bearded man added. "These three did yeoman's work to at least get the sheriff to do twice-a-week perimeter patrols."

"That's not enough," a man with a baseball cap yelled out.

"No, it's not," the association head agreed. "But at least it's a start. The journey has to begin with the first steps. But sometimes more ground is covered due to big shoes, too." He turned on his heels, searching the crowd. He then jabbed a finger at O'Conner, who stood toward the back and the side of those gathered.

"This man took one of those big steps. He stood down

some thugs who'd invaded our community and sought to do damage. This individual . . . O'Conner, isn't it?" He didn't wait for confirmation. "Mr. O'Conner took matters into his own hands, doing what our taxes are supposed to be paying law enforcement to do."

A veil of murmuring arose as Gwen Gardner walked back near O'Conner.

The association head enthused, "Let's give him a round of applause, shall we?"

There was light clapping and a few "All rights." Gardner held the plate she'd brought O'Conner in both hands and, bowing slightly, offered it up to him.

"Now who's the smart-ass?" he groused.

She winked at him. "Wave, Your Majesty. Wave to the peasants."

He made a weak attempt at acknowledgment. Usually, he was uncomfortable with this kind of attention. O'Conner was relieved yet a little let down that there was no half-assed part-time reporter there from some throwaway paper, doing his or her best to win a Pulitzer covering the barbecue.

But then what about bloggers? Had to be more than one of those bored house husbands or career women here who yakked online about the wonders of the latest colonic they'd experienced. But the clapping was over shortly, and no one seemed to have taken his photo with a cell phone, so no sense getting his boxers in a bunch over a transitory expression of goodwill, he decided.

"I gotta talk to Blanche about something," Stan Yamashira said, indicating the heavyset woman in the too-tight dress. "See you later, okay?"

"No problem," O'Conner said, figuring that was the sort of thing you said at gatherings like this. Yamashira walked over to the real estate agent and her hard-eyed companion.

"Mind if I have a bite?" Gardner asked, picking up one of the bratwurst she'd brought back. "I shouldn't but seems I can't help myself around you." She'd put mustard and relish on the sausage.

"Knock yourself out."

As she ate and they each eyed the other, Steve Brill, in a polo shirt, walked by, clapping O'Conner on the shoulder. "Way to fuckin' go, man."

"Oh, sure, yeah . . . Uh, thanks, Steve," O'Conner blurted as Brill walked past.

A bemused Gardner remarked, "Shy, huh?"

"Not so you'd notice." He quickly pinched the side of her thigh.

Before she could respond, someone else came over to him, an older woman using one of those walker sorts of contraptions with wheels and a seat.

"I applaud you, my good sir." What remained of her British accent was a lilt, but it was apparent. "How bold of you to show those louts the door."

"He thanks you, Cissy," Gardner said. "Stoic and all that business, a man of action, few words. You know the type."

The elderly lady nodded and rolled on.

O'Conner shook his head ruefully and enjoyed his bratwurst. It was good. So, too, was the sex later in the afternoon with Gwen Gardner.

"My, my, Mr. O'Conner," she breathed, thrusting beneath him. Moaning, she tightened her grip on his shoulders and bit the upper part of his chest as she orgasmed. His hand pressed the small of her back as she arched her body and shuddered. Reluctantly, Gardner let him go as he moved beside her in the bed.

He lay faceup, and she got a leg around his lower body, snuggling close. O'Conner put his arm around her, playing with the ends of her damp hair. They stayed quiet and still for several moments. A breeze came through the open window of her upstairs bedroom, the drawn shade curving in and out as the wind blew, then subsided.

"I suppose you expect me to make you some sort of snack," she commented.

"Only if I can watch you bending over in the refrigerator in your thong."

"Uh-huh."

"Isn't it customary for the man to buy the lady a meal after she's . . . you know?"

"Schtupped him?"

"Yeah, that." He laughed in his throat.

They were quiet again, until she said, "Do you have a first name?"

"What's wrong with Connie?"

"Nothing, except I don't think it's your name." While she talked, she turned his hand over, running a finger along his calluses.

"Yeah?"

"Mmm-hmm."

"Is Gardner yours?"

"Maybe you'll have to rough me up to get the truth out of me."

He got himself up on his elbow and put a hand on her. "I might demand you do all sorts of things."

She put her hand over his. "I know you will."

He gently squeezed her throat, and she reached below for him. They kissed and made love again. Afterward, as Gardner snored lightly on her stomach, O'Conner prowled about her house in his boxers and athletic tee. She kept a small decorative tin of cocaine in a nightstand drawer, along with a pill bottle of estrogen tablets and a double-headed, U-shaped pleasuring device made of smooth plastic. He examined this intently.

On a home office table were paperwork and printed-out business e-mails. Seemed Gwen Gardner made her money as the owner of the seven chain Fix & Go auto body and fender shops. He'd seen their ads on late-night TV. Was that a leftover from the first husband, or did she have a thing for the smell of grinding metal?

In a hall closet he found a loaded snub-nosed .38 in a shoe box underneath some linen. It was on an overhead shelf, and he had to stretch to reach it. There was no stepladder in the closet, so he wondered if the gun had been put there by the foot doc or a boyfriend. He was also curious to know if she'd shot the thing.

"Your daughter?" he said when Gardner's eyes opened from her slumber. He was sitting in a chair near the foot of her bed, his pants on, still in his undershirt. His bare feet were propped up on the knotted bed covers. He drank pomegranate-flavored lemonade in a mug and had pointed a toe at a framed photo on the Italian rococo-style dresser. The shot was of a pretty young woman in a silky blouse, arms folded, with a questioning expression on her face.

"Yes, my sweet baby, Harley Lynn. Can you believe it? Her father insisted we name her that. And said that way, together, you know, because it had been in his family for generations. Even though I argued it made her sound like a goddamn hillbilly." As she talked, she turned over, and, propping a pillow against the headboard, sat up and put her back against it. The sheet covered her lower half, but her tanned breasts were exposed. "What a maniac he is," she said affectionately of her ex.

Because he assumed he should show interest in a reasoned, older adult way, he said, "She's in college?"

"I wish," she huffed. "Made the brilliant decision to drop out after two years. Mind you, she was getting As and Bs, so it wasn't like she was failing. But no, she wants to be an actress or on-air personality." She blew air through her lips and noticed she hadn't pulled the sheet up. Gardner did so and continued. "She's in L.A. to pursue her dream. How brilliantly original, huh?"

"She having any luck?"

"Been in a couple of commercials. Actually got a few lines in one I saw about dish-washing soap." She hunched a shoulder. "At least it keeps her out of Chanchin's orbit."

"Who's that?"

"Asshole who runs with the Mas Trece. A shot caller, I guess they'd call him. Always going around in those oversize basketball shorts of his."

"She was going out with him?"

"They went to high school together. Met in, of all places, geometry class." She leaned forward, a lopsided grin on her face. "He became her tutor when she took algebra. Isn't that a pip?"

"Math whiz, is he?"

"Comes in handy when it's time to count his meth profits, I guess."

"Great. They keep house around here, do they? The Mas Trece?"

She gave him a look to match the one on her daughter's face. "Why do you want to know?"

"Ran into him and some of his crew a couple of times." He was also working out a theory as to why the Vandal Vikings were around, but kept that to himself.

She frowned. "What are you up to, Connie?"

He had more of his drink. "I'm a concerned Willow Ridge resident, aren't I?"

She made a face. "Don't go getting too full of yourself."

"Me? Never. But shouldn't I know where they are so as to avoid them? They're scary."

She removed the sheet and rumpled covers from her body and got out of bed, nude. O'Conner liked that she wasn't into overdoing waxing and what have you. He liked a bushy woman. She came toward him and stopped, putting her hands on her hips, looking down at him as he looked up at her.

"Don't be cute. It doesn't suit you. What are you up to?"

He considered a bullshit answer but said, "Learning what I can about them. It's been my experience one's percentage for survival is increased the more you understand the strengths and weaknesses of, shall we say, your opposition."

"And just how are they your opponents, Mr. O'Conner?"

He said evenly, "They don't obey the rules."

"Right, like you do."

He put his hand between her legs, caressing her inner thigh. He moved his hand farther up, and his finger then sought her clit. "There's one rule I adhere to."

She put her hand on top of his close-cut head, slowly moving her hips as he rubbed her. "What's that?" she whispered.

"Paying attention to the details."

"Uh-huh."

They pleasured one another on the chair and then

on the rug, the afternoon shadows lengthening in the
bedroom.

Three days later O'Conner was down on a knee,
peeping below the edge of the slats of a wooden window
blind. He was using binoculars Gardner had borrowed
from her friend, the Realtor. He'd been keeping watch on
a white, with gray trim, California Craftsman—complete
with a river stone chimney and intersecting gabled roofs.
The house was at the end of a cul-de-sac called Rio
Brava. It was the house commandeered by the Mas Trece.

Gwen Gardner didn't know the specific house the
gang was suspected of taking over. But she did know the
lowered Impala had been spotted coming to and fro on
this street, which was only three blocks long. O'Conner
had ventured out at four in the morning, after his time
spent with the cut-rate body shop magnate. He had
walked over here and scouted the area but hadn't spotted
the Impala. He had seen, though, that one of the houses
had blacked-out windows in a part of the second story his
grandmother would have called the sunroom. He had dis-
cerned the dark plastic taped to the windows once the
early light rose. There was a small open-air deck attached
to this room, as well.

O'Conner had then left, figuring he wouldn't return in
the afternoon, so as to reduce the possibility of being
seen by one of the gang. He had returned nearly twenty-
four hours later and had broken into a boarded-up, empty
house on the curve from the suspected Mas Trece abode.
There was evidence that squatters had been in this place,
as a section of the front room's hardwood floor was
charred from an indoor campfire. There was graffiti on

some walls, holes in a few of those walls, and copper pipes had been ripped out.

The slatted window in the upstairs bathroom provided O'Conner a roost to look out on the other house. The binoculars didn't have night vision, but he managed. By the third day now, he'd counted five times a Swift Trans delivery van coming and going from the house.

At first he'd assumed it was a different van each time, but he'd determined it was two different drivers, one making the trip once and the other twice. They'd picked up sealed cardboard boxes, several dollied out each time, but had made no deliveries. High-end meth was worth at least $150 a gram on the street, so O'Conner figured the Mas Trece product was hidden in small containers in the bigger boxes of freight. He had also noticed that kid Ian from the copier place, the Print Shack, bicycle over to the house.

He'd left his bike on the porch and had gone in and come out a few minutes later. O'Conner guessed the messenger bag he'd had on was filled with plastic bags of crystal meth or a mix of that and ecstasy. He'd learned the Mas Trece were a diversified drug-slangin' crew. He figured the kid sold on the college campus. Man can't make a living just jockeying photocopy machines, O'Conner empathized. Ian Childes soon pedaled away.

He still hadn't seen the Impala yet, but as he crouched on his knee, considering calling it a day as he was getting stiff and hungry, he heard the unmistakable low roar of a Harley. Arriving at the house, wearing her colors, was Inga, the Vandal Viking he'd previously encountered. He forgot about getting a sandwich as he watched her park her hog across the dead lawn and disembark.

Two Mas Treces came out of the house, and the three exchanged fist bumps and salutations. One of them had a prominent Z-shaped scar on the side of his lean face. They went into the house. Soon after the Impala drove up, and three men got out of it, including his buddy Basketball Shorts, Roberto "Chanchin" Saladago. This trio also went into the house.

O'Conner finally stood and worked the kinks out of his bones. He did some toe touching and bends, some push-ups and knee raises. He also made sure to peek through the blinds, but the Harley was still there. Forty-one minutes later Inga came out of the house alone, fired up her hog, and took off.

O'Conner had been operating on the theory the Vikings had been sniffing around Willow Ridge because they were looking either to muscle in on the Mas Trece meth business or simply to rip them off. But those ideas seemed moot given Inga showing up at their doorstep. This suggested an alliance between the gearheads and the cholos. But, he cautioned himself, there was another angle worth exploring.

Could be Inga was working her own action on the side. What if getting jacked around by one of her so-called brethren the other night had her ring up Chanchin for revenge? But that seemed awfully quick based on his casual observations. There was a familiarity she seemed to have with the two who'd greeted her. But clearly something was up, and O'Conner needed to find out what.

When he first got to the development, he figured he'd camp out a few days among the squares, then split for his destination in the Bay Area. But something about the development, even on the second night he was there, had wormed its way inside his head, he'd finally admitted to himself.

He wasn't getting any younger. Loath to admit it, but the knife's edge of his psyche, of how he approached the world, was, well, getting dulled. The brief dustup with Voss had confirmed this to him. It wasn't too many years ago, he would have pushed harder about his money with a guy like Voss—an arranger, not a doer like O'Conner. For him, O'Conner had used finesse with Voss.

He grunted. Instead of a slick sports car or a young hottie on his arm, maybe this was his midlife crisis. Putting down roots. *Shit.* Or maybe, he cautioned himself, climbing out a side window away from the Mas Trece house, he was just using new methods to get over like always. Still, wouldn't it be interesting to do something to shape his environment, rather than the usual of him reacting to circumstances?

Walking back to his house, he realized the praise he'd received at the residents' gathering had given him a charge. He'd already felt the simmer from Gardner in the supermarket, but he knew the deal was sealed after he was acknowledged as . . . Well, what was he?

O'Conner couldn't dredge up a name for what he was experiencing exactly, but he knew he couldn't let knot heads like the Vikings or whoever just run around loose and mess things up for him. It had been a whim to become a squatter, as he'd never had a house of his own before, and shouldn't a man his age experience that? So just the idea that the Vandal Vikings could bring the heat down on Willow Ridge was enough to want to keep them in check. He didn't know what he was going to make of this new situation he was in, but O'Conner was determined to be the one to call the tune.

At the house, his house, he used a key to unlock the new lock he'd recently installed in the front door. In fact, he'd replaced all the locks throughout the house. He opened the door and stepped inside, quietly closing the door behind him.

Chapter Seven

Four days later O'Conner accompanied Gwen Gardner on an errand. She'd asked him to come with her to one of her auto-body shops. This one was in Chino Hills. The drive was a little over an hour away.

"A man could get used to this," O'Conner said, readjusting his frame into the contour of the car's leather seat. Gardner's car was a late-model Cadillac CTS, which rode like it was on skis over the roadway—better than any heap he'd ever had, he noted. The factory air was on, and a smooth jazz number played on the CD unit. He actually didn't like that kind of music; it seemed like a halfway measure to him. If you're going to do a thing, do it all the way and don't fuck around. But Gardner smelled good, and he was comfortable, so he went with the flow.

"I'm not sure about this, Connie." Gardner briefly looked over at him, then back at the freeway.

He patted her leg. "That's why you brought me along."

She frowned, wetting her bottom lip with the tip of her tongue. "Not to go ape shit."

He mused, "Gotta show who's boss—in this case, you."

"You mean women shouldn't be involved in anything mechanical or technical."

"Women, men, cross-dressers, whoever, can be involved in any damn thing they want to be," he said. "Only this seems like a giant pain in the ass for you." Gardner had inherited the Fix & Go chain from her deceased father, an enterprising auto-body man who had started with one shop in Hawaiian Gardens in the late sixties.

She nodded. "Yeah, it's not like there's a lot of women in this line of work, except as order takers."

"But you do have a certain lifestyle, Gwen." He tapped the padded dash.

She put narrowed eyes on him. "Maybe you'd like to be a kept man in that lifestyle."

"Maybe I would. The prisoner of Flower Drum Avenue." He squeezed her leg this time. "But you might throw me over for some young stud on the cougar prowl."

"I like 'em seasoned, baby. I wouldn't be taking one of those boy toys on this kind of run, now would I?"

"Uh," he grunted satisfactorily.

The discrepancy had come up after the quarterly inventory report. The Fix & Go they were heading to had been through some personnel changes but had seemed to settle down when she hired the new manager. That is, until it was clear that the consumption of paint, Bondo, and other supplies didn't correlate with the number of vehicles serviced.

"They figure 'cause I'm a stupid broad, I don't know these numbers?" she'd groused to O'Conner. "I fuckin' worked, pulling dents and grinding fenders, in my dad's shop when I was in college."

"I don't think they use the word *broad*," he'd pointed out.

Incensed, she'd given him the finger.

He'd then suggested the site visit. "You ask him the questions, and I'll be just some guy in the corner."

"I should resent it that I need a man," she'd said, sitting on his lap and putting an arm around his neck.

"Never hurts to have backup," O'Conner had opined as they kissed last night.

The two arrived at the shop, located along a stretch of businesses that included a smog-testing outfit and a Thai restaurant called the Sunset Buddha, which anchored the far end of the block. She parked the Cadillac on one side of the shop's wide driveway. This allowed a view into a spacious cavity containing cars in various stages of disassembly and the workers involved in their repair.

"Hey, how you doing, Gwen?" the manager said as they exited the car. He was a heavyset man in a loose short-sleeved shirt, with combed-back hair and a full goatee. He had tattoos of the ace of spades and a black-bordered red diamond on one thick forearm.

"Mitch," Gardner replied. "This is my friend Connie."

"Good to meet you," Mitch Frane said, extending a beefy hand while assessing the newcomer.

"Same," O'Conner said, shaking the man's hand. He maintained a neutral appearance. He and Gardner had decided not to explain his presence to better keep her manager guessing. Let him wonder if O'Conner might be his replacement if matters didn't line up. As if he'd want to do that, O'Conner had admonished himself, though he did not express this to Gardner. Maybe Frane had sized him up as a lawyer, but he had his doubts.

Frane put his arm lightly around Gardner's shoulders, turning her away from the car and O'Conner. Softly he said, "So there's a problem you needed to discuss in person?"

"Let's go in the office," Gardner said.

As the two headed that way, O'Conner didn't follow but lingered on the shop floor. He watched a man in overalls, the top of which had been stripped off his torso and tied by the shoulder straps around his waist. He had on an athletic T-shirt underneath and was sweating as he banged out dents in a bumper using a sledgehammer and wood blocks of various sizes and shapes. The bumper was secured between two heavy vises set apart and bolted on to a work bench.

O'Conner watched the man work for a while, then turned to see two men pushing a redone Mercedes CLS into the paint booth—one pushed in back and the other was on the driver's side, his hand in the open window as he held the steering wheel.

Past the booth and to its left was the glassed-in office. A standing Frane was pointing at a seated Gwen Gardner.

"Now, that isn't right, what you're saying, Ms. Gardner."

"Something's not adding up." Calmly, she crossed her legs, eyes steady on Frane.

O'Conner, hands in pockets, stood before the office glass, looking in on the two. Frane looked from him back to Gardner.

"Who's he supposed to be?"

"Mitch, what you should concentrate on is how these numbers need to be reconciled. I'm not in business as a hobby, and my time is not so consumed by my next pedicure that I'm not checking the books. Times are real fuckin' hard, and none of us can afford to be coming up short."

Frane blinked. "I hear you, Gwen."

"Good," she said, standing. "Maybe you should have a shop meeting with the employees to remind them that not only won't I tolerate thefts, but I will also prosecute such to the full extent of the law."

"Understood," he said. Peripherally, he could tell O'Conner was still at the window, hands in his pockets, a blank expression on his face. Who the fuck was this guy? He didn't give off a boyfriend vibe to Frane. Or if he was, he certainly wasn't the fizzy water, Brie-eating type he figured she banged.

"Excellent." She held out her hand, and they shook. Afterward, she and O'Conner left the shop, Frane watching the pair go. The two had previously discussed whether it was the manager himself who was ripping her off or a specific worker. Gardner knew Frane had a well-stocked home garage, where he worked on custom cars.

"Doesn't matter, really," O'Conner had said. "The point is to let him know you know what time it is."

In the car, back on the 215 Freeway heading east, Gardner told him, "That made me wet." She looked over at him, designer sunglasses in place.

"Yeah, getting the blood up has that effect." He placed his hand on her upper thigh.

"You have an effect on me."

"Bet you say that to all the dudes under your thumb, Gwen."

She put those big dark lenses on him, puckering her lips and making kissy sounds. In Moreno Valley she bought them lunch at an Italian restaurant. On the way back to Willow Ridge, O'Conner half dozed. Gardner reached over him and opened the glove box. She felt around in there with one hand while she drove.

O'Conner sat up. "What are you looking for?"

"Got a box of mints in there. Too much onion with my peppers."

Playfully, he slapped her hand away and retrieved the box of mints. As he pulled the item out, a brochure dropped out onto the floor. O'Conner opened the box and pinched a round, white, chalky mint between an index finger and thumb. This he inserted between her lips, and she gently bit the tip of his finger.

He also popped a mint in his mouth and picked up the brochure.

"Aw, shit," Gardner said.

"Huh," O'Conner muttered, unfolding and reading the glossy, slick brochure. "The Anthem of Reason Institute." He turned his head toward her.

"Fuck you." She smiled. "Don't give me that superior look."

"When do we beam up to the spaceship, Commander?"

"That's not what they're about. And I only went to a few meetings."

"In L.A.?"

"No, out our way. They have a headquarters in Banning."

"Do they now?"

"Look, I was going through a bad patch. Harley Lynn was giving me fits, and, well, I hoped they might have some answers. Offer peace of mind."

The Anthem of Reason Institute was a quasi religion that advocated body and mind enlightenment, personal growth, and goal achievement. Sports figures and celebrities who were adherents proclaimed their virtuousness. As far as O'Conner and plenty of others could tell, the institute offered the self-help hustle in a new bottle.

He asked Gardner, "Is it like going to church?"

Snidely she said, "Like you would know about that."

He audibly sucked his teeth at her.

"Okay, no, it's not like church. It's more you come and talk about what's bothering you. Like group therapy."

"Or an AA meeting," he said.

"I suppose. You see, at the meeting there's always an Arranger—"

"A what?"

"That's what they call a certain level of staffer. Those who have come up through the ranks and are, ah, the gurus, for lack of a better term. They guide you on your journey to enlightenment and release. They help you arrange your mind and life."

"Son of a bitch." The term arranger had a different meaning for O'Conner. To him that was somebody like Zev Voss. A guy who was the behind-the-scenes type who got you the guns or acetylene torch, found a wheelman if you needed one for a job, that sort of thing. He said, "I'd bet the rent that if you have the ducats, then these Arrangers have a more hands-on approach with you."

"You don't pay rent."

"How bourgeois of you. Anyway, I'm sure what's-his-face, the dude who's one of their members, the one that does those action flicks—"

"Stef Agar," she interjected.

"Him," he agreed. "He must have Arrangers out the butt."

"He has his own section at the headquarters," Gardner said.

"Sweet."

"Uh-huh."

"How come you stopped going?"

"I don't know. I guess I got what I came for, but the Arrangers start to give you the hard sell, but you know, with subtlety. They knew I had the body shop chain and wanted me not only to give more, but also to recruit others to join."

She touched her sternum. "To me, that should be the choice of the individual. If you're getting something out of whatever it is, Zen Buddhism, yoga, primal screams—well, nobody does that anymore—but if you're getting helped, then it's only natural you'd want to share that with others. I shouldn't have to be pushed to pimp the process."

"Right on."

She slapped his thigh. He took her hand and kissed it.

Later they went to his house, that is, the house he was occupying in Willow Ridge. The first time Gardner had been inside.

"Early primitive," he cracked as she looked around. O'Conner had cleaned out the interior. The furnishings were spare, mostly chairs and a couch purchased from secondhand stores. There was also one of those coffee tables of lacquered driftwood, with a heavy sheet of glass attached, that decades ago had been all the rage in the front room.

In what was the dining room, there was no table or chairs, only his Kawasaki motorcycle. Several of its components were off to one side, atop layers of flattened cardboard boxes. Slowly, O'Conner was rebuilding the machine.

On the walls were a few framed reproductions, which, Gardner had the impression, weren't simply random selections. The works included a charcoal of a scene of Tahitian women at rest and one by Winslow Homer, called *The Gulf Stream*. In it, a shirtless fisherman in a small boat was adrift in rough waters as sharks circled. Yet the individual in the painting seemed unperturbed.

"This supposed to be you?" she commented, pointing at the Homer print.

O'Conner was behind her, hands on her shoulders. "That mean you're one of the sharks?"

She chuckled hollowly. "I might just gobble you up."

Later in bed, after making love, Gardner snored lightly as O'Conner lay on his back next to her, awake and contemplative. His fingers idly tapped a rhythm on his chest. The one new piece of furniture he'd bought was the bed. He wasn't so dense as to believe Gardner would go along with a futon on the floor, which would have been his preference. Now, when was the last time he cared about what anybody else might think?

O'Conner imagined he could easily slip into the guise of the kept man. To be sure, he knew he'd have to earn his keep. He could be her overseer, or assume some damn title. Make the rounds of her auto body and fender chains to let the workers know the owner was on her ones and twos. Hell, he could even scout a new location for expansion.

He snorted, dismissing these fanciful flights of becoming a civilian. If he did take Gardner up on her offer, he'd have to do it to play an angle. But never being in the hot car market, O'Conner couldn't envision himself conning her into letting him run one of her shops and turning it into a chop and ship front. He patted her firm backside reassuringly.

Easing out of the bed, he got into his clothes and took a stroll outside to review and plan his next steps. It was quietly alarming to him how matter-of-factly his complacency had crept up on him. What was he smoking, considering he could settle down in Willow Ridge? This suburban trip was for suckers. He wasn't that old. He was still a motherfuckin' stoker, as far as he was concerned. Chuckling quietly, he went on, curious to see what he might discover on this pleasant evening.

Walking in no particular direction, O'Conner wondered what else he could glean from keeping watch on the Mas Trece meth house. So far he'd seen Inga only that one time. Since then, there'd been only the comings and goings of the usual visitors. Time to switch up tactics, he concluded. He needed some background information, and that wasn't about to fall into his lap as he crouched down in the bathroom of an empty house. Anyway, he cautioned himself, the more he took up his post at the house, the greater the possibility he'd be spotted.

Eventually, he found himself toward the front of the subdivision, near the two-story Cape Cod–style house. The dark-haired young woman he'd seen the first night he was here was sitting on the porch in a beach chair, her feet up on the rail. She was toking on a joint, which she now held down at her side, the aroma drifting out to the street.

"Hey, man," she called out. "What brings you out and about?"

He came halfway up the walkway. The lawn still needed tending. "Looking for the purple haze."

She nodded her head rapidly. "You're a trip."

"You mean for a geezer?"

She smiled, showing pristine teeth. Then, joint to her lips, she pulled fumes into her lungs, squinting at him. She held the smoke inside for a few beats, then exhaled. "You all the time walking around here. Looking at this, looking at that."

"What if I was a sidewalk inspector?"

"Yeah, uh-huh," she said.

"What about you?"

"What about me?"

"This all you do?" He gestured quickly.

She managed a crooked grin. "Oh, I do a lot."

O'Conner came closer. "That right?"

The young woman rocked some in her seat, tipping back in it. "I asked you first."

"Guess I'm just restless."

"Bullshit."

"That's harsh."

"What are you up to?"

"Why I have to be up to something?"

"'Cause you ain't like the rest of these clowns in the Ridge."

"Do you say that to entice all the strangers?" He frowned. "This your house?"

She giggled. "Just like the one you're in is yours."

"What's your name?"

"I know they call you Connie." She let the chair down. "You want a beer?"

"Sure."

She stood and opened the front door, leaving it wide as she stepped inside.

O'Conner followed her. In the house he expected to find walls covered in graffiti, holes in the Sheetrock, and other evidence of the indifference of squatters. Instead, there were sparse furnishings, mismatched, but not busted up. Looked like they shopped at the same places he did.

The house's interior needed patching and a uniform paint job. But he could see where markings on the walls had been painted over with primer, and in a few cases attempts had been made to match the faded beige of the color scheme.

"Go on. Sit down," she said, calling from the kitchen.

He did. Stationed in the living room was a flat-screen TV anchored to one of the mismatched painted walls. There was one of those wireless video-game boxes near the TV, twin controls on top of it. There was also a fancy boom box on an end table. A CD case was on this, depicting a statuesque blonde in a leather dress, with exaggerated shoulders. The woman held a studded whip. The album was called *The Dreams of Grinquist*. He assumed the boom box was what had been playing music the night he got to Willow Ridge. Two iPhones were on the mantel of the unused fireplace.

She returned with two cans of imported beer and handed one to him. She sat on the couch, stuffing showing on one of its arms. O'Conner sat in a hard-back chair that looked as if it had been liberated from a school district warehouse.

He popped the beer's top and after tipping the can toward her, sipped the cold brew.

His hostess picked up a remote control and clicked on the TV, which was on one of the ESPN stations. A college football game was being rebroadcast from last Saturday. The dark-haired woman stared intently at this for a few moments, taking another hit on her joint. Maybe she was selfish, or maybe she figured O'Conner wasn't the marijuana type, but she didn't offer to share her weed.

"Did you have money on that game?" He nodded briefly at the screen.

She clicked off the set. "You moved the chair. Suspicious bastard, aren't you?"

He shrugged a shoulder as he took another pull on

his beer. He'd turned the chair so it afforded him a view of the front door and the open doorway to a hallway. He didn't entirely know what her trip was, to use her old-fashioned term, but he knew she wasn't coming on to him. She was sizing him up—but for what?

"Nice TV," he said. "One of those new Samsungs."

"You like it?"

"Can you get me one? I've got a blank wall in my place in need of dressing up."

Now she shrugged, stubbing out her joint. "You could go to Best Buy."

"Yeah. That where you got your set? Through the front or out the back?"

She grinned, and into the house stepped two young men, talking.

"I'm telling you, man," one said, "this is going to be sweet, like motherfuckin' Christmas for us." He had unkempt sandy brown hair and was tall and substantial in the shoulders. He was in his early twenties, like the dark-haired woman. His companion was the teen whom O'Conner had seen talking to the woman the night of their party. Both carried new DVDs, still in their boxes. There were household names printed on those boxes.

"The fuck?" the larger one said upon seeing O'Conner, who had his legs crossed, the beer in one hand on his knee. He glared at the woman. "This your stepdad, Mattie? Some kind of homecoming?"

She laughed in a burst. "Hardly."

The larger one exchanged a look with the teenager, and they marched into a back room with the merchandise. O'Conner was certain there hadn't been a sale at a nearby electronics store.

Momentarily, having established that O'Conner had

no family ties to the woman of the house, the brown-haired man returned and addressed the interloper. "You come in here to suck up my beer?"

"I was invited." Affably, he grinned up at the younger man.

"The fuck, man?"

O'Conner wondered was that the only expression he knew.

"He's the one my mom was talking about," the teenager said quietly. "She saw him fucking with those Vikings. Made 'em back down."

Big Shoulders turned to glare at the teen. "No shit?"

"No shit," O'Conner confirmed.

He regarded O'Conner, moving some to the side, shifting his tone. "What's your game?"

"Mattie was curious about that. You guys are nosy, huh?"

"And?"

"I'm not in your way."

Big Shoulders hooked his thumbs in the corners of his jeans pockets. "How would that be?"

O'Conner got up, looking from the challenger to Mattie. "Thanks for the beer." He put the empty can on the chair's seat.

"Sure we can't get you a rib eye sandwich? Some braised endives? Some shit like that?"

"Oh, I'm fine. Thank you."

Big Shoulders was an inch or so taller than O'Conner, and he leaned in. "I don't want to be inhospitable to a senior citizen, but don't make mi casa, su casa. Comprende, Grandpa?"

"Like I said, I was invited."

"You won't be again."

"That's what you say."

"You questioning my authority?"

"Not me, Chief. I'm sure to you we're all just squirrels in your world. Isn't that right?"

Big Shoulders looked at the teenager, who looked back at him guilelessly. "That supposed to be what? Funny?"

O'Conner was at the door. "Thanks for the beer."

Mattie gave him a smile and a half salute. Big Shoulders glared at him, and the teen, his arms folded, had a half smile on his face.

Outside he saw a red Corolla parked in the driveway. The trunk was closed, but there were several other DVD boxes with brand names he recognized on the backseat. Those DVDs hadn't been boosted from homes, but from a storeroom or right off the truck. But were these two part of a stickup crew or the crew itself, including the woman? And why the hell would Mattie invite him in, knowing the other two would be back with the contraband?

Was she keeping tabs on him while he was scoping out the doings inside Willow Ridge? O'Conner considered what the younger woman was up to as he let himself back into his house. He got undressed to his boxers and got back into bed, stirring Gwen Gardner awake with his movements.

"Hey," she said sleepily.

"Hey, yourself." Spooning her, he looped his arm around her midsection, pulling her closer.

She murmured and wiggled against him. "You're getting to be a bad habit."

"Don't take the cure just yet."

She made a sound, but it was unintelligible, as she was already falling back to sleep.

Lying there, O'Conner realized he had his work cut

out for him. This damn place was proving to be tricky, a territory that could have hidden quicksand waiting to suck him down.

After another scouting mission of the Mas Trece lab two days later, O'Conner entered his house as dusk settled over the subdivision. He'd done one more stakeout to convince himself there was little else to be learned from merely observing them. He needed to start asking around about the gang, but whom could he approach? Snooping could alert his boy Chanchin, and that wouldn't be a good thing. Conversely, it was important to know what was what.

If the Vikings were setting up the Mas Trece through Inga, then what he wanted to determine was if there was money to be made from ripping off the would-be thieves. Unless the motorcycle gang was simply trying to take over the dope concession from the other gang. In the various nefarious enterprises O'Conner had been engaged in over the years, he'd eschewed drugs. He wasn't a moralist. He'd witnessed the kind of profits to be had in that trade. But the lust of drug money seemed to breed a particularly corrosive treacherousness that infected everyone around the stuff. Logical behavior took a backseat to wanting more and more, and that was bad business as far as O'Conner was concerned. He dealt with professionals in a professional manner.

O'Conner stepped into the dining room to look at his partially disassembled motorcycle. He had taken the engine off and had dropped it off at the rebuilders. He contemplated working on the front fork, which required new shocks, but could not muster up much enthusiasm. He didn't need the bike and had taken on the rebuilding project as a way to keep his mechanical skills sharp. But it wasn't like his plan was to leave Willow Ridge the same way he got here. A tight smile came and went on his face.

As he came back in the other room, there was a movement to his left and the hall closet door swung open with a loud bang against the wall. A man wearing a ski mask and gloves came at him with a weed whacker. He wore plastic safety goggles, too, and he thrust the trimming head of the thing at O'Conner's face. Instinctively, O'Conner put up his hands, and the whipping nylon cord of the weed whacker tore into his palms and forearms, driving him back.

"Yeah, motherfucker," his attacker said. "Bleed, bitch."

O'Conner stumbled but didn't lose his footing. Too bad his furnishings were so few, or he'd reach for something to throw at this punk. They were in the living room, and the masked man was using his battery-powered weed whacker like a sword, swinging it back and forth, its nylon tendrils making multiple cuts into O'Conner.

"What? Don't have nothing smart to say, old man?"

He jabbed the gardening tool forward like a lance, expecting to make O'Conner do more backpedaling. But O'Conner went low, got his forearm up, and struck the shaft of the device. This knocked it upward, and blood dripping in his eye from a cut over his brow, he latched on to the shaft with his hand and jerked.

"Shit," the other man bellowed. "Stop that."

O'Conner lashed out with his foot as the man in the ski mask let go of his weed whacker, rather than being drawn forward and kicking in the groin. Fine by O'Conner. His attacker ran toward the rear of the house. O'Conner caught up with him in the kitchen.

Using the weed whacker like a baseball bat, he struck the man in the back with the control end.

The blow didn't stop him, but as the fleeing man got the back door open, O'Conner dropped on his butt like a player sliding into home base. His feet got entangled with the other man's ankles, and his attacker tumbled headfirst down the back steps. O'Conner leaped on him and socked him under the ear as he turned his head, eliciting a grunt.

O'Conner struck him again, this time with the whip end of the weed whacker, hitting his goggles, stunning the man. On his feet he hit him several more times, and the ski-masked intruder was done. O'Conner took off the mask and wasn't surprised to see it was the sandy-haired big-shouldered one from the Cape Cod house.

"Not bad for an old-timer, huh, punk?" he said through gritted teeth.

"Look, man," the other one began weakly.

O'Conner hit him under the jaw, silencing him. Standing over him, O'Conner worked the weed whacker on his face, then kicked his cut-up face. His chest rose and fell rapidly, and he left the younger man where he lay. He cracked the casing of the weed whacker over a raised knee and strode off toward the Cape Codder.

He banged on the door, and Mattie Dodd opened it.

"The fuck happened to you?"

"You know perfectly well," he answered, pushing his way inside.

"That right?" She closed the unlocked door quietly.

He pushed her against a wall with a thud. She grinned viciously. "You knew your boyfriend was coming home with those DVDs when you invited me in the other day. You wanted me and him to tango. Why?"

"Looks like you won."

"Yeah, so?"

"So you got any gas left, pops, or you just hot air in my grill?" She rubbed on his crotch, and it surprised him how quickly he got aroused. They kissed roughly.

O'Conner grabbed her by the shoulders and turned her around. She unbuckled her belt, and he pulled down her jeans, exposing a thong and a tramp stamp on the small of her back. The tattoo was a dragon partly curled around a rainbow-colored egg. She bent forward, pushing herself out some, and having gotten his own zipper down and his pants loose, he entered her from behind.

"Let's see if you can pound as good as you jabber," she taunted.

He pulled on her hair, and she mouthed a number of dirty words and phrases as they had loud and sweaty sex. O'Conner was light-headed when they finished.

Smiling crookedly at him, she hitched up her pants. "Not bad, Mister Greenjeans. You want a beer?"

"Oxygen," he murmured, bent over, hands on his legs, above his knees. "Crazy chick," he muttered.

He gulped down the beer she handed him, and they both turned as the teenager, Doug Brill, stepped into the house. He gaped at the two. O'Conner set the finished can on the arm of the couch.

O'Conner started to walk out, pointing a finger at the teenager. "I'm hardly one to give anybody advice, kid, but if you got half a brain, you better stay away from Bonnie and Clyde here."

Behind him the woman snickered. "Better get on now. Your Ensure's getting warm."

O'Conner stepped back outside, aware as his heightened state wore off how much his lacerations hurt. His right hand was swollen, and the cut over his eyebrow was dripping red into his eye. He returned to his house and took a slow soak in the bathtub.

Cody Bradford, the man who had attacked O'Conner, didn't return to the Cape Cod house. That is, he managed to get back to his car, parked across the street. He held some bunched-up used paper towels he'd gotten out of a blue recycling bin to his face. He saw Mattie Dodd and Doug Brill looking at him from the window. The teenage Brill came outside.

"Hey, man. What the hell's going on?" Brill said. "That scary dude O'Conner was here."

"I figured," Bradford responded.

"You . . . you need some help?"

"No. I got the message."

"What are you talking about?"

"Doug, get over here," a new voice said. It was Steve Brill, and he was walking quickly toward the Cape Cod–style house.

"Dad," the younger Brill began.

"Now," his father demanded.

Bradford shook his head and drove away.

Steve Brill stood with his hands on his hips, trying to make sense of the scene. His son looked back at the house, but Mattie Dodd couldn't be seen now. He walked over to his father.

"Who was that with the bleeding face?"

"Just a guy."

"My ass, Doug. What the hell is wrong with you? We've told you about hanging out here."

The son looked away, silent.

His father would save his lecture for when he got his son home. He knew better than to be doing such in public. It used to humiliate him something fierce when his old man used to do that to him. Gesturing for his son to take the lead, the older Brill walked behind him.

Back at their house Steve Brill said, "Go on to your room. I want to talk with your mother first. Then we'll meet with you."

"Whatever, man." Doug Brill went up the stairs.

Brill watched him go, then turned to his wife. She'd been sitting at the dining room table, helping their daughter, Millie, with her history homework. "When you're done, let's talk, okay?"

"Sure," Jane Grainger-Brill said. She looked at her daughter, who pretended to be reading about the War of 1812 in her textbook but couldn't keep the small smile off her face. Her big brother was in trouble again.

"You keep your mind on the Battle of New Orleans, got it?"

"Oh, yes."

Her mother kept a smile off her face.

Afterward, their daughter was allowed to play her Cheetah Girls Pirates Island treasure hunt game on the laptop. Husband and wife talked while seated in the breakfast nook.

"Good thing I got a heads-up from Blanche," Brill said. "I ran into her at the cleaners a few days ago."

"You mean about that house with the grandniece in it?"

"Yeah. She told me she'd seen Doug coming out of there last week. And when he wasn't here this evening, something told me our less than school-focused student wasn't over at the library, cracking the books, like he'd told his sister."

Grainger-Brill said, "So the older woman has put a spell on him?"

"I don't know exactly what's going on, Janey, but I

saw a man about the girl's age who Doug was talking to, and his face was bloody."

"He and Doug have a fight?"

"Didn't seem so."

"The girl, then? Mattie?"

"Who knows, Janey? But if he is attracted to this young woman, she can't be anything but trouble."

His wife nodded, recalling the sheriff actually sending out a car on a call about too much noise at a party in that house. They weren't clear on all the details, but the gist was that several months ago Mattie Dodd, the grandniece of the retired, widowed librarian who owned the Cape Codder, had come to live with her great-aunt Lori. In her seventies, the older woman was bothered by a number of ailments. Lori Stiglez subsequently had a stroke and was placed in a care facility by her grandniece.

"She's paying her great-aunt's mortgage some damn way," he added. "'Cause she certainly doesn't keep regular hours."

"What? She's hooking?'

"I don't think it's that, but she's up to something, and no doubt the gentleman with the hamburger face, who our son knows, is part of it." He didn't need to go on about how this was a danger to their son.

"Then let's get him down here," Grainger-Brill said.

Doug Brill didn't like being questioned and didn't like being pressed for answers. He did ask how his father knew he was over there, but he didn't get an answer. He also knew if he didn't cough it up, it wouldn't be too much for his parents to ship him off to one of these scared straight boot camps, or whatever the hell they were called.

It wasn't lost on him that at a dinner party his mom at first had been all aghast and such when her friend Erica

Parsons told her about making the hard decision to send her daughter Nicolette off to one of those outfits. He'd smirked because Nicolette was the chick you could always buy weed or meth from without fail. She bragged about a hookup with the Mas Trece. Her nickname was Nickel Bag Nicolette.

"Yes, I cried, but she came back a more aware person," his mom's friend had said.

Doug Brill knew the woman's daughter still smoked weed, but she had, it seemed, stopped selling the product. From what she'd told her friends about the experience, he damn sure didn't want a taste. He'd give up a name to his parents, figuring he'd direct their ire elsewhere. Plus, he was pretty sure that older dude O'Conner must have beat down Cody, and it must have been over Mattie. Because he was also pretty damn sure that bastard had banged her, so the motherfucker had it coming.

"Yeah, I get that I need to be more concerned about school," the teenager said. "But it's not like I'm going around jumping on people and squatting and what have you. Up to who knows what."

"Who are you talking about, Doug?" his mother asked.

"The wannabe Punisher of the burbs, who you and the other barbecuers are all hyped on."

His mother frowned at him, but his father understood.

"You know, your man 'Just call me Connie' O'Conner,'" he mimicked.

Steve Brill asked, "He did that to the one I saw driving off?"

"Hell, yeah," the younger Brill said confidently.

"And the one you say he fought, who's that again?"

Doug Brill squinted at his mother but knew he couldn't

weasel out of answering. "His name is Cody. He's a friend of Mattie's."

"And what's he do that he got into it with O'Conner?" Steve Brill asked.

Perfect. "Why don't you ask him, Pop?"

Mother and father exchanged a look.

Steve Brill briefly considered knocking on O'Conner's door but punted that idea in favor of informally talking it over with two members of the Willow Ridge Home Owners' Association.

"Far as I'm concerned, Connie is a positive addition to our humble subdivision." Stan Yamashira spread his hands wide and then dropped them flat on the tabletop. "If he did pimp slap this Cody, I'm sure he had it coming, just like that motorcycle gang member."

"Pimp slap?" the gray-bearded Don Spottiswood repeated. "Watching all those episodes of *The Wire* back-to-back on DVD is having an effect on you, Stan."

The three men sitting around Spottiswood's patio table chuckled.

The elderly man made a dismissive wave of his hand. "Aw, you know what I mean. Somebody has to step up to these punks if we want order restored."

"That's just it, Stan," Brill interjected. "This is not the Wild West. We pay our taxes."

"And we're not getting adequate services in return," Spottiswood said. "Headlines yesterday were about another round of cuts coming down from Sacramento."

"Isn't that what your Tea Party buddies want, Don?" Yamashira cracked. "Take away my Social Security, let the old folks and Section Eighters die off, and then strangle the government baby in the bathtub?"

Brill chuckled. "Jesus, Stan, you gotta stop watching Rachel Maddow so much, too." He went on, "So you two see O'Conner as the unofficial sheriff of our bucolic little hamlet? Our very own strongman?"

"That's a bit much, Steve," Spottiswood remarked.

"Not necessarily, Don. He's obviously a man used to dealing with problems in an overt fashion."

"He doesn't go overboard," Yamashira said. "Wasn't it your beloved Ronald Reagan who said, 'Peace through strength,' Don?"

"Something like that," Spottiswood admitted. "We know from Blanche that O'Conner is a squatter. It would be easy to get the bank to turn up the heat and send a deputy over there to have him removed," he added. "But I have to say, since the incident with the Vandal Viking, there's been renewed interest in the association." He picked up his glass of lemonade. "Some have even renewed their dues." He sipped.

"So what does that mean?" Brill asked.

"He's good for morale, Steve. Look, I'm not for rampant vigilantism, but I'm for people dealing with a problem when the bureaucracy can't or won't. As far as I can tell, O'Conner isn't involved in white slavery or luring underage girls into his clutches." He grinned. "Far from it, considering it seems he and Gwen are an item."

He continued, "I don't know anything about this Cody he whipped up on, but I have heard some tales about that great-niece of Lori Stiglez, and they're not something I'd put on the brochure advertising the Ridge's finer points."

Brill made a mental note to ask Spottiswood what he'd heard about the young woman. He said, "You gotta figure O'Conner stopped here because he understood a bunch of would-be suburbanites and retirees wouldn't stand up to him. Let him do what he wants."

"But he's the one standing up to the bullies," Yamashira pointed out.

"For now," Brill countered. "But a guy like O'Conner, a guy who's obviously been on the other side of the law, what's he really want here?"

"A quiet, safe place to live, like the rest of us," Yamashira offered.

"Steve's got a point, Stan," Spottiswood said. "He must be up to something. Why did he come here? Is he on the run, laying low?"

Yamashira said, "Isn't it enough that he's here?"

There were several silent moments.

"So what do we want to do?" Brill asked.

"Stan, you're his friend," Spottiswood began. "You can keep tabs on him."

"I look like Mata Hari to you?" Yamashira swayed a little in his seat, like he was doing an exotic dance. "I'm supposed to put the vamp on him and get him to spill his secrets?"

"I'm sure O'Conner is into older, wrinkled Asian men," Brill observed dryly.

Yamashira shook his head. "You two are hilarious. Martin and Lewis you are."

"We're just saying keep your ears open," Brill said. "Who knows what he might let slip talking to you? You could invite him out to lunch or something."

"Uh-huh. I'm sure Connie's got nothing better to do than watch me get the senior special at Carrows. Nothing better than us slurping spaghetti together."

"Precisely," Spottiswood commented.

"Shit," Yamashira said.

Brill laughed and clapped the old man on his arm. "Now you're getting with the program."

"So where are we at with Mr. O'Conner?" Spottiswood asked.

Yamashira and Brill glanced at one another and then at the head of the home owners' association.

Yamashira then said, "I guess we keep an eye on him. What else are we supposed to do? If it came to it, yeah, we could call the bank on him, but even then, it wouldn't be like the next day they'd get the sheriff to send a deputy out. More than likely they'd send some bank functionary to check, and Connie would know."

"You saying he'd retaliate?" Spottiswood ventured.

"I'm saying he'd be warned and would clear out in a heartbeat." Yamashira waved a hand at Brill. "That's what you want, isn't it, Steve?"

"But you think he's an asset?" Brill said.

"As far as I'm concerned, he hasn't been a liability," Yamashira responded.

"Okay, well," Spottiswood declared, "to the best of our abilities, we mark O'Conner's doings. But it's not like he's the only concern we have here in the Ridge."

"Not by a long shot," Brill agreed.

The three men stood and shook hands all around. Brill and Yamashira left, and Spottiswood remained on his patio. He looked out on the pH-balanced blue-green water of his pool in his backyard. The pool was in the shape of a lake, with irregular edges all around. Like something you'd see at some star's home profiled on *Entertainment Tonight*, Spottiswood reflected proudly. God bless those enzymes, he avowed silently.

Chapter Eight

O'Conner looked for a parking space near the Bleechwood Recycling concern, but there were cars and pickup trucks double-parked near the entrance, as well as various shopping carts spilling over with large garbage bags bulging with plastic and glass bottles and aluminum cans. He found a spot two blocks away and walked back. In the near distance was the Vincent Thomas Bridge, partially visible though the morning marine layer.

"Whatchu saying, hombre? That can't be right. I had me some real metal. Motherfuckin' computers and shit."

"The count is the count, Andre. How many times we been through this?" The recycling center employee was a medium-size, sturdily built individual with a goatee. A snap brim straw hat was pushed back on his clean-shaven head.

The man who felt he'd been shortchanged had on two mismatched shoes and pants too large for his thin frame. He had three shopping carts linked together by bungee cords and loops of twine.

O'Conner stepped past them on the overflowing lot. Two

other employees were hunched over, rapidly separating the recyclable material into massive piles of plastic, glass, and aluminum. Given the general cacophony of the place, no one paid attention to him as he wound his way around a glass-crushing machine to the rear. There he saw a large flatbed truck stacked with bins of crushed glass pieces leaving with a load for a bottling facility. Two unhitched truck trailers were also stationed in the area, one of them open, exposing the mass of plastic bottles inside.

"No, no, take it to Luna, not Mackintosh. Fuck that bandit," a wiry woman with stringy strawberry blond hair was saying into a cell phone. She stood near a makeshift desk, essentially a square of plywood atop a wooden box on a steel drum. "Damn. Look what done dredged his way out of the pit," she said in a hoarse voice upon seeing O'Conner.

"How's it hangin', Maeline?"

"Low, son, low." She laughed and gave O'Conner a brief hug after he stepped over. She noted his hands and the cuts on his neck. "What meat grinder did you fall through?"

"A story for another time."

"Heard about Rucka. Damn shame."

O'Conner said flatly, "Yeah, that was fucked up, but what you gonna do?"

"Ain't that right."

"You still up on the comings and goings of your old partners?"

"Hell no," she said, "and don't want to know. I haven't even been on a hog for seven, eight years."

"This is about a youngster. Goes by Inga. Can't be too many chicks using that handle."

Maeline Karlson had turned to talk to one of the men who'd been doing the sorting, then to O'Conner again. "That would be Brody and Sheila's kid, sounds like. Wild like her mother."

"Sheila . . ." O'Conner frowned. "The one who put the knife in the head of that boyfriend with the false leg?"

"Uh-huh."

"They around these days?"

"The old man's doing a bid in Mule Creek, and as for Sheila, I don't know and won't be finding out."

"I understand. What about this H she hangs with? He's a captain?"

"Miserable fuck is what he is," she offered. "Holbrook's his name, and he and Inga were tight . . . are tight. I don't really know."

"So you do keep in touch."

She showed nicotine-stained, uneven teeth. "I know enough to not be renewing acquaintances for you or any other goddamn body. But I'll give you this for free, slugger. H is unstable and is tolerated only because his brother took a shiv for Long Slim in the joint."

"Always a pleasure, Mae."

She winked at him. "Sure it is, Robespierre. Come back when you want to crack a bottle."

O'Conner gave her a mini-salute and left as she answered a call on her cell phone. Back in his station wagon he made two more stops and a phone call, eventually rolling past a set of old-fashioned courtyard apartment units in Santa Ana, in Orange County. He was on West 3rd, just past a cross street called Bristol. This particular barrio was unfamiliar to O'Conner. He knew there were parts of this town called French Park and Floral

Park, but that wasn't where he was now. Where he was now was considered the barrio.

He parked, and when he came to the closed gate fronting the courtyard, he didn't have to wait long, as a squat, muscular middle-aged woman came out of an apartment. She wore khakis and a heavy cotton shirt and had a backpack in place. She smiled at him as he pretended to have walked up just as she exited. They nodded cordially at each other as he went down a cracked cement walkway. He passed a child's plastic Hot Wheels tricycle lying on its side along the way.

The number he was looking for was around to the left, past the corner. A brown cat streaked with white was curled on the steps of an apartment where the inner door was open. Through a screen door with a dry-rotted wood frame came a *norteño* rap song. He wasn't entirely sure, but it sounded to O'Conner like it was a *narcocorrido,* a ballad about the attributes of a drug lord.

There was no screen on the door he sought, which was next to this one, and he knocked lightly with the knuckle of his index finger.

"Yeah," a gruff voice said from within.

"It's me," O'Conner said.

"The hell?"

The door opened on an older man. He looked to be in his mid- to late sixties and had bandy legs in a pair of worn jeans and sinewy arms sticking out of a loose black T-shirt. There was a scar that started on the back of the man's left hand and traveled a jagged course up to about midway on his forearm.

"Son of a bitch," the older man said, appraising his visitor. "Get on in here, I guess."

He stepped aside to reveal a front room with the

kind of elliptical shag rug usually found in a bathroom and pieces of secondhand furniture about. There was a compact CD/radio unit on a knickknack shelf, though no TV was visible. Several nonfiction books were stacked on a side table, under a lamp attached to the wall. Underneath the table was a toolbox. There were the sounds and smells of meat cooking in a small, sunlit kitchen.

"Take a load off. I'll be right there." He returned to the kitchen.

O'Conner glanced around and took a seat in a low-slung chair near the front window. The Venetian blinds were slanted open, the afternoon light washing across the dark-stained floorboards, some of them warped.

"What the hell brings you this way?" the man said from the kitchen.

"Just passing through. Figured I better see if you were still breathing."

That earned a harsh, quick laugh. "As you can see, I'm living like a sultan."

"You were never much for airs, Ben."

Ben Reynolds laughed again, and O'Conner could hear him taking the pan off the stove and running water in it, as the grease in it sizzled and crackled. Presently, he came out of the kitchen with a small plate upon which a paper towel absorbed excess grease from the sausage patties on it.

He came over to O'Conner, holding the plate out. "Dig in."

"I'm fine."

Reynolds lifted a shoulder and sat down in another chair, putting the plate on an upended plastic milk crate next to it. There was no couch or coffee table. He picked up a sausage with his fingers and took a bite, chewing thoroughly. "What you got going?"

"Not sure exactly. Trying to figure out the lay of the land."

"A score?"

"It's not that exactly." He filled him in on his current activities.

"Hmmm," Reynolds mused. "Sounds like there's some potential, this Mas Trece angle. But I hear some indecisiveness in the way you've laid this out."

"May be a function of age."

Reynolds had another sausage, wiping at the corner of his mouth with his finger. "Worried this might be your future?" He smiled broadly.

"Being upright is enough of a goal, isn't it?"

"Not if your pockets are empty," Reynolds said without rancor. "You say this chick you're squiring has got some scratch?"

"I doubt I'd get much knocking over one of her body and fender outfits."

"See, that's not where I'm going. I'm wondering if she has larcenous tendencies. You haven't tested her," he observed.

"Like how?"

"Like challenging her. But you're so sweet on her, you don't want to damage her feelings. That it?"

"All women aren't like my mother," O'Conner said.

"My point, Buster Brown. This dame is a civilian. She's not one of us."

"Meaning she's a mark?"

"Meaning she's an asset at least." He was about to pick up the third of the four sausages on the plate but paused. "Unless you're serious about her."

"I'm not sure."

The other man sat back, holding his hands out wide. "Shit, you know I'm no good at this Old Man of the Mountain bit. What am I supposed to tell you? What kind of advice I got living in this place?"

"You're too humble. That's your problem." He suspected Reynolds kept more than one abode, either in Santa Ana or other parts of Orange County.

"Uh-huh." He ate his sausage with intensity. "Since you're being all nostalgic and such, bothering to hunt me down, let it not be said I'm ungrateful. As you can probably guess, it's not like I've got irons in the fire."

"It's no big deal."

"Yes and no." Reynolds pointed at him. "Let's go hit a few. Get our minds right." He hunched a shoulder again. "I'd suggest doing nine holes, just like the old ladies, but that sounds like it might be too strenuous for you in your current delicate state. What about a driving range?"

O'Conner chuckled. "Okay, yeah, that sounds about my speed."

They took O'Conner's car to a range in Los Alamitos. Los Al, as the natives called it, was a mix of working-class folks, service personnel stationed at the Joint Forces Training Base, the largest civilian employer in town, and residents at an enclave called Rossmoor. O'Conner wondered if the upscale community was everything Willow Ridge aspired to be. He could see the emerald lawns leading up to big homes with big roofs on tree-lined streets. He couldn't imagine living there.

Reynolds swung his driver and sent the golf ball flush off the tee with a loud smack. His ball arched up nicely and came down against the far netting. A satisfied smile materialized on his lined face.

"You've been practicing," his companion said, stepping into position, adjusting his feet.

"Jealousy ill becomes you."

"Sheeet." O'Conner swung, but he could tell the way his shoulders felt that his follow-through was off. The ball went up, but it had an anemic arch compared to Reynolds's.

"It'll come back," the older man assured him.

Down the line from them a barrel-chested soldier in fatigues teed off. He cursed audibly as his ball went off course. If they'd been on the green, his shot would have gone into the bunker.

"Shooting them M4s ain't the same as the finesse this game calls for," Reynolds opined.

"Just as long as you or him don't start having a post-traumatic flashback and go after us, swinging drivers around," O'Conner replied.

Reynolds lined up his next shot and swung. It was as if he were an automaton and had been programmed to demonstrate how to tee off. "All day long, youngster, all day long," he crowed.

They practiced their swings for another forty minutes, then went to a local eatery Reynolds suggested, called Famoso.

"How you doing, Darla?" Reynolds said to the waitress when she brought plastic tumblers of water to their table.

"How's it going, Benny?" She was in her late forties or early fifties, a fading beauty with bleached blond locks but still an attractive, poised woman.

"This is, ah, Connie," Reynolds said, introducing his companion as if his name were unfamiliar with him. "I haven't seen him in a while."

"Good to meet you," she said.

"Same," O'Conner responded, tipping his glass of water in her direction as he picked it up.

"What's it gonna be today, gents?"

"Give me a slice of cheese and pepperoni and one sausage, will you?" Reynolds answered.

"Your usual beer?"

"Yeah. Thanks."

"And you?" She put her blue-green eyes on O'Conner.

"Sausage and peppers sandwich and an MGD."

"Okay." She finished writing on her pad, then said to Reynolds in a lowered voice, "We good for Thursday, sport?"

"Don't you know we are?"

She twisted her lips in an odd smile and walked away to place their orders.

"Seems like a nice lady," O'Conner offered.

"She is. She has this here part-time job and does some—what do you call it?—personal assistant, gal Friday hand-holding for this aerospace widow down there in Huntington Beach."

"That a fact?"

"Indeed."

She returned with their bottled beers and placed them on the table. She playfully pinched Reynolds's arm as she turned and left again.

"You two are right friendly," O'Conner said.

"We appreciate each other."

"Huntington Beach, huh?"

Reynolds had been about to sip his beer, but he stopped and looked at O'Conner. "What do you mean?"

"I mean, you and me hanging out, hitting some balls, having a couple of beers."

"You sound suspicious."

"Wary," O'Conner amended.

"That's a good word," Reynolds said, nodding his head and sampling his beer. "Suggests what could be several states of mind."

"What exactly are you and your blond bombshell lining up? And how is it you see my role?"

Reynolds pointed with the top of the beer bottle at the wall, indicating what was beyond it. "You seem to be in need of an activity to get you jump-started, give you a sense of purpose and direction."

"That's so kind of you."

"I do try."

"What sort of activity? Something nocturnal in nature or bold in the daylight hours?"

"Let me see how things align after Thursday, skippy."

"Okay by me."

Reynolds grinned broadly at him. Soon their food arrived, and they ate, discussing upcoming trades in the NBA draft. After their lunch O'Conner took Reynolds back home, then got back on the freeway to Hemet. The older man hadn't added information on what he was lining up—with the aid of the woman named Darla, it seemed—but O'Conner knew he would if the job was going forward. Was that the real reason he'd made the effort to look him up and then gone to see him? O'Conner questioned himself.

For some time he had known generally where to find Reynolds, and it wasn't as if—since he was originally on his way to the Bay Area—he'd intended to look him up. So what was different now? Had he sought Reynolds out because he figured he would be planning some scheme or another and he needed the tune-up? Had his escapade with Gwen Gardner got him hungry for real action? Was this a reaction to the fact that he was merely spinning his wheels in Willow Ridge? What the hell was it about the place that kept him there? Damn, it couldn't be the woman. It better not be, O'Conner warned himself as he drove home.

Home. Je-zus, that place must be getting to him.

Gwen Gardner studied her reflection in the bedroom mirror. She intentionally used harsh lighting so as not to hide her defects and age lines. So far, unlike her friends, such as Blanche Allen, she'd resisted the Botox way. She prided herself on a regime of exercise and eating right. She ate meat no more than twice a week, and even then it was usually fish or chicken, beef maybe three times a month, and pork only at a Thanksgiving or Christmas dinner—and then only one slice of smoked ham. Still, it was a treat she found herself lusting after a week or two before such events.

How sad was it, she wondered, touching a line on the side of her mouth with her fingertip, that she had come to a point in her life when a slice of ham was an object of desire.

"I'm going out," said her daughter, Harley Lynn, leaning into the bedroom.

"Where you off to?"

"See some friends. You know, Linda, Michelle."

"I should pry more, but to what end?"

Her pretty daughter batted her heavily mascaraed eyes and left in her hip-hugger jeans. Harley Lynn had called two days ago to ask if she could come out and stay for a few days, and her mother, of course, had said yes. It had occurred to her that this was the last few days of the month. Could it be that the light of her life was skipping out on a landlord she owed rent to in L.A.? She knew she'd lost her roommate a couple of months ago, another vivacious young thing looking to break into show business. She'd moved back to Trenton to take a part-time teaching job in a private school.

Gardner went into the kitchen and poured herself a modest glass of pinot grigio and then called O'Conner.

"Busy putting your scooter back together?" she kidded him.

"I'm so busy, I don't know if I'm coming or going."

"That right?"

"Uh-huh."

She wasn't too surprised later when she entered his house to see the cuts on his hands and face. She touched the scarring, eliciting a slight quickening in the act of doing so. She liked it that O'Conner was unlike other men she'd known.

"What exactly are you up to in our quiet little hamlet, Mr. O'Conner?"

"It's not like I'm going out of my way looking for trouble." They sat close to one another in the living room, on the couch she'd bought him. Gardner couldn't stand the threadbare one he'd had.

"But I bet you've caused some in your time."

"No matter how I answer that, it would just dig a deeper hole, wouldn't it?"

She wondered if he'd done time, but she didn't ask him. "You owe me nothing, Connie. I enjoy your company." She tucked her legs under her, putting her head on his chest.

He put his hand around her, and they stayed quiet with each other for several moments.

"My daughter's staying with me for a few days," she finally said.

"And?" he said, noting her wary tone.

"And I want you to meet her."

"Scare her straight, you mean." He recalled her telling him she'd been friends with Chanchin Saladago.

She chuckled. "Actually, that was not my intention at all. She's pretty mature for her age, and, well, it's not like I can keep her on a leash. My parents tried that with me."

"Leading to you running wild?"

She looked up at him. "That's right, baby." She kissed him.

As they got intimate, O'Conner decided Harley Lynn might be a source of information on the would-be Al Capone's activities, though he doubted he could be subtle enough to get anything useful out of her. Still, maybe Mom could be the one to do the probing.

Chapter Nine

The next morning he had renewed interest in taking up watch again on the Mas Trece house, to see if Gwen Gardner's daughter might stop by. What if she did, and what if she was there to renew her acquaintance and maybe get a free hit? Not like he had X-ray eyes to see into their house turned lab, but he'd been around enough tweakers to tell if she came rolling out of there acting in a certain way.

Normally, what people did to themselves was what they did to themselves, and he didn't give a shit as long as they were out of his way. But if she was a user, how could he not tell Gardner? What the hell was happening to him that he was even entertaining such notions?

"I hope you like your eggs scrambled, since that's pretty much the only way I know how to make 'em," he announced.

"That's fine." She came up behind him and put her arms around his midsection, her fingers kneading the compact muscles of his stomach and sides through his athletic tee. "You feel good," she breathed.

"What kind of example are you setting for your

daughter?" he said, lowering slices of sourdough into the toaster.

"For all I know, she didn't come home, either, though we did text each other last night." She didn't divulge if she'd mentioned O'Conner or how she might have referred to him.

He finished preparing the eggs, and they sat down to a breakfast of that, toast, and lox at the island in the kitchen.

"What are you up to today?" she asked as she swallowed more coffee.

"Research."

"Yeah?"

"Fact," he said, forking in food, "you might be able to help me."

"How's that, darling?"

"I'm trying to find a young lady by the name of Inga. Probably goes by Inga Brody." He described her, stating, "Has a kind of white highlights in her dark hair, like what's-her-name in *Archie* comics."

"Veronica, and it surprises me you'd know that. We gonna have a threesome?"

It was hard to read her expression, but he kept on track. "She might have a record. She's one of those Vandal Vikings."

She raised an eyebrow. "And you figure me for a one-time biker chick?"

"What I was thinking was this would be a way for your boy Mitch to get back in your good graces."

"You don't think he's one of them?"

"No. But I'd wager a steak dinner he might know of someone who knows of someone. There's a Viking chapter active in the Chino area, and from what you told me about him on our drive out there, him doing some street racing and what have you, it's not too far-fetched to imagine he might have found himself in a watering hole with some dude who knows them."

She chewed, eyeing him. "How do you know there's a Viking club around there?"

"I know a lot of things, Gwen." He speared a piece of lox with his fork.

"What kind of story would I give him for asking about this Inga?"

"She applied for a manager job at one of your other facilities, and you'd heard this rumor about her."

She ate more, running this over in her mind. "And who is this chick?"

"She may be up to mischief."

"Mischief."

"Um-hmm."

"Around here?"

"'Fraid so."

"What are you planning, Connie?"

"Isn't it enough to want a safe environment for the residents of Willow Ridge?"

"I'll ask it another way. What is it that you know?"

He told her he had suspicions that the Vandal Vikings might be looking to move drugs through the subdivision.

"I don't get it."

"What better place to have a stash house than in a bucolic setting such as this?"

"You must be squinting when you look around here, Lone Ranger. Another house just went belly up on this block."

"Then it's time to shore up our defenses," he responded.

She regarded him, then said, "This some kind of test? You want to see if you can scare me off?"

They were sitting on stools, and he pulled hers closer by one of its legs. "What if it's my way of seducing you?" he asked, his face nearing Gardner's.

She looked at him steadily with a crooked smile on her unmade lips. "Maybe I don't scare easy."

"Good." They smacked lips together, then finished their breakfast.

Afterward, she left for her exercise class and O'Conner got a call from the motorcycle shop that his engine was ready. The cylinders had been resleeved, the head milled, and new valves installed. He told the mechanic he'd be right over to pay for the work and pick up the engine.

As he stepped outside, Stan Yamashira was coming toward him along the sidewalk. The older man raised a hand in greeting. "I guess I caught you at a bad time," he said.

What would a suburbanite say? "No, come on. I'm just running an errand."

"Sure, okay." He got in the station wagon on the passenger side, and O'Conner backed the car out of the driveway. O'Conner told him then where they were heading.

Yamashira asked, "You looking to hit the road again?"

"Not unless you're running me out of town, Sheriff," O'Conner replied. A beat then, "Why? What's up?" He had an idea, but better to have the other man spell it out.

"There's been rumblings from some quarters about your latest escapade." He'd registered the condition of O'Conner's hands and face. "Though it has been noted, there hasn't been any loud partying at Mattie's house since then. Rather, her great-aunt's house."

O'Conner absorbed this. "How come you're telling

me this, Stan? Why not blow the whistle on me and force me out?"

The retiree hunched a shoulder as he looked out the side window. "There's degrees of ambivalence about that. It's not like there'd be a rush from the authorities to move on you." He looked over at him. "And it's not like we haven't tried before to remove the, you know, undesirables."

"Me, undesirable? Heavens," O'Conner intoned flatly.

Yamashira gestured, continuing. "As I said, the association is undecided when it comes to you." His eyes held and lost a mischievous glint. "Do you know the term adverse possession?"

"Sounds like bogarding to me."

Yamashira frowned. "I don't quite get you young folks and your slang, but yes, it means possession of real estate that is actual, open, notorious, and so on."

Now O'Conner frowned. "I thought you used to work for Water and Power, Stan."

"I did, but when you get old, you have a lot of time to read up on a variety of subjects. I don't spend all my days down at the lake or watching *The Price Is Right*." He quickly amended, "Well, not every damn day." Both chuckled, and the older man added, "Plus, I pick up on this property stuff from Blanche Allen."

It took O'Conner a moment to recall she was the Realtor. "You do, do you?"

Yamashira either chose to ignore his double meaning or simply didn't perceive it. "What I'm saying is, I happen to know the house you're currently in is in a kind of limbo state. It's been foreclosed on, but seems Patterson, even though he was behind by months, hadn't been sent papers to show up in court."

O'Conner knew from Gardner that Arthur Patterson,

fleet sales manager at Garwin Motors, had occupied the house before him. "You know this because your girl is selling the house?"

"My girl?"

"Blanche."

"Aw, cut it out, Connie. She's no kid, but she's young enough to be a daughter, and you saw her at the barbecue with her girlfriend, Didi. That one is the jealous type."

"Kind of heavy, but in a shapely way?"

"Yep, that's Blanche. She used to be married to an attorney, Martin Hurwitz. Fact, I believe she used to be a mouthpiece, too."

"But she discovered she liked houses and women better."

"She's a switch-hitter but is currently batting for the other team."

O'Conner grinned at the old man. "You get that from watching *The View*, something like that?"

"I couldn't say."

They drove along some. Then O'Conner asked, "Is it Blanche who's selling the Larkspur house?" The FOR SALE sign he'd removed from the lawn had the name of the realty company on it and a phone number but no name.

"No, not her."

"But she'd looked into its status."

Yamashira looked over at him. "Checking up on the competition, I guess."

"And you asked her about what was happening with it on my behalf?"

Yamashira hunched a shoulder again. "Like I said, I try to keep myself busy."

"This adverse possession means if for a period of time I occupy the house and no one comes along to claim it or the deputies rap their batons on the door to throw me out, I could claim this right when the owner does show up?"

"If there's an owner."

"And if I wanted to stay."

"There is that."

They got to the motorcycle shop in San Jacinto, not far from a junior college. The two entered, and O'Conner waited in a short line at the parts counter. Stan Yamashira wandered about, looking at various helmets and accoutrements for the motorcycle enthusiast. He stopped at a bulletin board to read the flyers posted on it. There was one announcing the upcoming annual Kruisin' for Kids event. This was a public relations program put on by bikers cognizant of their less than savory image among the public. As with a 10K run for charity, a rider got sponsors to donate toys and gift certificates for underprivileged children. Though in this case, the cruising was more of a parade and rally.

O'Conner paid for the work and, with the help of two employees, loaded the rebuilt engine block and the twin heads in the back of the station wagon.

"You're not expecting me to help you get that out when we get back, are you?" Yamashira asked seriously when they got going again.

"You look pretty buffed to me," O'Conner cracked.

"Ha-ha. Everybody figures I'm their straight man," he said, referring to the joking Brill and Spottiswood had aimed at him. Yet here he was, palling around with O'Conner, as they'd requested.

"Assembled, the engine's a little more than five hundred pounds. I've got one of those circular drum dollies and a ramp I rigged up. That's how I wrestled the engine into the car and out here to begin with."

"Once you get your bike back together, then what?" Yamashira asked.

"Not sure," O'Conner answered. Better to have it ready, he concluded.

The old man didn't say anything to that.

Gwen Gardner's exercise class was led by a woman who called herself by one name, like Cher and Madonna. She went by Barclay. She was in her midthirties and was willowy, though she had sizable breasts for a woman with a sinewy frame. Playing to the cliché, she talked to her classes about the need to eat the proper amount of fruits, raw vegetables, and legumes, including lentils and certain kinds of peanuts. Countering this sort of proselytizing, she would also mention that a well-prepared turkey burger now and then couldn't hurt, either.

Barclay's regime was a mixed bag that included Tae Bo, hot house yoga, and tai chi. At the moment a sweating Gardner, along with the other participants, was on her back in the corpse pose. She was bringing her knee to her chest, relaxed but estimating where matters were going with O'Conner. Rather, how far would she let things go with him? She didn't feel he was conning her in any way, romancing her to swindle her out of her money. She smiled at the image of O'Conner as an aging gigolo. Legs lowered again, she bent her upper body up and, arms stretched out, grasped her toes with her fingers. O'Conner was certainly not conventionally handsome. His face wasn't unpleasant, and it didn't hurt that he had a solid bod for a man his age. But he was no graying pretty boy. There were etched lines at the corners of his eyes—eyes she just knew had seen things that would probably give her nightmares.

No, this new man in her life wasn't like other men she'd known. Maybe one or two of them might have cheated on their taxes, but she had the very distinct impression O'Conner was the sort who might dangle a chap who had tried to cheat him by his ankles out a window. He was thrilling and unpredictable. But was he too out there for her? What was he up to, looking into the Vandal Vikings? The good of Willow Ridge? Muscle in on their action?

Back on her feet, bending over, grabbing her upraised leg behind her, she certainly did not envision becoming O'Conner's gun moll, or whatever the modern term was. Though she didn't imagine he saw her playing such a role—or so she liked to believe. Begging the question, she reflected, just where did the closemouthed Mr. O'Conner see their relationship going? Was that even on his mind? Was he killing time until his next big score, and why wasn't she more worried if he really was up to something of a criminal nature?

Barclay started the tae kwon do phase of the class, and they all got into their modified martial arts stances. They began the rhythmic movements of their arms and hands. The design of this particular exercise regime wasn't about self-defense but about conditioning. As Gardner's heart rate and sweating increased, she considered she might want to look into some supplemental training of the offensive variety. If she was going to be a gun moll, she better be good at it.

Returning to Willow Ridge, O'Conner and Yamashira passed by a nondescript apartment building among several other like structures. This particular dingbat-style building was called the Mayfair.

In the front room of apartment 14, Chanchin Saladago and Harley Lynn Demara were fencing with two wooden back scratchers. He was nude and sweaty, and she was in her Victoria's Secret women's lace boxers. Both were nicely buzzed on some primo weed called Purple Passion, and T.I.'s "Get Back Up" played on a CD unit on a shelf.

"Watch out now, baby girl," Saladago said, waving his back scratcher at her as he weaved his torso from side to side.

"Watch out, son. I'm the Queen of Swords." She thrust the claw of her back scratcher forward, lightly dusting Saladago's chest.

"The who?" he asked, the whites of his eyes red and glazed. He was mesmerized by his fencing partner's pert breasts.

"You don't remember that show from when we was youngstas?" She drifted back into affecting what she perceived to be street slang when she was around Saladago. It helped to be high, too.

Saladago seemed to go out of himself, then return with the sought data. "Oh yeah, that fine-ass heina with them hips. She was like, like a female Zorro or something."

"Big hips, huh?" She put her hands on her sides and did a bit of a vamp. "What's wrong with these?"

He hooked his wooden claw in the waistband of her underwear and tugged. "Ain't nothing wrong with 'em," he said, leering. "I especially like it when I got my head buried between them."

She smiled and got her legs around him, grinding against Saladago as he held her close. He had his hand on her upturned backside as they kissed and tongued.

"You miss me, baby?" he breathed.

She was gnawing on his tattooed neck. "I missed your two-toned, crooked dick in me, vato."

"You're just saying that because you know how heated that makes me."

She bit down hard. "Show me."

There on the rug he did his best to do so. Afterward, they transferred to the couch, sprawled about, both sipping from the same can of malt liquor.

Demara asked, "So there's no problem with me handling the shit, right?"

Saladago had a beatific shine on his face. He was blitzed out from the marijuana and the sex. Life was so goddamn good. "Yeah, baby girl, I can hook your little Hollywood wannabes up."

She had some brew. "It's more than that, Chanchin. A few of those skanks I'll see at the party play in bigger pools, feel me?"

He snickered. "You're funny, trying to talk all down and shit."

Annoyed, she playfully hit him in the chest. "This is not about me just trying to look cool to these fools. This is about how I get my career on. Shit."

"Yeah, I got it, Harley Lynn. I got it."

Her initial plan was that she would supply some blow and X to the showbiz types. She figured meth was out, since it aged you, causing your gums to recede and messed up your teeth, and that wouldn't do with the in-front-of-the-camera crowd. But upon further research, which meant asking a couple of druggie friends, she determined she could offer crystal meth, too.

In her sights was a cutter, a film and TV editor named Reo Culhane, who was on the low-budget, direct-to-DVD slasher-horror movie rung. Recently, he'd directed a couple of these efforts as well. He was going to be at

this party, and he liked Demara and his coke and meth.
She was looking to get a featured part in his first direc-
torial effort for the Syfy Channel, a wonder of CGI and
limited horizons called *Curse of the Flying Piranhas*.

Saladago's smartphone chimed, playing a few bars
from an old Kid Frost rap number. He picked it up and
answered.

"Yeah, yeah," he quipped, then listened. "I know, fool.
Who you tellin'? They all the time fuckin' with vatos on
that." After listening some more, he added, "Right . . .
You tell them we'll sit down with Yano and quell this
chisme. Right, right . . . I'm out." He severed the call and
tossed the instrument onto a counter.

"Goddamn farmers," he groused.

Demara knew his condescending reference was to La
Familia, the Mexican Mafia. "They all up in your business, baby boy?" The Mas Trece, like most Chicano and
Mexicano gangs in the Southland, had a monetary relationship with their so-called godfathers.

"They be, but Jimmy P is a lieutenant, so he has to
handle it."

Jimmy P was Jaime Prado, also known as Jimmy
Puppet. He was called that due to being peppered in the
leg when he was eleven by a clerk when he tried to boost
a computer printer. Jimmy Puppet didn't have a computer but had heard how valuable printers were. He was
running from the discount electronics store with the
device and got tripped up by the trailing cord. His pursuer got within range as he got up to flee again, and
blasted the juvenile. Since then he had had a peculiar
gait—his wounded leg lifting and descending in a way
that suggested the limb was being pulled by invisible
strings.

Afterward they lay there, content, his hand inside her

cute boxers, fingers rubbing her thick curls. Eventually he said, "Your mom's going around with that O'Conner dude?"

She nodded, saying, "Gonna meet him tomorrow night. She's fixing dinner."

"She tell you anything about him?"

"What do you mean? He's just some guy."

"No, he's not."

She regarded him through her narcotized state. "What do you mean?"

"There's talk about him all over the Ridge. He's not just some civilian. He pushed up on H, this whacked-out Vandal Viking, and didn't blink." Saladago didn't tell her about their confrontation in the backyard of the house O'Conner had taken over. He didn't like the way it made him look, and he wasn't going to appear weak or indecisive to this woman—or any woman or man, for that matter.

"Huh," she said. "What? Like, he's a retired cop, you mean?"

He slowly shook his head. "Aw, hell no. This motherfucka has been on the other side of that fence."

"So what's he doing in the Ridge?"

He stopped rubbing. "Right. What is he up to?"

She fixated on the question, then dismissed it, wiping a sheen of sweat off his chin.

"No, but wait." Hope, reaching for what little breath remained to her, "Your dad is going to read a toast to O Coop?"

She nodded. "Why not. Mama must have one too."

"Nuh, But's Doing there—"

"I'll tell you something about being—"

"What is happening? This isn't your girl?"

"No, but not—"

She laughed into them, into her relaxed smile. "What do you expect?

"There's a girl that I met over the ridge." He then just sort of shrug. He leaned to the ground, his face in his hands. "I got to get to that road." "And so go and try her dad over the corner of the book and at his house to either he, what over the little thing I heard was talked with luck, and because I have to turn to you well, or once, she to this company on my account or close. For that matter.

"Huh," she said. "Now." Like she'd started to not listen.

"Dan," she said to him. "As though impossible to let her hear it more, or the sound of her voice.

"So what's he doing in the house?"

He spoke, curious. "Well, what can she say?

"She has said her question, then placed her fingers without a word on his chin.

Chapter Ten

Gwen Gardner stood at the meat case of the Earth Harvest supermarket. Initially, she was going to roast a chicken, but she liked the way the grass-fed flanks of beef looked under the cool glass. She made a sound in her throat, surprised at how easily she was slipping back into the role of the happy homemaker. But her daughter would be around only for a few more days, and playing house with Connie was pleasant and adventurous, but he didn't seem like the settling-down type—maybe she wasn't any longer, either.

She chose her cut of marbled meat, deciding on making a roast. While she was in the produce section, selecting some red potatoes, she saw Blanche Allen having an argument with her girlfriend. What is her name again? Didi. But Didi what? Crawford. That's it.

"Relax, will you?" Blanche Allen was saying to the younger woman. Both were in jeans, Allen's the stretchy kind, which fit her heavier frame well.

"Don't tell me how to act," Crawford growled. The two stood among the piles of oranges and apples. "You think this is a fuckin' game, and it isn't, Blanche. This shit could backfire."

Allen looked over at Gardner, who'd put her potatoes in a plastic bag, smiling weakly. "Hey, Gwen."

"Blanche," Gardner responded, "Didi," she added, nodding briefly and turning her head to finding a tie for her bag.

"How about we talk about this at home and not entertain our neighbors with our trivial disputes, darling?" Allen smiled and touched the Maori tattoo encircling Crawford's forearm.

Her girlfriend suddenly seemed to realize they were in public, and her features softened. She put an arm around Allen and gave her a quick hug. Crawford then put a container of strawberries in her hand basket, and the two walked away. Gardner considered if this was a sign she shouldn't become complacent when it came to O'Conner. That put a smile on her face, a smile mirrored by her daughter's at dinner that evening.

"So what exactly is your first name?" Demara asked O'Conner at the table.

"Harley Lynn," her mother scolded playfully, enjoying a sip of wine and wanting to see if O'Conner squirmed.

She squinted her eyes at her mother, then looked back at O'Conner. "Well? You spending time with my mama, and what do we know about you?" She said it lightly, but there was a force of meaning behind the words. "You're already getting a reputation around here," she went on, indicating the cuts healing on his hands and face.

How he'd got them had been the topic of several versions of gossip in the subdivision, including one story alleging

O'Conner had had a run-in with a lawn-conscious, jealous husband.

"I'm just trying to fit in." He cut another piece of roast. "Have I mentioned how much I like this here supper you done fixed?" He gestured with the piece of meat speared on his fork.

"You have, kind sir," Gardner said.

"Harley Lynn," O'Conner began, "is there something in particular you want to know about me?" He looked directly at the young, pretty woman, who favored her mother in terms of her cheekbones and full mouth.

"Have you done time?"

"I can honestly say I haven't. But I have associated with some who have been locked up."

"Associated how?"

"Yeah?" Gardner piped in.

O'Conner displayed a tight smile. "I have had the occasion to be owed money from such individuals."

"That right?" the daughter said. "How would that be . . . Connie?"

"You mean, did I pull a heist with these individuals?" he stated bluntly.

Demara twisted her lips. "Like that."

He looked at the mother. "What if I said yes?"

"Yeah, Mom, what if he said he did?"

Gardner chewed and swallowed. "Was anybody hurt?"

"No, not the civilians."

"Then I say leave room for dessert and coffee." She stood and took her plate into the kitchen.

Gardner was at the head of the table, and O'Conner sat opposite the daughter. He sat back, holding his wineglass in one hand. "Since we're coming clean, Harley Lynn, what's the deal with you and Chanchin?"

"How do you mean?"

"You know damn well the Mas Trece aren't Jehovah's Witnesses."

"Chan is different."

"Is he now?" her mother said, returning from the kitchen. She carried a tray with cups, utensils, saucers, a full coffee carafe, and a peach cobbler she'd bought.

"Oh, we're not making this about me," Demara said testily. "What I do is my business. I'm a grown woman."

O'Conner made room for the tray, which Gardner placed on the table. She sat, pursing her mouth as she regarded her daughter. "Are they baking meth or cooking it, or however the hell you refer to what they do with it here in Willow Ridge, Harley Lynn?"

"How would I know?"

"I know he's not good for you," her mother replied. She pointed at O'Conner. "But he is for you?"

"He's not a drug dealer."

Her daughter got up and walked out of the dining room. "Later."

O'Conner had cleaned his steak knife and used that to cut into the cobbler. They both remained quiet as he served her and himself, while Gardner poured coffee for each of them. The front door opened and closed.

"I realize this might put you in an awkward situation, but please, whatever you're up to, make sure it doesn't suck my daughter down, too, Connie." She hadn't touched her dessert but drank slowly from her cup. "You might need to protect her despite herself."

"I will, Gwen. She's a pain in the ass, but I will."

She nodded curtly. After they cleared the table and put the dishes in the dishwasher, she straddled him as he sat on a dining room chair and they made love.

As they did so, she said, "Connie, I'm not fucking you to make you feel beholding."

"I know," he said hoarsely. He took hold of her backside and thrust himself deeper in her, causing both of them to shudder with pleasure.

Afterward, they sat in her study, on a plush couch, to watch a TV show Gardner followed on her flat-screen. She'd recorded it the day before. The program starred two female investigators in L.A. One was a werewolf plainclothes detective, partnered with a superstrong female android.

Crazy shit, O'Conner reflected as Gardner slept, her head on his thigh.

The following morning Mitch Frane, the manager of the Fix & Go in Chino Hills, got a call from Gwen Gardner.

"The inventory's going to be on track for this month, Gwen," he said after pleasantries.

"I had no doubts in that regard," she stated. "But I have a somewhat different request for you. Now, don't take this the wrong way, but I was wondering if you'd had some dealings with the Vandal Vikings."

"Motorcycles aren't really my thing," he said. "Or numbnuts like those Vikings, if I can be frank."

"I understand, Mitch. I do. Yet is it a stretch to consider you might know some people who know these types?"

"I'm not sure what you're getting at here."

She chuckled, and he couldn't tell if it was out of nervousness or contempt. "I'll just say it straight out, then. I'm looking for this biker babe named Inga. . . . Uh, Brody would probably be her last name." She relayed to him the description O'Conner had given her of the younger woman. "Obviously, I don't want you to put yourself in harm's way, but if it was possible for you to ask around some and not set off an alarm, I would be grateful." She added quickly, "Of course, I don't want you approaching her. Just if you could get an idea on where to find her, places she might hang out at, that sort of thing."

"This for your friend Connie? If you don't mind me asking."

"Not at all. And yes, it is for him."

"I'll see what I can do, Gwen."

"Thank you, Mitch."

"Right." Frane hung up the phone and for a moment stared at the calendar tacked on the wall near his desk. The image above the fold was of a tree-lined lane blanketed with rust-colored leaves. He stared at this for a moment more, then got up from his desk. Frane went back onto the shop floor, hands in his pockets.

In her kitchen Gwen Gardner clasped the flats of her hands together and bowed slightly, sitting on a stool. "I've done as you wished, my master."

O'Conner was pouring another cup of coffee. "Thank you kindly."

"What do you have planned for today?"

"Oh, I don't know," he hedged. "Probably work on my bike." Initially, he'd planned to scope out the Mas Trece house to see if her daughter showed up, but what good would that do him or her? It wasn't like he was going to go bang on their door and demand she leave with him. He wasn't her stepdad, and she was of age, at least chronologically. He knew what he'd promised Gardner, and he wasn't bullshitting her. But sometimes you had to let these strings unwind and see where they took you.

"Well, I've got a full day of my yoga class and taking a friend to lunch and a movie." She got off the stool.

"A male friend?"

She presented a lopsided grin. "That's the first time I've gotten a rise out of you."

"Not so," he said, then sipped.

"You know what I mean, Herman Cain. And no, it's Kim Schmitz. She and her husband divorced, and she's out of work. Laid off after eleven years as head of HR for Heyden Glenn."

"What the hell's that?"

"If you were the mother of a teenage girl, you'd know that Heyden Glenn is the shit when it comes to fashion and accessories for the stylish young woman." She pointed toward the north. "They used to have a store over here in the shopping center, but that one closed a couple of years ago, when the households started going belly up around here."

"Aren't the HR people the ones they need to tell the other poor suckers in a soft and gentle way they're being let go?"

"Until they outsourced the HR department to an outfit in Utah. Mormons work cheap and long, it seems."

O'Conner shook his head and had more coffee. "Is nothing sacred?"

As he was leaving Gardner's house, after they kissed and said their good-byes, a familiar lowered Impala rolled up, letting her daughter out. She walked past O'Conner without a word and on into the house. Chanchin Saladago was driving, and he briefly looked over at the other man, who looked back, then drove off.

Behind him, O'Conner could hear the raised voices of mother and daughter. He walked toward his house.

* * *

"I don't know, Kim." Gwen Gardner moved bits of her salad around with her fork, uncovering a piece of braised chicken.

"It makes sense," her friend said. "Blanche pools our money together into an LLC, and the entity buys property cheap. There's this area, naturally, and in Vegas you have beautiful homes going for half or even a quarter of what they once went for. Look at Detroit. The whole damn city is shrinking."

"I'm sure various people are doing this," Gardner commented, chewing slowly.

"My dickwad ex is," Schmitz added.

"Tim's in this investment Blanche is setting up?"

"Oh, hell, no. He's in one with some of his precious USC frat brothers."

Gardner put her fork down. "I'm certainly no financial whiz, but you better make sure you've examined the angles in this, and you're not just doing it to take a shot at Tim."

Schmitz snickered. "There's nothing wrong with showing Tim I can do well without him."

"This will tie up your savings."

"Blanche isn't snowing me, Gwen. She's told all of us it's a gamble, but in the long run we'll see returns."

"Maybe I'll chat her up about her enterprise," Gardner said.

"I'm a big girl, Gwen. I know what I'm doing. Stan Yamashira, he's no dummy. Jenny Warren and a few others we know in the Ridge are in on this."

"Look, I'm not saying different. Could be I want to get in on the action, too."

Her friend chewed and said, "Not going to have your man slap her around, are you?"

"What are people saying about him?"

Schmitz replied cheerily, "He's your rough boy, isn't he? And he looks like he can do it rough as you want it."

Gardner wagged a finger at Schmitz. "Behave."

"Come on, Gwen. Give. Who is Mr. O'Conner, and what are his intentions?"

"Intentions?"

"He doesn't talk much but clearly has a big swingin' dick he don't mind whipping about." She twitched her shoulders, as if chilled, and made a happy face.

"Girl, you got them men folk on the brain."

"I got their privates on my mind. I itch bad," she cracked. "You know Tim and I hardly touched each other those last six or seven months. Your Connie got a brother, younger . . . older? I'm not picky. Just, you know, a little wanton."

They both giggled, and Gardner was glad Schmitz didn't push it about what O'Conner was up to, as she had no idea. And after the round with her daughter at dinner and this morning, maybe she liked it that she didn't have a lot of details.

"Tell you what," Gardner said. "Let Blanche know I want to talk with her about this opportunity of hers, and I'll work on hooking you up with your own steely man."

"You better."

While the two continued talking and enjoying their lunch, O'Conner was driving along a residential street in a hilly area overlooking the water in Laguna Beach. Nothing was too far from the water in Laguna, he was discovering.

"That's her place," Darla Ballard said, pointing a

finger with a chipped purple nail. She was the waitress friend of Ben Reynolds.

She'd told O'Conner on the way out here, she'd gone to Laguna High School in town. "When you could still get a shack for a song around here. Shit," she'd lamented. "If only I had done that."

Ballard had finished smoking and was stubbing out an unfiltered Marlboro in the Sable's ashtray.

"Okay to stop in front, or is this restricted parking?" He didn't care about a ticket per se. He still didn't know what the pitch was that Ballard and Reynolds were up to, so he didn't want to leave a record of his being here.

"No, they need to have us peasants be able to come and go on their goddamn errands. Go ahead." She popped a peppermint in her mouth.

O'Conner noted there were several large homes being built or renovated in this part of the canyon of the one-time artists' colony. The design of the aerospace widow's house, to which she'd told him to drive, was reminiscent of the clean lines of Gregory Ain. It was constructed with flat surfaces and had subdued detailing that should have given off a sense of sterility but somehow suggested comfort and stability. Two gardeners were at work, trimming and cutting.

"Here you go," he said to Ballard, the station wagon idling at the curb.

"If you're not in a hurry, why don't you come in a minute and see the place?"

"Sure. Why not?" He figured this was her way for him to size up the interior.

He turned off the engine, and together they traipsed to the front door, a large portal of heavy wood. As they did so, it was opened from within on silent hinges by a chubby but pleasant-looking young Latina in attire similar to Ballard's—jeans and a loose top. Ballard, too, looked good in her getup, given her age, O'Conner approved—Ben that old dog.

"Lourdes, how goes it?" Ballard said. Incongruously, they knocked fists.

"Aw, you know," Lourdes MacShane replied. She took in O'Conner but didn't block the door, waiting for Ballard to explain who he was. She stepped away from the door, and they entered.

"I'll introduce you to Barbara," Ballard told him.

He nodded. "Yeah, okay."

There was a large modernist metal sculpture in the airy foyer. O'Conner couldn't make out much about it. It looked to him like it was some guy's idea of birds in flight, but for all he knew, the thing symbolized triumph and despair. The woman called MacShane had gone away, and as he and Ballard stepped past the sculpture, he could see other art pieces—framed paintings and photographs—along the walls.

"She's loaded," Ballard pointed out unnecessarily.

He followed her along a hallway. The wall facing out was composed of glass brick, letting in a diffused, warm light that showed the freckles on Ballard's arms. Down another hallway and on into a large room framed on two sides by sliding glass doors and with various big leaf plants about.

Ballard addressed the room's lone occupant. "Barbara, I want you to meet someone."

The widow wasn't what O'Conner was expecting. She was a tall, handsome woman, about his height, and she was wearing slippers. She'd risen from behind a sleek-looking desk, where she'd been reading over a sheaf of papers, mumbling as she did so, red pen held in a manicured hand. She was in a simple dress. An arresting jade and silver bracelet matched the jade and silver necklace she wore.

"This is Connie. He's kind of Ben's stepson once removed," Ballard said. "Or something like that. Ben used to date his mom before she died."

"How you doing?" O'Conner said, playing along with the light tone.

She and O'Conner shook hands. "Pleased to meet you."

"Same," he said.

She had expressive violet eyes. "You visiting Ben?"

"Kind of. I was passing through Southern California and hadn't seen him in a while." He knew not to go on, as Ballard hadn't briefed him on what to provide as a cover story.

"Well, I just wanted you two to meet. Connie gave me a ride to work. That sled of mine . . ." Ballard didn't finish. As far as O'Conner knew, her Camry was running fine.

"Maybe I'll see you again," the other woman said.

"Cool," he answered.

"I'll show him out, then get back to my research," Ballard said, putting a hand on O'Conner's upper arm.

Walking out, she asked him, "What do you think of her?"

"Okay, I guess. What am I supposed to think?"

"She's working on her memoirs."

"Good for her."

"There's a file folder I put under the front seat. Study up."

O'Conner frowned and was about to ask what the hell was going on, but MacShane appeared again, gesturing to Ballard to come with her.

"I'll see you," the waitress and part-time personal

assistant said to O'Conner. She went off with the maid, or whatever the other woman was around here, and he let himself out. The two gardeners continued their chore of taming the many swaths of greenery about the house. O'Conner didn't flinch as he passed one of them edging the lawn with his weed whacker.

Sure enough, under the station wagon's front passenger seat was a nine-by-twelve envelope, the clasp holding the flap down. O'Conner hadn't noticed Ballard putting the envelope there when she was in the car. Of course, it made sense that she wasn't a civilian, given that she and Ben Reynolds were going around together. He put the envelope on the seat and drove away.

Back at his house O'Conner sat in the backyard, before his empty gray pool, as he'd painted over the graffiti. He was on a swaybacked lawn chair, an open beer at his feet, and he read through the material amassed by Ballard and Reynolds on Barbara Giffords, née Ryderson. There was all the usual biographical information, including the fact that Giffords was a product of Surf City, USA, Huntington Beach, where she'd been a volleyball champ in high school and college. After graduating, she'd attended law school and passed the bar, trying mostly civil cases and a few criminal ones, but the law wasn't for her. She'd saved her volleyball endorsement monies and invested in an antiques shop, employing her mother, who had an eye for those sorts of items. Eventually, the two had four such shops in tony areas of the Southland.

Her deceased husband had been some twelve years her senior, one of those by-the-seat-of-your-pants types, O'Conner determined, reading through a photocopied article on him from an aviation magazine. He was a decorated helicopter pilot in Vietnam, and after that he was a commercial freight pilot with the Flying Tigers, which also did a good deal of military contracting work. The husband, Neal Giffords, was something of a tinkerer and had patented several devices used in the aircraft industry. When he passed from a rare blood disease, he'd long ago sold his Double Wing Aircraft Manufacturing concern to a large outfit for a healthy profit.

O'Conner halted his perusal and had more of his beer. He put the file aside, bored with the material. Was the point about this that the widow Giffords kept a cache of money hidden from the IRS in her basement, and Reynolds and Ballard needed his help in boosting the scratch? Or maybe the husband had invented an antigravity machine and they wanted to sell it to the Russians. He yawned and stretched.

"Must be good being you."

He turned to see Mattie Dodd standing there in cutoffs and a T-shirt with the logo of the band the Foo Fighters on it. It was easy to tell she wasn't wearing a bra. She came over to him, a crooked smile on her face.

"Where's Cody?" he asked.

"You're so damn suspicious."

"With you, yes, I am." He made an effort to keep his eyes on her face. "What you want, girl?"

"Why I got to want something?"

"Because you're a schemer, Mattie."

"Look who's talking." She undid her cutoffs and let them slide down to reveal the tiny sheer black panties underneath. She stepped closer and guided O'Conner's hand between her legs; then she squeezed them together, gyrating some.

"I need you to do me a favor, Connie. And this isn't a job for sweet Dougie."

"You can't buy me with sex." Funny how he seemed to be saying that, or a variation of those words, lately.

"I bet I can," she answered.

She went on her knees before him in his seat, O'Conner willingly opening his legs wider. She undid his zipper and took him in her mouth until he moaned and climaxed. Dodd got to her feet and finished what remained of the beer.

"What's my cut?" he said coolly, also standing and zipping up. The phone rang inside.

"We'll go over the job and work that out." She put her shorts back on. "It's a knockoff hustle, designer purses and other sort of accessories, to answer your unasked question." She began to walk out of his backyard. "I've got to get some details straight, but I'll be back in touch soon."

"I could tell you to go to hell."

She smiled. "You could." Dodd quit his abode as the phone rang again.

It was Gwen Gardner, and she'd heard from Mitch Frane. He had a lead on where to locate Inga Brody.

"I'm going to see you tonight?" she asked after delivering the message.

"Sure," he said. "Want me to bring some takeout? How about from that Thai place you like?"

"Aren't you the homebody?"

"That's what they say about me."

"I say more than that about you, Connie."

"You know, you're all right, Gwen," he said softly. "Damn all right."

She let a silence grow between them. "See you round seven, okay?"

"For sure." He hung up the phone, watching his diffused reflection in the sliding glass door. The chair he'd been sexed down in was tipped over on its side. Hands on his hips, he decided he'd reseed the backyard, see if he could get the grass to grow again.

Chapter Eleven

Kim Schmitz sat at her dining room table, talking on her smartphone to Blanche Allen. She was being reassured, having put her cashed-out 401(k) into the real estate venture.

"I understand how the market works, Blanche," she went on. "I just want to be clear we're going to get quarterly reports, as you outlined in the agreement. Because let me tell you something. Your girlfriend, partner, whatever she is, Didi, is not what you'd call a people person when it comes to answering these kinds of questions." She listened to the other woman's response, with a few "Uh-huhs" spoken at intervals.

"See, now, that's a good idea, Blanche," Schmitz said at length. "A meeting of the investors is only right and proper. Good, good . . . I look forward to it." She clicked off and got up to make herself some tea.

On the table was a notice from the bank about her falling behind on the mortgage payments. Schmitz was four months in arrears, but she knew people in the Ridge who were much further behind than she was. She had calculated, as well, that the bank wouldn't be sending out the sheriff for at least another three months, and even then she figured the substation had placed forcing people out of their homes low on their list of priorities.

She'd seen on YouTube a rally by a community group called Urban Advocacy in which they had their supporters surround a house in East L.A. to prevent the law from evicting an elderly couple. Too bad there wasn't a similar group like that out this way, she lamented.

After she put the kettle on the fire, there was a knock at her door. She knew who it was and opened the door to reveal Ian Childes standing on the porch, his messenger bag slung across his slender body. His bicycle was propped against the porch's low wooden railing.

"Mrs. S, what it bees like?"

"Ian," she said, indicating for him to enter.

The part-time college student walked inside, stepped into the dining room, and put his bag on the table. He unzipped a section and extracted a small plastic Baggie of Mas Trece brand crystal meth. He placed it on the polished surface, and she handed him three folded-over twenties and a five. There was a discount for Ridge residents.

"Want some tea? I have a blueberry scone we can split."

"I appreciate that, Mrs. S, but I better stay on my rounds. Next time, huh?"

"I'll hold you to it." Didn't hurt to keep the motor in tune with a bit of innocent flirtation practiced on a younger man, she reasoned. He waved good-bye to her as he rode off on his bike.

Loading her glass pipe, she then fired up her concoction and sat on her fenced-in patio, the sun glorious on her face as she indulged in the euphoria-inducing narcotic. She also sipped on a merlot. Knew she was using too much, as the rush wasn't like it was when she first started, or rather picked up the habit again after twenty-some odd years of not doing any drug other than marijuana now and then. Well, booze was a drug, wasn't it? But who counted that? she reflected, taking another drink, the near beatific meth stare on her face.

Schmitz smiled, her head back on the cushion of her beach lounge chair. What was the opposite of being a vampire? Being afraid of the sun? She welcomed the sun, its rays shining on her and through her, empowering and fulfilling. She closed her eyes, and the meth told her she wasn't broke and worried about money. That she hadn't sent out countless résumés while prowling job lists, like all the other suckers. High, Schmitz fantasizing about making love to Gwen Gardner's aging beefcake boyfriend, O'Conner. She could almost feel his muscular arms encircling her from behind as he pressed his body to her, and she shivered just a little from pleasure, despite the heat of the day.

Incongruously, it wasn't at a biker bar or a tattoo joint where he'd been told he could find Brody. Rather O'Conner watched her coming out of Acorn continuation school in San Jacinto, where she was the shop teacher. These sorts of schools were public entities set up as a last chance effort for students who'd gotten kicked out of regular school for fighting, truancy, drug use, or being pregnant. He imagined Brody maintained a tight discipline in her class, teaching her teen charges how to properly mill the barrel of an AK and so forth.

Parked opposite the school, on the residential side of the street, he smiled at this notion. Rowdy teenagers walked by, cursing and laughing, O'Conner watched Brody get on her motorcycle in the school's parking lot and ride off. A couple of young men watched her go. These two no doubt were fantasizing mightily and lustfully about the teacher. He was in the Sable station wagon, but he didn't think she'd remember it from seeing it several nights ago. The vehicle was fairly nondescript, and her attention had been on other matters.

He knew he couldn't follow her on the bike; she would spot him for sure. He might be able to dummy up paperwork of some sort to try to buffalo the admin staff to get a home address for her, but that took time and risked exposure. One of these numbnut slackers might know. It wasn't hard to imagine one of her hormone deluded charges trying to follow her home one lazy afternoon—and gotten socked in the jaw for his efforts by Brody. Or could be there was a Vandal Viking offspring among the student body. But that didn't get him an address.

O'Conner drove away, a slight smile on his face. Time to put it to Gwen Gardner, as Reynolds had challenged him.

"You want me to pretend I'm calling from another school district," she repeated over her cell phone after they'd discussed his plan.

"I think it'll sound more convincing if it's a woman," he said. "Don't freak them out. This is about a job in the summertime, so you're not stealing her from them."

"They might ask to call me back. What then, Lex Luthor?"

"Cloning a like number for, say, the Inglewood schools isn't too tough. Then we set up a digital answering voice to make you sound bureaucratically official and what not. In fact, this works better if you request the information, then tell the secretary, or whoever you're talking to, you have to get to a meeting and leave your return number."

"Make it sound like this is normal business, no big deal."

"Precisely."

"You've done this before?"

"I have indeed."

"You intend to make me do all manner of bad things, don't you?"

"This is of your own free will, baby."

"Get it ready. I'll make your damn call." But she didn't sound annoyed.

O'Conner could ask Reynolds to help him set up the subterfuge, as it was a specialty of his, but he didn't want to be indebted so quickly to him again—not until he had to, he concluded. He made a few more calls and drove back into the Los Angeles area. He found the man he was looking for at an informal neighborhood meeting in the Richland Farms section of Compton when he finally got off the 91 Freeway.

O'Conner had to park several blocks away and walk back into Richland, a roughly ten-block square section that was a rural outpost inside the hardscrabble birthplace of gangsta rap. The section dated back to when the city was founded by Griffith Dickenson Compton in 1898. Plenty of old-timers maintained that it had been stipulated Richland would remain agricultural—though no such records existed attesting to that assertion. He passed kids watering and feeding goats and llamas, and a man and a woman in cowboy hats talking affectionately as they slowly rode their horses side by side.

"Okay, but a meeting with her aide is better than no meeting at all," Arceneaux, the one he was looking for, was saying in the neighborhood meeting.

"It's a stall," said another person in the small knot of them. He was a man in an Obama as superhero T-shirt, a vest, and cowboy boots.

"We make the best of it," said another.

O'Conner hung back, and in a few minutes the discussion ended with each person assigned specific tasks before and after the meeting with the councilwoman's aide.

"Arcie, what it be like?"

"Damn, they let anybody in here."

They shook hands, and O'Conner followed the other man, a beefy sort with old-fashioned, black horn-rimmed glasses, along a path weaving between a house and a plot of land bordered by wooden fencing. Fresh replacement slats contrasted with weathered planks.

"Really, you have to do this now? I mean the smell, man."

"Please, don't act like nobody in your family ain't from the country," Arceneaux quipped. He'd stepped into the fenced-in area to the excited squeals of several hogs, who ran around the man's legs. He'd brought in two plastic five-gallon buckets and proceeded to shake loose the meat scraps, apple cores, bits of corn, and O'Conner couldn't tell what all else, the feed for those pigs.

"Sure hate to interrupt your nature hour and all, but I've got work for you."

"Let me tend to the chickens and water the horses. Then we can sit a spell."

"Aw, Jesus," O'Conner griped.

"Fact, you can help. It'll make it go faster."

O'Conner scattered grain around for the chickens, who scratched about a bare yard in front of Arceneaux's two-story house. In contrast to its surroundings, it was a redone McMansion of stucco and brick. A rooster gave him the snake eye but didn't come at him.

After the chickens were fed and the horses tended to, Arceneaux had to give some medicine to one of his goats, which naturally balked at this, and they had to run after her for a few minutes to corall her. Thereafter the two leaned on the pigpen fence and talked about what O'Conner needed. They also agreed to a price, and the two shook hands again.

"Shouldn't take more than a day," Arceneaux assured him. Despite outward appearances, Arceneaux had spent more than two decades as an electrical engineer for Boeing in El Segundo.

It was late afternoon, and traffic back to Hemet would be unbearable. O'Conner briefly considered going back to the Takeoff strip club, which he'd gone to with Voss, to see if he could chat up that heavy-hipped, green-eyed blonde in her thong. He chuckled. What was wrong with him getting so oversexed at his age?

Instead, he took the streets and went to San Pedro, to the water. He got turned around a few times but finally found this seafood restaurant he'd last been at over a decade ago—then to plot a job robbing a set of specific cargo containers in a Long Beach storage yard. What his crew had been after was not what was listed on the bills of lading for those containers.

O'Conner had a meal of red snapper and grilled shrimp, with pasta in red sauce on the side. He had two beers and was feeling mellow by the time his coffee arrived. After paying his check, he walked along nearby Signal Street, looking out on the harbor. He could hear a freighter chugging out there, its lights clear in the thin fog rising up. At his car in the parking lot, a woman about ten years older than he was appeared. She was carrying a plastic bucket of flowers, which thumped against her leg as she walked. She thrust one of her plastic-wrapped bouquets at him.

"Beauties for your sweetheart?" She was tired, her voice was without affect, like that of a Thorazine patient.

"Naw, that's all right." He handed her a folded-over five. He watched her shamble away in the gathering pall. Not much of a drinker, he nonetheless found a neighborhood bar called the Captain's Keep and had two whiskies, not being able to shake the image of that woman and her bucket of flowers.

"Fuck that," he grumbled, as if it were a talismanic phrase he invoked to ward off a lonely, poverty-stricken future. He pounded down another drink and at some point got back in his car, which he'd parked on the street. The next thing he knew, it was dawn and the fog was gone. Fuzzy-headed but alert, he drove home and got into bed, ignoring the ringing phone.

Later he watched Gwen Gardner making sandwiches for both of them in his kitchen.

"How're you feeling?"

"I remember why I don't drink much." He yawned and scratched his side and had more of his coffee. He wore a T-shirt and a pair of lounge pants she'd bought him. She handed him a plate containing a roast beef sandwich on a French roll, with peanut coleslaw an added bonus.

"Thanks, sweetie." He turned on his chair to the

kitchen table and started to eat. On the table were sections of the *Los Angeles Times*. She kissed the back of his neck and sat to the left of him with her food.

"What's new and exciting with your daughter?" he asked.

"She makes sure when she's talking to Chanchin on her phone that I'm not in earshot."

"Once we get a line on Inga Brody, I think this'll also give us a better picture of what, if anything, the young lovers are up to."

"How's that?" she said.

"I saw Inga talking to our would-be John Gotti." This wasn't exactly true, but close enough to being accurate. He continued, "Of course, the guy I know setting up the phone bit can sell me a couple of bugs, if you're really curious. Put one in her favorite purse, that sort of thing."

She twisted her mouth. "That would be going a little too far, wouldn't it, Connie?"

"I read parents do it all the time." He didn't mention that this would also aid him in getting the lowdown on the Mas Trece. Better to be the concerned, overenthusiastic boyfriend.

"I don't want to take it that far." She ate some, then said, "Is your point that these kinds of"—she gestured—"these kinds of situations mean either you're willing to do what's necessary or don't half ass it, as you might say?"

"Something like that." He touched her knee. "Everything is not a scorched-earth scenario with me, Gwen. I know about moderation."

She eyed him mischievously. "Oh, that's too bad. 'Cause Kim has a thing for you."

"Thinking about renting me out for stud services?"

"I told her I'd ask if you had a friend."

"Might be a bit much for her to handle," he said, reflecting on the sort of men he'd done jobs with in the past.

Gardner got an odd look on her face.

"What?" O'Conner said.

"You'd be surprised about what goes on here in quiet Willow Ridge."

He chuckled dryly. "So I'm learning."

She chewed, then said, "I'm pretty sure she's a Mas Trece client."

"No."

"Yes," Gardner said, ignoring his sarcasm. "We were at a cocktail party not too long ago, and she offered me a bump, as she called it."

O'Conner folded his arms. "You chicks around here are running wild. You need a firm hand."

"Do we now? And you know when to apply the iron fist in the velvet glove and when not to, Muammar?"

"Are you mocking me?" he intoned lightly.

She held a slice of pickle and, leaning over, fed part of it to him. He chewed animatedly. They smiled at one another. O'Conner picked up his mug, making a mental note to do some research on Ms. Schmitz. The residue from the mug's moist base had created a wet crescent atop an article in the Calendar section of the *L.A. Times*. The piece was about an upcoming movie based on the harried existence of a personal assistant to a B-list actress. The movie was called *The Sherpa Wore Silk*.

An actress up for a small speaking part in *The Sherpa Wore Silk* was kissing and tonguing Lilly Nash at a party two nights later in Studio Village, in Los Angeles's San

Fernando Valley. Nash's tattoo of an iguana, curled around part of her neck and upper shoulder, was exposed due to the spaghetti-strap tank top she wore. The ink drawing had gotten appreciative stares and comments. These two were busy in a hallway populated with several others. Harley Lynn Demara weaved through this knot of bodies to get to the other side.

"What's happening?" Reo Culhane said when she'd gotten through. He took her by the shoulders and planted a kiss on her cheek.

"Got the Tina." She grinned.

"Well, let's not stand on ceremony. Gotta give it a taste test, don't I?"

The two went through another hallway and through the kitchen to a service porch area containing a stacked washer-dryer combo. Culhane closed the door to this small area as Demara took a metal sunglasses case out of her purse, along with a plastic bag of the meth crystals. In the case was a glass pipe. She removed it. He held the bag to the light, examining it like an intern staring at an X-ray.

"Looks like you got yourself a good cooker," he commented.

"This is the real deal, Reo."

"Cool."

She put some pieces in the pipe and lit the contents by waving the oblong flame of a disposable lighter back and forth under the pipe's bowl. The stuff liquified rapidly, and they took turns sucking the vapors into their lungs.

"Nice, nice," Culhane enthused. "Man, when I partake, it's like . . ." He held up his hands, his fingers wiggling, as if each was attached to electric wires sending pulses through it.

"Yeah, I know." She giggled. Demara felt like she could do anything.

"Oh, yeah, I get these great ideas when I'm like this. Like I just know how I can do this movie I'm supposed to shoot in Bulgaria for the Syfy Channel. Shot by fuckin' shot. See, it's all about how we follow a King Arthur after Camelot, who's wandering the American West, looking for a dragon that's taken the form of this gorgeous woman."

"Huh," Demara said, nodding and having more. But cautioning herself not to take it too far. She prided herself on being able to control the urge, not let it master her like she'd seen it do with others. *Fuck that.*

"Might be a part in it for you, Harley Lynn."

She tapped the crystals. "You mean a trade?"

"Along those lines, yeah."

She crooked her finger. "Can I tell you something?"

"Sure, baby," he said eagerly, moving closer in the close space.

"I'm not stupid, Reo, so don't try and play me. This is business. I supply, and you make a cut by getting me clients."

"Sure, but this is Hollywood, babe. You know how it goes. You do favors, and favors are done for you."

"How it goes is, this yesca doesn't just grow out of the ground. Understand? I'm responsible for the product. I get jammed, you get jammed. If it serves me to give a little away, I make that decision, not you, Reo. You don't make me promises. But that don't mean we can't talk about, you know . . . A producer wants some shit for a party or his side squeeze, we negotiate. That's what we do in Hollywood."

Culhane had focused on her words. "I got it."

"Sweet." They bumped fists and exited the room.

Back in the living room Demara made a few low-key sales and saw at one point Culhane texting on his smartphone. She hoped it was to the connection she wanted to make through him. Several years ago he'd been a second unit director on a modestly budgeted movie about a girls' finishing school that was actually an academy for training assassins. At the wrap party he'd befriended the producer, a man named Tug, Tugwell Hintton, who'd made his money back during the dot-com bubble, before it went bust.

Hintton also owned a piece of L.A.'s pro basketball team, the Comets, and had been fairly successful in the movie business. This Demara knew, as it was common knowledge in the industry. What wasn't common knowledge—but Demara also knew it because of the shared vice with Culhane, who liked to gossip—was that Hintton enjoyed getting his bump on now and then, too. Naturally, Culhane was always looking for a way to get in good with Hintton, whose parties he attended.

A personal assistant of Hintton's about two months ago had been arrested for attempting to buy some meth in a sting operation the LAPD had conducted. While everyone assumed the stuff was really for Hintton, the assistant had taken the hit. No doubt an under-the-table payout had been made to him to do so. Hintton had been maintaining a subdued lifestyle, but she figured he had to be hurting to get his tweakness on regularly and was desirous of having a steady pipeline.

Later Demara was chatting up a husband and wife who were packagers with a direct-to-DVD deal when Culhane appeared beside her. He let her conclude with a promise from the couple they'd look at her reel from her agent.

"You free this coming Tuesday?" Culhane asked.

"I could be. What up?"

"Take a spin out to Malibu for brunch. Want you to meet my boy, Tug."

She faked like she'd maybe heard of Hintton, and let him fill her in. They made the date, and Culhane went off again. Demara sent a text to Chanchin Saladago. He was driving to L.A., and they'd meet up later at her apartment—she'd made enough in sales in the last week to cover the rent for another couple of months. He also had a crash pad in town, but he'd hinted it would be occupied for the next few days by a dude who had to lay low over some beef in Riverside.

Her plans went beyond Saladago's rep to the glitter and loafers crowd. She was a glorified pusher. That was a dead-end ambition and sure to get you ratted out by one of these poseurs sooner than their mamas could get their next lip-plumping Botox injection. If there was anything her toehold in Hollywood had taught her, it was you better get yours when the opportunity presented itself, because the merry-go-round usually gives you only one ride and then your'e yesterday's flavor.

Resting her head against the wall in the hallway, Harley Lynn Demara closed her eyes and fantasized about how she would landscape the backyard of her plush home on the hill overlooking the peons of Los Angeles. She then went and had another hit on the pipe.

Chapter Twelve

Mattie Dodd wiped at the corner of her great-aunt Lori's mouth with the paper napkin. She was having her breakfast, and they sat together in the sunny cafeteria area of the Garden Shores senior care facility. After her stroke, her auntie had been able to regain her speech due to ongoing therapy. She also had limited mobility on the left side of her body. Depending on her level of energy on any given day, she was able to use a four-pronged cane to walk, very slowly, instead of her wheelchair. Today was such a day.

"How's the house?" she asked in her halting way, each word carefully formed. There was a slight slurring of the hard consonants and a sibilant quality to the s's, but Dodd was used to this.

"Fine," her grandniece said as she used a fork to spear more eggs and inserted the utensil in the curved hand of the older woman. She watched, transfixed, as her great-aunt got the food aloft and into her mouth.

"Ha. Didn't spill," Lori Stiglez said. Small things were major triumphs to a woman in her condition.

Dodd smiled at her. Her great-aunt then shifted her eyes to a plastic cup with a straw in it. Her grandniece held this for her so she could take a sip of the orange juice.

"How's your job?" her great-aunt asked after she had had more of her breakfast.

Dodd had told her she was working part-time as a checker at the Earth Harvest supermarket. What were the chances she'd ever find out the truth? It was not like she was going to improve any more than what she had, Dodd had glumly concluded.

"It's going okay, Aunt Lori. I'm getting to be an expert at my Arctic Glos and my Zephyrs." She touched her arm as she told her the lie about knowing the differences between the varieties of nectarines. She did know one from the other, just not in the context of working at the market. "I think they're going to give me more hours."

"Wonderful, dear. I'm so glad you're taking care of me and the house."

"Of course," Dodd said, willing herself not to look away.

Her great-aunt finished, and Dodd helped her out to the patio. There she sat in a chair, her saucer-brimmed straw sun hat on to shade her eyes and face. There was a folded-over front section of the newspaper, and Dodd passed this to her. It helped her great-aunt's mental mechanisms to read, and she still enjoyed doing so. When it came time to turn the page, one of the attendants would eventually spot her efforts and help. There were men her age and older who had some mobility who would help her, as well. One, Mr. Mills, a World War II vet of the Battle of Arnhem, had told Dodd, winking, that her great-aunt was a hot tamale.

She got her settled, then kissed her cheek. "I'll see you next week, okay?"

Stiglez nodded slowly. "I'm looking forward to it, sweetie. Be good. . . ."

"Be safe," her grandniece said, finishing for her. It was an expression the older woman used to say to her when she was small. She was leaving to meet with O'Conner and take him with her on a trip into Los Angeles.

O'Conner and Mattie Dodd stepped into the alley off Santee Street in downtown L.A.'s fashion district. She was dressed conservatively in jeans and a pressed shirt, sunglasses over her amber eyes. The rear area of the buildings was open to these alleys, where items such as multicolored scarves on spinning racks, luggage sets, and skirts folded atop small tables were on display. They came to a beefy individual in cargo shorts and a tank top, bulked arms prison tatted up, sitting on a chair beside a closed riot gate.

"Hey," Dodd said. "Vi's expecting us."

"All right," the guard answered. He took in O'Conner but didn't say anything else. He produced a cell phone and spoke into it in a quick burst. The riot gate rolled up, and O'Conner and Dodd stepped inside the cavity of a room.

On either side of them were stacks of boxes taller than O'Conner. An older Asian woman, of Chinese ancestry, O'Conner surmised, came through a door in the rear of the space. She handed a purse to Dodd. The young woman slipped her sunglasses on top of her head as she turned the purse over and over, feeling the surface of it carefully.

"Very nice," Dodd said.

"Louis Vuitton, Kate Spade, and Gucci," the older woman said. "Depending on the brand and make, there's on average twenty-five in a box."

The boxes stacked about them were of varying sizes, so O'Conner assumed this woman dealt in various kinds of knockoffs, given he understood everything from shoes to DVDs were such commodities.

Dodd said, "I can start with five boxes, mixed, and then step that up once I get my reps going."

The other woman considered this, then looked beyond the two at the guard in the alleyway. O'Conner turned his head and saw the man gesturing. He came into the space and, pressing a button on a wall-mounted control unit, began bringing the riot gate down again. Dodd put a hand on O'Conner's arm.

"A raid?" he asked the older woman.

"Mas Trece wannabes," the guard answered in a whisper, shaking his head. "They come around shaking down the paleteros and sidewalk sellers."

"Little gnome bitches is what they are," the other woman added. "Ought to bust some caps in their asses."

The guard chuckled silently. Outside loud voices in Spanglish could be heard as the group of junior gangsters gave grief to several of the merchants along the alley. Soon these dissipated, and the riot gate was raised again.

"Let's talk percentages," Dodd said.

"Seventy-thirty."

Dodd slowly shook her head from side to side. "I'm broadening your customer base, Vi, new territory and all that."

"Sixty-five, thirty-five. You talk a good game, Mattie, but you don't have the numbers to back that up yet."

"Okay, how about this? You consign ten boxes—

mixed labels, like we said—and if I can move them in a month . . . no, a month and a half, then we renegotiate our terms."

Vi Moon and the tattooed guard, who'd remained in the room, exchanged a look. Then she said, "We'll agree if you can move the goods in that kind of time, we'll talk some more."

The two shook on it, with Dodd handing over some money as advance collateral. The guard loaded six boxes of bootleg handbags on a dolly, and with O'Conner carrying three and Dodd the last box, they walked back to where he'd parked his station wagon in a pay lot. It was one of those lots where you paid at a machine for your numbered spot, an attendant coming around at intervals to catch any scofflaws. They loaded the boxes, and the other man left.

"Are there enough women in Willow Ridge who have the disposable income for these bags?" O'Conner asked her.

She smiled at O'Conner over the rim of her sunglasses, which she'd placed over her eyes again. "Women like your sweetie Gwen, her friend Jane, and some of these other broads know other women with their tastes who live outside of the Ridge." Dodd headed toward the passenger door. "Some of these chicks have fashion night parties, sex toy parties." She pretended to be shocked, widening her eyes. "So the word will get around that I have designer bags for cut-rate prices."

"You give them a cut out of your end?"

"That or usually trade, giving the hostess a couple of extra handbags or sunglasses, whatever." He unlocked the doors from his side, and she got in the car, too.

He put the key in the ignition. "But they must know these are knockoffs."

"See, that's the thing. The same factories in China where the legit labels are outsourced to also turn out these versions. Leather is leather, Connie—"

She was suddenly cut off by the tapping of a gun muzzle on the passenger window. This action was duplicated on O'Conner's side of the station wagon, too.

"Damn," Dodd muttered.

"Here we go." O'Conner opened his door slowly and got out, as did the younger woman. The two gunmen had stepped back some in case either of them tried to open their door quickly and broadside them. A van had pulled onto the lot, blocking the rear of the Sable. The sliding side door of the van was open, and a heavyset woman in a low-cut, stretchy top was at the wheel of the idling vehicle.

"You know what to do, homies," one of the robbers said. He was a compact Latino with a shaved head and a diamond stud in his left lobe.

O'Conner went to the back end of the Sable and swung the hatch door to the side, allowing access to the cargo area. He put one box on top of another and took both in his arms. One of the robbers stood near him; the other was on Mattie Dodd, chatting her up while they stole from them.

"Girl, what you doing with this old-timer? You need some young, hard stuff. Know what I'm sayin'?" He grabbed his crotch to emphasize his come-on.

"You're probably right," Dodd replied. "I feel sorry for his wrinkly ass, is all." She got closer to the vato with the gun on her and put her hand where he'd just rubbed. "I bet you can show me a rockin' time."

"Da-yum," his partner exclaimed.

"Hugo!" the woman yelled from the van.

Hugo was getting into it. "Oh, shit, yeah, baby girl."

Diamond Stud's attention was momentarily focused on the soft-core antics. O'Conner dropped the box he was holding. There was a small knife in his hand. He stabbed Diamond Stud in the arm of his gun hand, deep in the muscle of his bicep.

"Oh, fuck," he screamed. O'Conner put his heel on the other man's foot, simultaneously grabbing his wrist, twisting the wounded arm.

As this was going on, Dodd kneed Hugo, the crotch grabber, in his favorite area, then followed with an elbow to his nose, causing him to loosen his grip on his gun. She took it from him.

The big woman in the van had a gun and took a random shot through the open side door, causing everyone to duck.

"Don't be stupid, Lina," Diamond Stud said, holding his wound. "You know you can't shoot for shit, and that'll only bring the hoota." There were people walking by the lot, and though none had come over, that didn't mean one of them wasn't dialing 911 on their cell phone.

"Put those boxes back in the car," O'Conner ordered Hugo. The robber advanced slightly, hunched over, and did so. "Now, both of you chuckleheads get in your van and get the fuck out of here."

The two did this, as well, and the van drove off.

"We gonna go teach that slippery bitch a lesson? Like we're supposed to believe these fuckers were Mas Trece," Dodd muttered, boiling.

"I'm sure Vi and her tattooed boy toy have cleared out by now."

"Leaving their shit?"

"You have a point. But that would also mean us trying to get through that rolled-down door of theirs, and what chance would we have before the gendarmes showed up?"

"Yeah, I guess," she said.

They got in the station wagon, and O'Conner backed up. He patted her leg. "I appreciate that you don't like somebody trying to make a chump out of you."

She glanced at him, then back out the windshield, as he righted the car and headed toward the 10 freeway.

"But it's not like you're not coming out ahead. How much can you get for one of those gussied-up purses?"

"Two hundred, two-fifty a piece, and that's a bargain," she revealed.

"See?"

"I put up eight hundred on good faith."

"You'll still come out a winner. And, anyway, you recruited me 'cause you figured she'd pull something like this."

"Cody's the one who made the connection. This was weeks before you kicked his ass," she said. "Vi is, like, somehow related to him, an aunt through marriage to an uncle, something like that. But after you two went at it, I figured she might try some kind of payback."

"Ah," O'Conner remarked.

She studied him with a snide glance. "It's different when it's you, huh, big daddy?"

"You goddamn right." They both snickered. But he knew she knew enough about him to realize that his veneer of detachment was only surface gloss when it came to him being the object of a setup. After some moments of silence, he asked, "What do you know about her operation?"

"Not a lot. I think she has a direct pipeline to mainland China. The way I understand it, there's towns over there that specialize in producing the knockoffs. Particularly in the southern part."

"Seems I've seen something on TV about how the sales of the counterfeit goods account for a noticeable percentage of China's GNP," he commented.

"You're smarter than you look, old timer," Dodd cracked.

"Occasionally. You think Vi has a hookup at the port? This stuff is smuggled in those shipping containers."

"Check this," she added. "Like I said, you have some factories turning out legit and bootleg. So in some cases you can have shipments of both kinds in the same freight load."

O'Conner mulled that over. "Is that just bribing the right official, or does that mean you have some companies who profit on both ends? They make their designer brand for the Brie and wine set, and turn a blind eye to the ghetto-fabulous stock?"

"Which would mean they still get their cut of that," Dodd noted.

They drove along some more. Then O'Conner asked, "I suppose Cody's so smitten with you, he'd fall for you making up with him?"

"I don't know exactly. You really don't like anyone trying to punk you, do you?"

"You don't, either."

"You figure we can rob Vi like she tried to rob us?"

"The idea's growing on me. But we have to be realistic. Even if we did find out where she gets her stash or, let's say, hijack a shipment heading to her, what would we do with it? A truckload of . . . I don't know . . . more purses or tennis shoes." He looked over at her. "You're a one-woman operation. That would be a lot of merchandise to move."

"I have a network," she noted. "Got this singer. She goes by the name Grinquist. Big, good-looking Amazon chick. She was on one of those sing-off TV shows last summer. She got voted off in the second-to-last round, but she went on to have a couple of downloaded songs that got her a following and a record deal."

"So?" O'Conner remarked.

"So she likes her some shoes and handbags, that's so. She tweets to her followers about my goods."

"You know phones can be easily hacked into," O'Conner said.

"I know," Dodd replied. "She uses a kind of code the insiders know. We're even setting up an underground thing where she would do some of her new numbers, and she'll be decked out in limited edition bootleg designer wear."

"That her gal pals will know to buy from you."

"That's right."

"How do you know her?"

Dodd smiled. "We played basketball together in high school. Her real name is Sally Herberts."

"Grinquist is much sexier," O'Conner acknowledged.

Another silence dragged on. Finally Dodd said, "Look, what if it was you and I doing it together, O'Conner? I'm sure you'd like to get out of the strong-arm hustle you've been doing."

"What with my advancing years," he quipped.

She was getting wound up. "If those motherfucks on Wall Street taught anything, it's white-collar crime pays so much better."

He half turned to her, then fixed his eyes on the road again. "Awfully wise for your tender age."

"Look," she went on, "any of those greedy shit heads who got us in this mess ever go to jail?"

"What about Madoff?"

"He bilked his clients, but he's not one of those short-changers who made their money legitimately by screwing just everyday chumps."

"What're you talking about there, Angela Davis?"

"It would surprise you I know who that is."

"You're just full of wonder."

She elevated her middle finger, smiling. "Asshole. So, like I was saying, I don't just sit around getting high and daydreaming, O'Conner. I've been studying up on this predicament of ours."

"Have you, now?"

"Yes. You know what a collateralized debt obligation is?"

"Hip me to it, Professor."

"Well, sport, since the financial crisis, CDOs have been responsible for something like six hundred billion in write-downs."

"A write-down being you reduce the value of an asset because it's been overvalued in the market," O'Conner said. "But a lot of times this was because the bank or financial outfit was responsible for the overvaluing to begin with." He grinned. "See, you're not the only one who's been watching the educational channels."

"And a whole bunch of people made money betting those paper assets would tank. Shitty collateral affected these values 'cause a lot of subprime mortgages were being issued to people who lied or went along with bull-shit being written up about their worth on a blizzard of applications. That house in the Ridge is my Aunt Lori's place. She damn near lost her home 'cause of a messed-up second mortgage she had to take out."

Dodd paused then added, "The company that developed the subdivision was part of something else that was in turn a subsidiary of a real estate entity that had ties to Lehman Brothers. So when they tanked, taking our money with them, that's how the funds dried up to finish Willow Ridge. Shit, Lehman kept doing what's called Repo 105, hiding billions in assets from the SEC while the ripple effects of their bullshit fucked up the finances of tens of thousands of people like my aunt."

"What happened to her?" O'Conner asked.

"She had two strokes and is in a rest home now. My aunt . . . her daughter, I mean—Aunt Lori's my great-aunt, really—had to hire a lawyer, but she managed to have her declared indigent so the state couldn't seize her crib. She'd created a trust a while ago, which actually was Auntie Lori's idea. She was a legal secretary."

"And you took over the mortgage? Heck of a thing for a youngster like you."

She leaned over and rubbed a hand on his thigh. "What were you doing when you were my age, pops?"

"Wouldn't you like to know, whippersnapper?"

She gave his crotch a squeeze and sat upright again. "I know something else you don't know."

"What's that?"

"The bi broad, Blanche, she's up to some shit. Property swindle bamboozling, I'm guessing."

"How do you know that?"

"Her muff buddy, Didi, got busted for it in the past. She used to be a member of one of those cults. They got a place over here in the Santa Monica Mountains and a big honkin' compound out in Riverside someplace, too."

O'Conner frowned. "The Anthem of Reason Institute, the ARI, you mean?"

She grinned crookedly at him. "You heard of them?"

"Yeah. Who hasn't?"

"Like I said, O'Conner, you're more full of surprises than a shopping bag with a pissed-off scorpion in it."

"Are you telling me ole rose lips Didi was doing some kind of real estate scam for the institute?"

"She caught the case, but the talk was she'd done it on orders from her bosses."

"Again, you know this how?"

"Didi hit on me."

"Damn," he said appreciatively. "Where?"

"In the supermarket."

"Earth Harvest?"

"Uh-huh." She pointed at him. "But I'm no ho. This was a few months ago, and Blanche and her hadn't really hooked up yet."

"Good to know. Now wait. She hits on you and all of a sudden tells you this shady business to impress you?"

"We went out for a drink. Plus, I already kinda knew."

"You swing both ways?"

"What if I do?"

"I'd want to watch next time," he said seriously.

"Pervert creep."

He grinned broadly.

"I don't, but I knew this story about her and the institute. A friend of my auntie writes for the local throwaway, the *Inland Gazette.*"

"They covered the swindle story?"

"They did," she answered. "It was about four years ago, and Didi and some others were cheating HUD out of subsidy money. Inventing pretend tenants for low-income-qualified apartments, that sort of thing. This case was not just in the local papers out our way, but in the *L.A. Times,* too."

"The ARI's pretty damn well off. Why would they need a few thousand that kind of scam could produce?"

"You sound like an expert."

"Stick to the subject, homegirl."

"If I remember right, it was suspected the ARI had various groups doing this all over the place, so that's hundreds of thousands, maybe millions. Anyway, it's only Didi and her little crew that get busted. And really only because one of them was into knuckleheads and was banging this slanger living in one of the apartments who gets busted on a dope charge and rats out this stupid chick."

She continued, "So Didi does her time, and when she gets out, being from the area and all, and now being on the shit list with her ARI buds, she gets a job over at one of those chocolate chip outlets in the shopping center."

"Which is where your great-auntie's friend, the reporter, recognizes her."

"Yeah. She interviews her. Didi goes on about how she learned her lesson, blah, blah. But peep this. Joan—that's auntie's friend—has a background as a producer in local TV news. She doesn't for a minute believe squat what Didi's going on about, and lets her doubts be known. She does a column for the paper. Anyway, the institute loves to sue, so they don't run the story."

O'Conner absorbed this, then said, "But you read the story?"

"She was proud of it and sent it to Aunt Lori and a few others."

"It occurs to me, Mattie, maybe it was you who approached Didi. Pretending like you were interested in her and then seeing what you could pry out of her if you got her hot and bothered and liquored up? Looking to diversify your crime portfolio."

"You have a devious manner about you."

He eyed her sideways and said, "The way of the crab is sometimes called for, sunflower."

"Whatever that means. Anyway, it's not a month later and she's hooked up tight with Blanche, and, well, you know, she's sniffing around."

"So you two have a drink, and then you got her nose wide open, huh?"

"I'm pretty sure I know what your outdated expression means, and it's not that. But she chats me up a time or two, and I can tell she's angling about maybe I can help her and her new girlfriend out. But Blanche puts the quash on that."

"The jealous type, is she?"

"They're both type As, so they must trade off tops and bottoms."

"Maybe they wrestle for it each night."

"I'm sure you'd like to believe that," she cracked.

"You can't imagine."

"Uh-huh."

They rode along for a while in silence, until Dodd asked, "You seeing Mrs. Gardner tonight?"

"I probably should."

"Wouldn't want to mess up your good thing."

Her voice was neutral; he couldn't read anything into it. He said, "Besides, you've got some homework to do on Vi."

"Yeah, I guess I do."

"Damn straight."

She smiled at that and asked, "What did you mean about crab-like? Like sneaking up on somebody?"

"Sort of," he said. "See, one morning long ago, I woke up on a beach after a night of how you say . . . ?"

"Revelry," she answered.

"That's the word. Anyway, my bleary eyes open, and

the side of my face is in the sand. It's painful to move, so I'm just laying there, watching this crab move in on a lizard laying on a flat rock. He's just lazing away, the rock heating up as the morning breaks. The crab was cool, you know? Easing over, over . . . no hurry but steady on his prey."

"Fascinating," she drawled laconically.

Unperturbed, he continued with his story.

She laughed at him after he was done. "Okay. Thanks, Zen master Cool J. I get it about being patient. Great advice. Especially from you." She laughed some more.

"Damn youngsters." O'Conner kept driving.

Zev Voss had two nephews in their twenties, sons of his sister. The diligent one, Barry Franzen, worked for him at Channel Marine Machining while attending night school. The other one, Curt Franzen, was a chucklehead who liked his weed, but he didn't like to work—or rather, work hard. Curt Franzen happened to be driving through the Inland Empire after an interview at the ARI compound for a job as a security guard. He could think of nothing better than sitting on his ass, watching monitors and munching on Ritz Crackers. Having to get up now and then to help some drugged-out celeb, there to dry out, back to the room as he or she wandered around, stumbling and mumbling, in a robe.

Franzen happened to be driving past Willow Ridge and remembered going to a party there at a big-legged chick's house. This dude he knew, Cody Bradford, had invited him. She'd had some good weed. He drove in and looked for the Cape Cod–style house he recalled. But things looked different in the day, and the place was more spare looking, he noted. He got turned around, but what the heck? He didn't see too many people out, and these suburb types were so careless.

He parked and strolled around, trying this or that side or back door. At a nicely kept-up home down the street from the frame of one not yet completed, the back door was unlocked. It was Gwen Gardner's house, and her daughter had left the door unlocked. He looked around for jewels or cash, but found neither. He did cop a snubnosed .38 from a shoe box on a shelf in the closet and then quit the house. He tried a couple of other homes, then left the housing complex.

Later, back at Willow Ridge, O'Conner and Dodd went their separate ways. O'Conner was self-conscious about them being seen together. It wasn't a good idea to be hot and heavy with two women in this kind of proximity to one another, he estimated. But Dodd wasn't Gardner. He understood their deal to be simply—how did the saying go?—friends with benefits. Huh, he reflected. These modern chicks.

Their connection, he reminded himself while he parked in his driveway, was about them putting a score together. That they dug each other physically was cool, but it wouldn't do to get all in a knot emotionally, he advised himself. Particularly given he was old enough to be her father, if he'd been like so many of those hapless high school man-boys who knocked up their cheerleader girlfriend. And as long as he understood the young woman was all about Mattie, he wouldn't get confused. His cell phone rang, and he answered it. On the other end was Ben Reynolds, who needed a favor.

* * *

O'Conner didn't notice Steve Brill, who'd come home after dinner with other managers from his office. He passed by on the cross street. He noted the troublesome Mattie Dodd standing near the driver's window of the Sable station wagon belonging to O'Conner. Noticed, too, as she pushed on the back of his head and briefly ground her crotch on his face as Brill drove on, a rueful smile on his face. Goddamn O'Conner had it going and coming.

At Gardner's place there was a problem with the trap under the main bathroom sink. O'Conner went right to work, got it undone with an adjustable wrench she had and unclogged the pipe, backed up with hair and sludge. When he was done and had cleaned up the area under the sink, he sat for a moment on the edge of the bathtub.

"What would I do without a man like you around?" Gwen Gardner stood in the bathroom doorway, elbows braced on either side of the frame.

"I'm sure you'd manage."

"Getting me ready for the letdown?"

"I'm not going to lie to you, Gwen. But I really don't know what my plans are. Fully, I mean."

"You'll keep me abreast, won't you?"

"Most assuredly."

She lingered for a moment longer, then walked away. O'Conner sat, looking at the normality of his surroundings, feeling quite comfortable.

In bed after making love, O'Conner slept quietly on his side. Gardner was snuggled behind him, her arm draped over him, her eyes closed, but she was awake. She felt the slight rise and fall of his body as he breathed.

She opened her eyes. Light came into the room through the half-shaded bedroom window. Enough so that by moving her head back some on her pillow, she could note the scar tissue and grown-over areas where the skin had a sheen to it on his upper back. Here the skin didn't quite match his natural color. She idly rubbed her fingers over several of those coarse patches of flesh. Not for the first time she wondered how he'd gotten each mark, and not for the first time she imagined they weren't earned in home-repair accidents.

She pulled herself tighter to him, nuzzling his neck and putting her leg partly on his, as well. He made a low sound. It occurred to her that might be what a large animal, the kind with fangs, sounded like as it rested—readying itself for the following day of stalking and attacking. She chuckled a little in her throat and fell asleep, her body matching the rhythm of his slumber.

Chapter Thirteen

O'Conner rolled his rebuilt motorcycle down the walkway and put the kickstand down. He wasn't the most experienced rider, so he'd asked the guys at the motorcycle shop about the best way to break in the redone engine. He keyed the electric starter and turned the bike on but didn't crank the engine. The motor turned over but didn't start. He turned it off but then clicked it to on so that he squirted more gas across the tops of the four pistons. He clicked the ignition off again, then on, and cranked it this time. The motor's crankshaft turned over again and again and again and then caught. The Kawasaki came to life, and unlike in its previous incarnation, the machine wasn't belching oily smoke. He left it running to warm up and went back in the house, momentarily returning wearing sunglasses.

Once the rocker arm cover was hot to the touch, he got on the bike and eased it down to the street. He took off in low gear, not for the highway, but to an alleyway. The alley ran for several blocks and was located in the eastern part of the subdivision, where a series of juncture boxes were situated, as well. This was where a lot of the fiber-optic wiring and the like came together, as Willow Ridge had Wi-Fi and the other cyber and digital amenities the modern home owner demanded.

He used the straightaway so as to open up the bike to fifty and sixty miles an hour. He went back and forth several times, earning some scornful glares from a few residents at their back windows. This was a way to seat the piston rings, he'd been told. Finished, he then took a more quiet tour through the housing subdivision. He rode past places he'd been on foot, passing FOR SALE signs, some with FORECLOSED rectangles affixed to them. The lawns of these homes were overgrown and yellowed. He went on past houses that were occupied and tended. However, a few of these were next to the stark wooden skeletons of planned but unfinished abodes, silent testament to the elusive quality of normalcy here in Hemet, or anywhere else as far as O'Conner could determine.

He cruised about as if the quaintly named thoroughfares of Willow Ridge, such as Blue Mountain Way and Palm Grove Lane, were on his private estate. He grinned at that notion as he went on the path bordering the artificial lake, a few heads turning to watch him. No doubt the populace was relieved to see he wasn't festooned with the Vandal Vikings colors but was merely some middle-aged weekend biker with a day off enjoying his fine-running machine. O'Conner didn't see Stan Yamashira out and about as he made his circuit and turned off to take the motorcycle into the other confines of the Ridge.

Going along a street called Vista Rio, he noted a female jogger up ahead. The woman wore shorts and a sports top, an iPhone strapped on her arm, the earbuds in place. Her running shoes were stylish but worn, having many miles on them. O'Conner had started to pass when the jogger looked over at him and called his name. It was Jane Grainger-Brill. He used his foot to click the clutch into neutral.

"How are you?" he said in a neighborly manner, straddling the idling machine.

"Good, Connie." She jogged a little in place, having removed one of her earbuds. It sounded like a waterfall was playing through them. "So you got your bike back together? Gwen said you'd been working on it."

"You know how it is. Like to finish what I start."

She nodded, then said, "With this and your station wagon, you're kind of in between, huh? Either it's back to the open road or in your family car, you're a regular Hemetian."

"Hemetian?"

"One who lives in Hemet." She jutted her jaw upward. "What I've heard them call us flatlanders up there in the mountains of Idyllwild. A crack-up, isn't it?" Idyllwild was a picturesque hamlet where people from L.A. kept places to get away to for quiet weekends.

"That's for sure," he said.

"Gotta go," she said, inserting her earbud. "Let's try to get the four of us together. I'll talk to Gwen."

"Sounds great," he called back, and she jogged away. Taking off on his bike again, O'Conner was tickled by the notion of him and Grainger-Brill's husband sitting around, having a beer and watching the game on TV. Brill worried about the point spread in his office pool, and he contemplated the details of the upcoming takedown.

Oh yeah, he kidded himself, he was getting to be a regular Hemetian, all right. He rode on, consciously avoided the Mas Trece cul-de-sac. No sense raising a red flag if he didn't have to. Though it did flash through his mind to wonder what Gwen's daughter might be up to.

* * *

They met for lunch at a place in Malibu overlooking the ocean. Down below the deck they were on was a knot of men and women surfers lazing in the sand, as the morning waves had smoothed out. Reo Culhane eyed a beauty in a blue bikini, then returned his attention to his companions and his mimosa. His second one.

"Give it some serious consideration, will you?" Tug Hintton said to Harley Lynn Demara. "What's the downside?"

"Dignity. I could be labeled a flighty lezbo," she said.

Hintton made a gesture. "Come on, Harley Lynn. You know those men and girly girls will tune in to a show like this. A personality like yours, you're sure to break out. I mean, for goodness' sakes, if that damn Snookie can become a household name, then it's gotta be your turn."

She said, "You're not tweaking, are you, Tug?"

He chuckled. "Not yet." He had more of his raspberry iced tea. He was a stocky individual with workingman's hands and a pleasant, heartland kind of sunburned face. He wore pressed jeans, loafers, and a heavily starched pale blue button-down shirt, and there was a Chinese character for success on a thin gold chain around his thick neck. "Well, don't dismiss it out of hand. The mix is getting put together now, so a decision will have to be made shortly."

Hintton had pitched her a project his production company was looking to do for MTV. It was a reality show where a group of young women, gay and straight, were thrown together. The twist in this scenario was the straight women had to actively hang out and court the gay women and vice versa. "It's a show about shattering our illusions," Hintton had stated.

"It's a show about watching girls kiss and grope each other," Demara had countered.

She wasn't averse to the prospect of making out with another woman on camera. But she was concerned about the long-term effects it could have on her career. The program could well go down in history as just a somewhat more sedate version of a Girls Gone Wild video. But then, given the endless parade of faces and bodies and silliness on all those channels you could get on your satellite dish or cable, maybe it didn't matter. You were just part of the assembly line of titillation. They were also discussing a component where the participants would work with the staff writers to transform their inner thoughts into animated word balloons that would appear over their heads at given intervals.

"All right," she said, holding up a hand. "I'll let you know soon. Cool?"

"That's what I'm talking about." Hintton rubbed his hands together like an old-timey serial villain. He nodded approvingly at Culhane as the three continued their lunch.

It always amazed Demara that the rangy Culhane ate heavily yet didn't put on weight. His steady infusion of meth treated him right. He methodically ate his Cajun-style rib eye with a double portion of intentionally lumpy mashed potatoes. With surgical care he cut his meat, chewing each piece thoroughly. It was as if he was practicing restraint, and should he let his will slip, he'd pick up the meat in his hands and go at it lustfully with his incisors.

"Shall we take a test-drive?" Hintton asked when they were finished. He placed his black American Express credit card on top of the bill in its plastic tray.

"Oh, yes," Culhane said. He wiped his mouth with

his cloth napkin. He briefly looked at the residue he'd removed, then tossed the napkin aside.

Demara and Culhane in his aging Camry followed the producer in his shiny forest-green Land Rover. His multileveled house was up a gated road, and they passed a pair of gardeners going about their tasks of trimming and caring for a large xeriscaped swath that featured mountain currant, bayberry, succulents, and various other plantings where there had once been a rolling lawn.

Entering the abode, Demara asked to use the bathroom and was directed to one on the second level, accessed by a staircase with a chrome railing. As she reached the landing, she looked to her right, through a sliding glass door. Outside was a slightly raised concrete terrace with two large white circles, one inside the other, painted on its surface. A large white plus sign was painted in the middle of the inner circle. Domed landing lights bordered the outer circle. Demara was pretty sure this was a helipad, as she'd seen something similar on some cable TV show about fabulous mansions.

"Damn," she mumbled and found the bathroom.

Afterward, in the sunken living room of the house, as Demara heated some crystals in her pipe, a tall blonde in butt-hugging cutoffs and a loose, plunging V-necked top clacked into view in high heels.

"This is Tomika," Hintton said, introducing her.

"Hey," the beauty said, plopping down next to Hintton on his white leather, U-shaped couch. She picked up a copy of *Wired* and listlessly leafed through it.

She looked awfully damn Aryan to Demara to be a Tomika, but this was Hollywood and you could be anything you wanted as long as they paid for it. "She gonna be on the show?" She studied her handiwork and judged it ready. She put a flame to the pipe's bowl.

"Yes," Hintton said, bobbing his head up and down and smiling.

Tomika put the magazine aside. Demara passed the pipe to the other woman, who reached across Hintton's torso.

"Thank you," Tomika said. She had an accent, but it wasn't a European one, Demara decided. The blonde took a pull and handed the pipe to Hintton, who duplicated her actions. He sat back on the cushions to let the rush overcome him. He held the smoking pipe on his thigh.

"Ahem," Culhane said loudly.

"Sorry, brah." Hintton handed the pipe over, and the director sucked some fumes into his lungs.

Soon Demara cooked up more meth, and the four sparked up and lazed on the large couch, Hintton and the tall blonde huddled together, with Culhane sitting in the curve and Demara a foot or so away from him. At some point the producer picked up a remote control on the coffee table and put on music, which played from hidden speakers. At first he had on a driving techno beat, which brought forth groans of displeasure.

"Everybody's a goddamn critic," he groused goodnaturedly as he switched the sound to mellower smooth jazz riffs.

The four remained still, enjoying their collective euphoria. Demara looked at Culhane, his eyes half lidded, a slight smile on his face. She closed her eyes, remembering the drug-aversion class she took in high school. Their teacher, the with-it Mr. Griffin, had run through the effects of numerous drugs and had shown them a video supposedly of a man freaking out on crystal meth. This guy paced about a room in what looked like a middle-class abode. He would stop now and then, his hands upraised, fingers twitching like insect antenna, and launch into another paranoid rant.

"It's not black helicopters, man. It's like these invisible, these floating platforms, man, that swoop over our roofs when we're asleep or in the can, man. They've got these scopes, these machines with which they can tune in to our brain waves like you would a radio."

Of course, the kids guffawed at this clown, as did their teacher, who nonetheless did his best to impart the proper warning to his charges about the dangers of the drug. Demara had yet to see anybody hallucinate on meth, though she certainly knew those who manifested shitty attitudes when coming down from their high.

She opened her eyes and looked at her companions. Each was enwrapped in his or her personal enjoyment. She had expected Tomika to be lying across Hintton. But she'd curled her supple body into a fetal position on the couch and lay with her now bare feet next to his leg. Her purple-painted toenails had sparkles on them, and this fascinated Demara. She giggled, then closed her eyes once more.

Two hours later Culhane and Demara were again in his Camry, heading back to Los Angeles. She felt good. She'd been worried that Hintton would hedge about wanting her to supply him with meth based on whether she said yes or no to the reality-show idea. But she could tell he liked the Mas Trece shit too much, and they agreed that she would be his candy girl. Addicts were so predictable, she told herself. And well-off ones liked the idea of their stuff being delivered to them by those they deemed underlings—be it drugs or a seared ahi tuna sandwich. That reminded her she was hungry again. She better watch her caloric intake, she warned herself, but she was also comforted knowing her old man liked an ass he could grab on to when they went at it.

"You think much about fate, Harley Lynn?" Culhane suddenly asked her.

"That Tina makes you philosophical, huh?"

"I'm serious."

Her forehead crinkled. "I guess I try not to, Reonaldo." She called him by his full name to demonstrate her irritation at his question. "Life is complicated enough without worrying about some power sitting up there, looking down on us, moving us around like chess pieces."

"That's not exactly what I mean. To me fate is this cosmic force that doesn't overtly manipulate us but rather offers us a choice."

"Like what's behind the door," she stated.

"Exactly. Fate puts the choices before us, but it's up to us to make our own opportunity."

"But there's a tiger behind one of those doors, Reo. That's not an opportunity. That's death."

He hunched a shoulder. "That's fate, babe."

"Sheeeet."

"Just saying. You want to recognize when opportunities are there."

"Well, isn't Hintton an opportunity?"

"Yeah, he is."

"But?"

"But you want to strive for better, is all."

"Gee, Reo, getting all big brotherly. You are the one who set this up. Wanting to get in good with your boy."

"Understood. I . . . you know . . . don't want you to set your sights too low."

She laughed heartily. "Damn, you sound like my mom."

He glanced over at Demara. "She knows about you and Chanchin?"

"So?"

"He could be blocking your path."

Echoing her mother's words, she said, "He's no good for me, you mean."

"Hey, I'm just saying he's of the moment."

"You ought to tell Mom that about her boyfriend."

"Yeah?"

"Shady type," she said with a bemused grin.

"Bullshit."

"No, really. Chanchin and him had a little run-in. Fact, he saw him the first night he showed up at the Ridge, the night he started squatting."

"He's homeless?"

"Now he's not. And he's practically moved in with my mom. Shit, she's all enamored with him." She shook her head disapprovingly. "He could be trouble for her."

"What? Like he's going to rip her off?"

"Not like that. But he practically admitted he's done armed robberies."

"He's younger than your mom?"

"No," she said, then amended her statement. "He might be a couple of years younger than her, but he's in shape. Chanchin says he walks like a dude that's been on the razor blades, as he calls it. Been inside, he means. But O'Conner says he hasn't done time."

"O'Conner," he mused.

"That's all he goes by, or says to call him Connie. But he looks about as much a Connie as Big Blondie back at Tug's fits her name."

He snickered. "What's he look like?"

She described him.

Culhane frowned, watching the roadway as they went along Pacific Coast Highway.

"Why that look?" Demara asked him. "You couldn't possibly know him, Reo."

"Saying I'm not down?"

"Oh, no, homey, you the downest motherfuckah I know."

"It's just that he sounds familiar. About seven years ago I was doing second unit on this cable movie for the Syfy Channel. It was a pretty good effort, all about a prison revolt at a max prison built on the moon."

"All right," she said, encouraging him to continue.

"So we had some extras who'd been gangbangers who were now part of a talent agency specializing in guys like that. Tatted up and so forth, able to ad-lib in the right slang and like that."

"He wouldn't have been one of the bangers."

"Yes, I know. But there was some older dudes the casting director found to play other prisoners, and I remember this one time a couple of the younger ex-gang members were bothering one of the second-billed actresses. I think she got faded on some weed with one of them, and naturally, they figured this was an invitation."

"Of course," she responded dryly.

"Anyway, I remember this guy getting in their faces one time. This was toward the end of the day and near the trailers. I was just watching, but this guy doesn't come to blows with the other two. They're puffing up their chests and talking smack about what they're gonna do to him and his mama, and he's cool, quiet, and shit. Not getting bent, not thumping himself or anything."

"Just talking," Demara commented.

"I can't really hear him, but this cat deflates the two saggers and they walk off. He's not gesturing wildly or raising his voice. But whatever he tells them gets them to back the fuck off. He then walks back my way and gives me a quick look and keeps on. That's why I remember his face. The actress didn't have any more problems."

"I bet he hooked up with this chick."

Culhane nodded. "Indeed he did, now that you mention it, but that's not my point. The point is this dude was one of a few ex-cons the casting director got for minor roles, and if memory serves"—he tapped his forehead with an index finger—"the one I think was your boy O'Conner had done time for manslaughter."

"He said he wasn't in the joint."

"Like he wouldn't lie? I'm sure he doesn't want to rock the boat with your mom."

"Maybe." She shrugged a shoulder. "It doesn't seem to me he'd give a damn one way or the other, though."

"But he's been cagey about his past, right?"

"That's true. Yeah, he could have been covering up." Demara's thing with Saladago didn't give her pause. She could handle him. But her mother involved with a man like O'Conner got her beside herself. She didn't want her mother hurt psychologically, and she certainly did not want her to get in trouble with the authorities. That wouldn't be good for either of them. "Was the one you're talking about on-screen in this epic?" she asked.

"He might have even had a line. I have a copy of the film. It's called *Lunar Riot*. I'll get it to you, and you can take a look."

"All right," she said. They were on the Santa Monica Freeway, heading east. He was dropping her off near Century City and her gym in one of the high-rises. There was a film and TV agent she'd started a friendship with at the treadmills. From the few choice words she'd said during their runs, Demara had a suspicion she was into X. No sense not feeling her out, given she was a full-service provider of vice.

"You do appreciate the irony of this situation, don't you?" he asked.

"I know what the fuck I'm doing. It's Gwen I need to watch out for."

"Right on."

"Uh-huh," she drawled.

That evening Demara and Saladago had a pizza with three kinds of meats, along with roasted red peppers, as toppings from nearby Scorchy's Pizza and Hot, Hot Wings and drank several imported beers. They were in one of several apartments the Mas Trece kept in L.A. The apartment was in one of those dingbat buildings ubiquitous to the Southern California landscape. This building was called The Windcaster, and the sign included a large plaster starfish alongside the title. It was in a part of the city west of nearby downtown, where the multicolored neon signage was in hangul, the Korean written language, but the language you heard on the avenues was Spanish. The apartment had been recently occupied by one of their soldiers on the run, who had since snuck into Mexico, heading for Michoacán. For their aperitif, the couple shared a blunt.

On a square flat of plywood on the dining room table, Saladago had begun assembling a cityscape. It featured structures made out of cut and glued together pieces of cardboard, roadways fashioned from black construction paper, small metal trucks, motorcycles with plastic army men on them, and animal cracker boxes taped together to form a rectangle, which he'd redecorated with a marker to indicate windows and doors. There was also a built-up section at one end, composed of several pieces of plywood cut in semicircular shapes and then tiered one on the other. This represented the amphitheater above Willow Ridge.

She asked him about the model, and he answered, "Ever see *The Dirty Dozen?* This great fuckin' war picture with Lee Marvin and Charles Bronson? It's about these condemned prisoners who have to take this castle with a bunch of Nazi high rollers in it."

"No," she said. Though she did have a vague idea who Charles Bronson was.

"You ought to," he responded indignantly. "Me and Pops would watch that flick when it came on TV. He loved that movie and knew the lines from that bad boy." He stood and did a quick imitation of Jim Brown running to throw grenades down the air vents as a machine gunner cut him down. "Big Jim almost makes it. Then tat, tat, tat, bitch ass Nazi motherfuckahs cut him down." He fell back onto the couch, laughing.

"And?" she said impatiently.

"It's about being prepared, baby girl." He shook a finger in the direction of the model. "You just wait. You'll see. Okay? This ain't no bullshit."

"Whatever."

She lost interest, but later, blitzed, she asked him another question. "You do any checking into O'Conner's background?"

"No. What for?"

They sat next to each other on the couch, their clothes on. On a sheet of graph paper, Saladago was drawing an organizational chart with the meth lab house near the top and rectangular boxes off of that connected by lines. In the boxes were various names, including Demara's. One of the boxes had the tag Biker Girl in it and was off to the side, in its own area. He'd written the word Rally over the box.

Saladago looked up from his handiwork at her. "You think he's up to something?"

"What do you think, Chan?"

"Think you need to tap your mom's bedroom so we can get the lowdown."

She hit him in the upper arm. "Ugh. You don't need to be hearing that, and neither do I. He don't tell her anything, anyway. Nothing that she don't want to hear."

"Yeah, you sure about that?"

"You don't tell me shit." She pointed at the hand-drawn diagram. "Who's Biker Girl?"

He didn't hesitate. "Inga Brody."

"Who's that?"

"She's a—what you call it in those spy shows?—an asset."

"A booty asset?"

"It ain't about that, Harley Lynn. This here is bid'ness."

"I'm just your mule bitch. You don't have to tell me nothing. Ain't that right?"

It cracked him up when she tried to sound like a heina. She was so cute. "You'll know when you need to know."

"That right?"

"You know I'm on the real."

"Building your version of a cartel."

"The American way, baby."

"Where do I fit in that?"

He glared at her with glassy eyes. "Where do you want to fit in? You the one about pushing product to get your career on, and I'm good with that. Shit, at least your clients pay on time and they don't have to be regulated like them corner fools. But you talkin' about bein' crewed up for sure? For being really down?" Now he had let his diction slip, as if he were talking to her like she was an eight ball chick with a teardrop tattooed on her cheek.

"I'm an earner."

"That's right. You are." He spread his hands, by way of asking if she wanted more. But nothing came free.

She was on the payroll because she was his squeeze. If she wanted to be part of the organization, that meant all the way in. She couldn't be straddling the fence like she was now. She finally said, "I don't know that I'm ready."

"You let me know, Harley Lynn. Okay?" Tenderly, he touched her face, then returned to plotting out his chart. Afterward, he studied it intently, eschewing any more beer or weed.

Since they were teenagers in high school, Demara had known Saladago was one of those people who had a faculty for vectors and numbers. She'd struggled through geometry, and one time she was trying to finish up some homework during lunch at the outdoor benches. That was why he'd come over from his clique of homeys on the quad and taken the pencil from her hand. "Check this out," he'd said. Standing next to where she sat, he'd then completed the correct depictions of her trapezoids and isosceles triangles. She'd huffed. He'd been triangulating ever since.

Before they went to bed, Saladago crumpled his chart into a tight ball and set it alight in the sink and washed the ashes down the drain.

As they lay together after making love, Demara snuggled against his back, an arm around his muscular shoulders. They slumbered as one, and Saladago dreamed about his father. Among his tattoos was one for him, Octavio, done in a style that was a cross between Gothic and skateboarder. Unlike the typical barrio story,

Saladago's father hadn't disappeared and was a hard-working man who made his living at a firm that produced double-glazed windows in various shapes and sizes for houses and apartments. Must have been something in that that made his middle son so good with shapes and figures, his old man would joke. He got along okay with his dad.

The old man never laid a hand on his mother and did his drinking mostly with fellow workers at a bar near the factory. One night he was sitting there, joking and laughing with the others, when a car jumped the curb and plowed through the front of the bar, the Lion's Den. Octavio Saladago died instantly, upon impact with the out-of-control Mazda family van, it was determined later. The driver wasn't drunk or high. She was fond of cats and had swerved to avoid one skittering across the road.

The older brother and younger sister of Chanchin Saladago grieved along with him and their mother. This was his junior year in high school. His mother had gone on about God's will, but the middle child understood the true meaning of his father's untimely exit from this world. He understood that if there was a God, He or She left the day-to-day running of the universe to flunkies like Fate, Death, and all the rest of them crafty pendejos. That you better get it in your head there was no certainty or reason. If there was, a good man like his dad wouldn't have died like he did. His siblings got themselves lined up in desk jobs like any other wage slave, whereas he was about getting what you could the best way you could.

In his dream as the two painted the side of the family's house, his father shook his head disapprovingly.

"What will you become, Roberto? One of those hard men who forever looks over his shoulder? No one to trust? Who offers pain in one hand and suffering in the other?"

"I don't make anyone do nothing they don't want," he said.

His father looked away from him and, using his scraper, returned to chipping away the old paint from the wood. He chipped and chipped, and the cloud of old paint and wood dust that was kicked up was so thick his son suddenly couldn't see his father. He tried to call out to him, but he'd lost his voice. When the dust subsided, his father was gone from his ladder.

Saladago shifted on the bed, but he continued sleeping, as did Demara. Her face was serene.

Chapter Fourteen

Chanchin Saladago didn't get the fascination with motorcycles. Bikers talking about the wind in their hair and face, the freedom of being on their hog and the open road. Knotted about how helmet laws were forced on them by a bunch of pussy-lipped bureaucrats—another sign of the erosion of our freedoms. He snickered at this as he leaned on the side of his car. It wasn't the Impala, but a Nissan cut low to the ground with black, sporty rims.

At one of the outdoor benches near them, Jimmy Puppet and Emilo "Zacca" Alvarez munched on burgers and fries. Zacca Alvarez's nickname was derived from the Z-shaped scar on the side of his face. Once, when locked down in what was then the California Youth Authority, he had the opportunity to receive plastic surgery to eliminate the mark. He steadfastly refused, as the scar made him stand out, he reasoned. It also made him easier to point out in a lineup, but there it was.

Saladago would admit, though, that Inga Brody looked good on her Harley as she rode onto the parking lot of the Sonic fast-food outlet. In her jeans and form-fitting black tee, the silver streak in her hair highlighted, she was like an advertisement for a grind-house film with plenty of T and A, playing only in his head. She parked and got off her machine.

"What it is, what it could be," she said.

"Funny lady," Saladago replied.

She'd put her hands in her back pockets, looking around the lot. The wind blew parts of her dark hair across her tanned face. She shook her head to clear her vision. "They're going to be moving about seven hundred large during the run."

"On the bikes?" he asked.

She smiled. Her teeth were crooked, but it made her look endearing. "The Vikings have a float in the parade. The haul will be hidden on this, and when they get up to the amphitheater, there'll be a truck waiting for the final stage of the delivery." She removed her hands from her back pockets and gestured with one. "Collectors will be making collections and tallies a couple of days before."

"The feria comes together, then, the night before. Where the float is built, right?"

"Shit, don't even think about hitting them there, homeboy. The float's being assembled at the ironworks in Chino. That place will be hip deep in club members in from Fresno, Arizona, and what have you, itching to shoot and hack any pepper picker's face that pops up."

Saladago remained placid. "They're around during the run, too."

"And the cops," she noted. "'Cause the weird thing is that the only damn time Hemet gets a heavy police and sheriff presence is during this damn event."

"Meaning the Vikings leave a lot of their firepower at home," Saladago concluded. This made sense given any number of the club members were facing third strikes. Of course, the same harsh penalty hung over the heads of his crew, too. That was why Brody's inside information was invaluable.

"We good on the supplies?" she asked.

"Hooking that up today over in Orange County."

She looked away, then back at him. "We can't rehearse this. We've got to do it right the first time out."

"Who you tellin'?"

"Funny man."

"Ain't I?" He grinned but then added, "We still better meet to go over what everybody's supposed to do. Got an apartment in L.A. where we can do that. Even did up a model."

"What?"

"You know, like the streets and buildings and shit." Because of his math skills, Saladago had been guided into an architecture class in high school. He had found the practice of drafting elevation plans and designing pools boring. He had liked the part when they got to make models of structures, such as auditoriums and office buildings.

"What for?" she asked.

"So we can go over who's supposed to be where. We can see it, see?"

Brody huffed, but they agreed on a time and she rode away. Saladago had two money drops to make; then he and his men got on the freeways and were out in Santa Ana before 2:00 p.m. He'd been in the barrio out this way a few times and found the address he'd been given easily enough.

Saladago admired the restored houses outside the windows of his car as he went along in the Floral Park section. Along an oak-lined street he parked, and the three got out and followed a pristine driveway, no oil stains or cracks in its surface. It was the kind that had an island of grass in the middle. The grass was immaculate, as well.

In back of the main house was a garage with an apartment over it. A set of narrow steps led up to the garage apartment, and taking the lead, Saladago started up. The glass-paneled door above him opened, and Ben Reynolds stepped out.

"Downstairs," he said, pointing that way.

Saladago groaned, but the three reversed course and went back the way they'd just come. The Mas Trece trio stood around the garage door as Reynolds unlocked the padlock on the latch, then swung the door upward. Inside overhead fluorescents were on. There was a man in coveralls standing under those lights. He wore an opaque George Walker Bush mask under a watchman's cap. He also held a Remington semi-auto pistol grip shotgun at half mast. There were thin blue rubber gloves on his hands, like the ones mechanics wore. His wrists weren't visible, as the gloves went up some into the sleeves of the coveralls.

This hombre did not appear unfamiliar with the workings of the shooting item, Saladago estimated.

"The fuck," Alvarez exclaimed, reaching for a pistol tucked in his waistband under his loose shirt.

"It's just a precaution, gentlemen," Reynolds said calmly.

Jimmy Puppet had put a hand on Alvarez's arm. He knew Saladago wanted to see what kind of a leader he was when the unexpected happened.

"We come vouched for, man," Saladago said.

"Then let's get to it," Reynolds replied.

The garage was outfitted as if it were for hobbyists, only there were no hand or power tools in it. Four plastic patio chairs were atop one another in a corner of the space. A plastic picnic cooler was over there, too. The floor was spotless. No oil stains here, either. There was an empty workbench with only a roll of paper towels standing on end on it.

Underneath the bench was a metal equipment case, like something used for housing a rock band's gear. Reynolds tapped a toe on the case and stepped aside before Zacca Alvarez and Jimmy P picked it up and placed it on the workbench. They unlatched it to reveal several cylindrical canisters bedded in foam.

Alvarez picked up one, making a face at it as if it were a giant insect. "What this funny writing on it?"

"That's the Cyrillic alphabet, youngster," Reynolds answered. "These goods are Russian military issue. They use this quicker than tear gas on the unruly types they got over there." He didn't add the information about vomiting, disorientation, and possible death from the stuff, which was covered in the warning label the Mas Trece member couldn't decipher. Besides, he was sure his buyers couldn't care less.

"How we know you ain't selling us empty cans, huh?" Alvarez shook the canister, holding it up to his ear.

"Keep that up and you'll find out," the older man warned.

Zacca Alvarez looked at Saladago, who looked at Reynolds and the other one. He was now farther back in the room, the gun still at the ready. He didn't seem to tire holding the weapon, and Saladago knew from experience that it wasn't like in the movies, where you saw dudes shooting shotguns one-handed. Those things had a weight and kick to them.

The spray from it would surely catch him—and he doubted he would be as lucky as Jimmy not to have his head blown the hell off. But he wasn't here to fuck around, anyway. Saladago took out folded-over hundreds and flicked them down onto the bench. The money was held together by a thick rubber band.

"What about gas masks?" Alvarez asked as he buckled up the metal case.

"That's what them Internets are for," Reynolds said, picking up the money.

Alvarez was about to argue, but Saladago cut him off. "Let's go. We got what we came for."

The three left. The man in the Bush mask then walked out front, along the driveway, the shotgun down at his side. He returned, taking off the mask, to reveal his face. It was O'Conner.

"How'd you know I knew them?" he asked, snapping loose a paper towel from the roll on the workbench and wiping his sweating face. Little air had circulated underneath the mask.

"I didn't. I needed you for backup. You didn't ask what for the other night."

O'Conner had left Hemet in plenty of time but had arrived only twenty minutes before Saladago and the others. A big rig carrying tomatoes had overturned on the 91 freeway, and traffic had been backed up for three miles.

"What if I had told you I couldn't make it when you called?" Not particularly worried about leaving his trace DNA around, O'Conner discarded the used paper towel on the workbench.

"Darla's pretty handy with a gat. But you know these macho types. Just seeing a woman in this context, they'd be duty bound to flex and see if she'd jump or not."

"You got it all covered, don't you?"

Reynolds held the money aloft. "Out of this I gotta give Barry his cut. Then there's you."

"Barry? Barry Nichols, Bent Nickels?"

"Yeah. He was the broker."

"Good God, he's ten, fifteen years older than you."

Reynolds smiled crookedly.

"What the hell is a man who should be concerned about polishing his dentures doing hooked up with the Mas Trece?"

"Bent's got a hustle going among the seniors," Reynolds said proudly. "What with Cialis and Viagra keeping these old degenerates in the saddle, some of 'em are also getting their kicks with that ecstasy. He supplies 'em, and he in turn is supplied by a Mas Trece, ah, representative."

A disturbing image of wrinkly couples high on X, and the men primed on erectile dysfunction pills, careening around rest homes flitted, unwanted, through O'Conner's mind.

Reynolds continued. "The Mas Trece homeboy found out Bent had been in ordinances in the Korean War and asked recently whether he could obtain the bye-bye gas."

"Which is where you came into the picture."

"Indeed."

O'Conner lifted two plastic chairs off the stack and sat in one while sliding the other one over to Reynolds. As he did this, he said, "Right, like I expected to be justly compensated for the trepidation I no doubt instilled in Chanchin and his knuckleheads." While there seemed to be no threats imminent, he nonetheless leaned the Remington on the chair to facilitate an easy reach.

"Aw, don't pout, I think highly of you."

"Thanks for looking out for my self-esteem."

"Naturally." Reynolds pulled the small cooler over and flipped the top open to reveal the ice and the two beers inside. He handed a can to O'Conner and also sat down. Reynolds popped the tab of his beer and had a pull. "So what do you think those ruffians are up to?"

"Something soon, that's for sure."

Arceneaux had been able to back trace an address for Inga Brody. He'd also offered to set it up so O'Conner would be able to listen to her calls on a smartphone, but he didn't think that would be necessary. That was too much sitting around. Plus, he was pretty sure Brody wasn't a gabber. The Vikings had certainly learned the lessons of other bike gangs, like the Hell's Angels and the Huns, who were both busted by the DEA and ATF. He was sure she was always circumspect over easily tapped phone lines, be they traditional or wireless. Still, there was her visit to the Mas Trece lab. He told Reynolds about that.

As he did, Reynolds smiled knowingly. "And here you are, a motorcycle owner."

"What are you talking about?"

"The Kruisin' for Kids rally. It's a week from this Saturday." He explained its purpose and noted that the Vandal Vikings would be prominent, with their members riding in the rally.

O'Conner had more of his beer. "The Mas Trece gonna fuck with them during the parade, or is there some sort of tailgate party and what not?"

"There's gotta be more than that, obviously. But I bet your girl, this Inga, knows. Why else would she be palavering with the enemy? You said you came on them messin' her around."

"That's usual biker bullshit for them. That wouldn't be a reason for her to turn on the club. Which, if she's found out, is a death sentence." He sipped more.

"Arcie got you into her phone," Reynolds said. "Play detective, and have him bring up calls she made. Go back a year or no more than eighteen months, let's say. It would have to be an incident fresh enough to be current but old enough that she would have the patience to plan."

"She's not the kind to kiss and tell," O'Conner opined.

"Clues, baby, clues. Why am I watching all those *Rockford Files* reruns on cable for, if not to pick up some pointers? If it was something that happened to turn her, there may be a hint of that in a phone call she made . . . or received."

"Makes sense," O'Conner said. "I'll see what I can find out, if only to satisfy you."

"Do it quick, okay? What you discover might be good for our thing."

"What thing is that?"

"The score Barbara is financing," Reynolds answered flatly, having more of his beer.

"The woman in Laguna Beach? The one Darla had me drive out and meet?" He remembered the file, too. "Wait, she's not the mark?"

"She's the guv'nor. That's what they call 'em in the British underworld." He smiled, pleased with his international take on nefarious subcultures.

"And here I figured I was sizing her up. But she was checking me out. The file your girl laid on me for what? Show me she was legit?"

"Barbara's new to the undertakings of crooks like us. In her world, that's how you establish bona fides."

"You really have been cracking the thesaurus, haven't you?"

Reynolds raised his eyebrows over the rim of the can to his mouth.

"What's the job?" O'Conner asked.

"You remember Barbara has those antique shops? Four, to be exact."

"Yeah."

"So she has a fifth store she opened about three months ago in a swank little mall in Orange. But this isn't an antiques shop. It's a pet food and supplies outfit. Sells reptiles and turtles, too. But she didn't open the store because she did a business plan and determined this was a new market for her. The store, given the rent and the overhead of the two staffers, is a losing proposition."

"But it's about the location, isn't it?"

Reynolds ducked his head slightly. "That's right. Two doors down from her, there's a company called Felcor. They're a full-service provider to nonbank ATM machines. Convenience stores, swap meets, even a few Indian casinos out your way. There's a lot of these damn machines around. Each time there's a transaction—and the average withdrawal is sixty bucks a pop—there's a surcharge fee."

O'Conner said, "Felcor supplies the twenties and fifties to the ATMs and splits that fee with the store owners."

"They do," Reynolds answered. And in most cases, the stores only rent the machines. They don't buy them outright. Anyway, twice each month, in the middle and at the end, there's something like two mil collected and redistributed through their facility, an unmarked building. Their name isn't even on it. Most of the tenants in the mall have no idea what Felcor does, anyway. They purposely have the armored cars coming in the early hours."

The end of the month was approaching. "How does Barbara know what they do? I can't imagine she was at the shop at three in the morning, changing the filters in the turtle tanks, and saw an armored car roll up."

"She knows one of the investors in Felcor. A trust fund baby."

"He approached her about investing?"

"I'm not clear on all the particulars, but this cat tried to bamboozle her mother, Catherine. He tried to muscle her out in some kind of assets grab. For tax reasons, the bulk of the money Barbara earned when she sold off her late husband's aerospace firm is in Mom's name. It's a philanthropic institute she controls. Catherine must be close to seventy-five or so, but she's not a bad looking chick for her age."

O'Conner snickered. "You lookin' to squire the mother, too, Ben?"

"Just sayin', is all."

"Huh," O'Conner grunted. "So this is a revenge bit?"

"Cold-blooded payback. Barbara wants this fool hurt."

"Felcor's money must be insured."

Reynolds smiled. "We're to plant evidence against this guy, Paul Stevenson. Make it seem like an inside job."

"That's fuckin' devious. What? Paul did the gigolo bed hop with Mom?"

"It's that kind of burning insight you bring to the table that I've come to rely on," Reynolds deadpanned. "It was Barbara who approached Darla."

"Well, well," O'Conner said and had another drink.

They finished their beers and worked out the particulars needed for the heist. They then restacked the chairs and quit the garage. Reynolds was anxious when it came to DNA. He retrieved the paper towel O'Conner had used and, along with the empty cans, put it in the cooler, which he carried out by its handle.

Out front they set a time to meet for the takedown's prep, which would include Darla Ballard and Barbara Giffords. Reynolds would secure most of the equipment they needed, but left it to O'Conner to obtain some items from Arceneaux, though he knew him as well. He said he was going to talk to Voss about an item or two, but when O'Conner told him about their run-in, Reynolds decided it was best to use someone else.

"I know he's a pro and all, but he could still be festering about getting back at you," the older man said.

"You're the boss," O'Conner replied.

"Try to keep that in mind," Reynolds cracked.

The two went their separate ways.

The house Reynolds and O'Conner had commandeered was underwater. While foreclosures were less abundant in Orange County than in the Inland Empire, there were still plenty of homes where the owners had simply walked away from their overwhelming debt. This one had belonged to a friend of Ballard's and had been taken over by the bank some months ago. Reynolds had removed the FOR SALE sign embedded in the front lawn and had stuck it inside the empty house.

Reynolds had used spurts of liquid nitrogen in an aerosol can to gain entry. The can's spray nozzle had a small tube attached to it, for accuracy, and he'd frozen out the mechanisms in the locks to get into the house and the granny flat above the garage. If the Mas Trece returned, they'd find it empty. Even though the bank was fastidious about the upkeep of the premises, the house had been on the market for eighteen months. Given the economic conditions, it wasn't going to sell anytime soon.

Good thing, Reynolds reflected as he drove off. He wasn't a man who'd gotten used to punching a time clock. Criminal undertakings weren't seasonal or dependent upon customer relations. You planned, you did, and you were gone.

He looked in the rearview and watched O'Conner's station wagon recede. If he had any regrets about not being a traditional example of a father figure to him when he was a teenager, it didn't show on his face. He put his eyes back on the road and continued on.

Chapter Fifteen

Gwen Gardner rounded the corner in the Earth Harvest supermarket with her handheld basket and ran into Stan Yamashira. He was pushing a cart and had on his floppy fishing hat. His nose was peeling from over-exposure.

"Stan, how goes it?" she said.

"Fine. And you . . . and Mr. O'Conner?"

"Good," she said. It tickled her that the older man was fond of him. Inwardly, she hesitated to refer to O'Conner as her boyfriend.

They were in the produce section, and Yamashira touched his index finger to the brim of his hat. "Well, there's some nectarines over there I'm eager to try." He began to walk off.

Gardner blurted, "Stan, it's not my business per se, but have you put some money into Blanche Allen's investors' pool?"

"Yes, but a conservative amount. I didn't go over-board. Why? You thinking of putting in some money?"

"I was."

"But?"

"But Connie advised me against it."

"What'd he say?"

"He said Blanche's girlfriend, Didi, was involved in a real estate swindle once before. Did a couple of years in the joint."

Yamashira almost laughed. O'Conner's influence was evident in her choice of the slang term for prison. "Come on, Gwen."

She moved closer, lowering her voice. "I Googled it and found a couple of pieces in the *Orange County Register* and the *L.A. Times*. It involved the Anthem of Reason Institute." She didn't mention she'd been attracted to the ARI once. She knew their reputation and wanted to make sure he understood she shared his wariness about them.

"You're shitting me."

"I'll send you the links. Didi is Deidra Crawford. And no, it's not a case of mistaken identity. There's a pretty clear picture of her in one of the articles."

"I'll read 'em." He was about to go to his nectarines but stopped again. "How did Connie find this out about the girlfriend?"

A hand on her hip, proudly she said, "He was looking out for my interests, Stan."

"As he should. But how did he find out?" he repeated.

"Tell you what. You check out the links, and then you can ask him."

"Thank you, Gwen."

"You judge for yourself."

"Okay." They said their good-byes to each other, and he walked over to the produce. As he considered his choices, he ruminated on what Gardner had told him.

She wasn't given to malicious gossip, so he was certain the e-mail he'd get from her would be legit. What he particularly wondered was how O'Conner had obtained the information about Didi.

Selecting his fruit and putting it in a plastic bag, Yamashira considered what if O'Conner was some sort of secret operative for those damnable ARIers? Maybe they'd sent him into Willow Ridge to ingratiate himself with the residents, get in good by standing up to the bikers and gang members, like he had, and it was all a ruse. Wedging himself into their community, he'd sown dissent from within. What was that show from the '50s called?

His hand reaching for the strawberries, Yamashira recalled the title, *I Led Three Lives*. It was about an undercover FBI agent posing as a communist to infiltrate various cells out to disrupt and overthrow our precious democracy. He pictured the actor in his mind. He couldn't remember his name, but he was always on edge, sweaty, and near paranoid about getting found out. Placing his selection in his basket, Yamashira chuckled. O'Conner was the opposite of that guy in the TV show. Cool and collected, Mr. Removed, he was.

But hadn't he gotten in good with the fetching Gwen Gardner? His money girl. Hadn't he gotten on the good side of an old duffer like him? Oh, yeah, the two of them would be his strike team for sure when the shit went down. This notion amused the hell out of Yamashira, and by the time he was finished shopping and back home, he'd worked out the steps O'Conner would take to engineer a takeover of the Ridge. The subdivision would be remade as a gated enclave of the ARI, where their celebrity members would be sent to dry out from whatever affliction was ailing them—from falling down drunk on the red carpet to flashing their junk in public.

Absolutely hilarious. Yamashira felt so pleased with his scenario, he lived it up and ate two nectarines.

Chapter Sixteen

Cody Bradford absently picked at a scab on the lower part of his jaw as he reached inside the refrigerator in Ian Childes's studio apartment. It was one of the lacerations that bastard O'Conner had administered to his face via the weed whacker he'd initially attacked the older man with before he took it from him. Pointedly, he didn't offer to get a beer for Childes or Doug Brill, who was also in the apartment. Nor had he brought the beer. He closed the fridge door and had to use a bottle opener to get the cap off the foreign-made brew. He took a pull, watching the other two, blank-eyed.

"Oh, shit," Childes exclaimed, working the control of a video game. He was first-person shooting and slicing on the TV screen as Rip Torrent, hero of *Mortal Death II*. Childes had just wiped out a truckload of zombies with a flamethrower and several MLB worthy, expertly pitched grenades.

The two gamers sat on Childes's worn couch, its stuffing erupting from the cushions and its sides. There were several posters taped to his walls, attesting to several fast-held conspiracy theories among the left and the right.

One of the posters depicted a crosshairs circle over the Twin Towers as they were destroyed on 9/11. It advertised a past conference organized on the theme that the attack was an inside job of a hyper-secret government agency and Wall Street.

"So, did you see about that slot with Chanchin?" Bradford asked Childes.

There was more clacking away on the controls hooked to the Xbox. Both Childes and Brill leaned and jerked their upper bodies as they battled each other in the game. Brill was King Zombie.

"Man, I told you it isn't like that," Childes said, not letting his attention lapse as he spoke. "It's not as if me and Chanchin hang." Reactively, Childes pulled in his shoulders as his avatar, Torrent, ducked in the game. "Like, I tried to ask him if he wanted another, you know, campus rep, but he didn't seem to hear me." In truth, Childes had asked Saladago about bringing Bradford on, but the gang chief had laughed, saying his friend was too much of a fuckup.

"Yeah, well, ask him again, okay? I got to get something going." Bradford sat splayed in an upholstered chair. He put the beer beside him on the floor.

"I'll try," Childes lied. He wasn't about to piss off Saladago, endangering his part-time job selling X and meth, and the income it generated for him.

There was more mayhem and bloodletting in the game. Then Brill asked Bradford, "You gonna make up with Mattie?" Bradford not being around the Ridge lately meant he didn't have a reason to see her. Plus, that O'Conner was around now, and he was scared of him. He might be his dad's age, but he was clearly not concerned about maintaining middle-class niceties. He'd come up to you and knock the shit out of you if he felt like it.

"Double fuck that ho," Bradford growled. "I know you're all infatuated with her 'cause she has a nice ass, D, but believe me, that chick is larcenous." He picked up his beer and, after another swallow, pointed the top toward Brill. "She's bangin' O'Conner, isn't she?"

"I don't know," Brill said sullenly. But he was pretty sure she was. He'd overheard his father talking to his mother about seeing O'Conner and Mattie Dodd being cozy. His dad had sounded kind of impressed, and his mom had given him some lip about that.

"Sheeet," Bradford swore. "That motherfucker is top doggin' it all over the Ridge, isn't he?"

"I guess," Brill said. He tried to concentrate on the game.

"You know that's so." Bradford wiped the back of his hand against his mouth. "The Mas Trece looking to put him in check?"

"What for?" Childes said. "They stay out of each other's way, and if you ask me, Chanchin likes it like that just fine."

"He's hardly worried about some dude closer to fifty than forty," Bradford sniffed.

"Chanchin's not doing anything special to get up on him is what I see," Childes remarked.

Talking ceased, the sounds of laser fire, brains being eaten, and death screams from the game filling the space. Then Brill observed, "What do you suppose Mattie's up to with O'Conner? She's not giving him fellatio for the taste of sour dick." The three of them guffawed.

"I got an idea," Bradford answered eventually, nodding. "Mattie had talked about it before, but I'd stalled her."

"What are you talking about?" Brill said.

"Vi and her bootleg designer gear hustle." He pointed

at the floor forcefully. "She bugged me a couple different times to get in on that, so I sorta introduced them."

"Yeah, so?" Childes veered his torso to the right as Torrent ran up a wall, like in a *Matrix* movie, then back flipped off its surface and out of the way of the swing of an energy-crackling scythe.

Bradford hunched. "Because even though Vi was once married to my dad's half brother's cousin, kinda making us like family, that bitch is more treacherous than Mattie."

"Does your dropout ass know any bitches who aren't treacherous?"

Taking Childes's snarky comment seriously, Bradford estimated he did not and said so.

"You think Mattie's using O'Conner as an enforcer, something like that?" Brill said, his Zombie king dropping down a shaft lined with robot octopus tentacles.

"For sure." Bradford chewed his bottom lip, frowning. "But I bet I could fix it so Vi doesn't do business with her."

"Look, Cody, you might want to leave her alone." Childes inclined his head slightly at Brill. "What D says about O'Conner sounds like he don't play. The one time I met him, you could tell he was, you know, serious."

"He don't scare me."

"Maybe he should," Childes said. "You know at the conventions I go to, you meet older dudes who said they were in the Gulf War and saw the file the military had on the results of the squalene in the flu shots they gave the troops. Shit like that. But then you find out they only know some guys who were over there and only read about the experiments, the same way I did. Posers is what I'm saying." He paused, then added, "'Cause I'm pretty sure O'Conner isn't about posing."

"Yeah, that's for sure," Brill grudgingly affirmed.

"He can fall down like anyone else," Bradford shot back. "And break them arthritic knees of his."

"Apparently, he didn't have no arthritis when he was handing out your beat down." Childes snickered.

"Ha-ha, motherfuckah." But Bradford had made up his mind. He had to come up with an excuse to contact Vi, which meant it better be about money—her money. Goddamn, he and Mattie had been friends with benefits once upon a time. But the last half year or so, they'd been only crime partners, working the knockoff electronic goods hustle. What had changed? It wasn't like he'd been any more or less himself these past six months. *Chicks.* Who the hell knew what went through their minds?

Staring at Childes and Brill, who continued to play the video game, it occurred to him it was Vi who'd turned him on to the thing he and Mattie had going. An Asian dude down in Alhambra, in the San Gabriel Valley, near L.A. They got the shit from him on consignment, then sold it at a markup to swap-meet contacts, soccer moms, whoever. It was a sweet deal, but he needed Mattie to work it, as having a pretty, smart girl like her involved just seemed to make the customers come running. He knew enough about himself to know that Mattie's way of smiling and being friendly was not his thing.

He got another beer and mapped out his next steps. He was going to fix it so she'd see he was invaluable. He was also for damn sure going to take care of that joker O'Conner. Absently, he picked at the scab again.

Chapter Seventeen

Along with several workers at Pearson Plastics, Marci Vickers was eating lunch in the factory's lunchroom. Chewing on her tuna fish sandwich, spiced with sliced jalapeños, she jutted her jaw at a group on a tour filing past the doorless doorway.

"Who's that with Mike?" she asked. Mike DeFord was the plant manager, and he was leading the group.

"Some kind of sports trinkets outfit," her coworker Nina Reyes said. "I think we might be getting a contract with them. Which is a good thing."

"You ain't lying," Vickers replied. "Get us some overtime."

"Girl, that's what I'm praying for."

They smiled. Vickers's cell phone chimed, playing a ringtone of a Kanye West number. She removed it from her pants pocket, recognizing the all-too-familiar number on the screen.

"Shit," she muttered, answering the call. It was from the front office at her son's school.

Reyes looked on with a jaundiced eye as Vickers talked.

"Yes," she said wearily. "This is Marci."

"Mom," her son said.

"What is it this time, Cullen?" Like in a lot of public schools, the kids were forbidden to use their cells on campus during school hours.

"Why you got to be a hater, Mom?"

"If you don't—" she began.

"I'm on the debate team," he blurted, happily interrupting her.

"You're shittin' me."

"Naw. This here is real. We gonna compete with other schools and everything. We get to travel out of town, whatever."

"So all that mouth you give me finally pays off."

"I guess, yeah," he said contritely.

"I'm proud of you, Cullen. I'm looking forward to seeing your debates. Call your father and tell him."

"I will, Mom. We've got to, you know, rehearse our speeches, learn new words, and what have you after school. See you at home after that."

"Okay, honey."

"Good news, huh?" her friend said when Vickers clicked off.

Vickers told her and added, "Maybe 'cause he's so excited about this, he'll actually get some homework done."

Reyes, who had two children of her own, raised a juice bottle. "Here's hoping."

When she'd finished her lunch, Vickers went to the restroom. In the stall next to her she overheard another woman talking on her smartphone.

"Look, motherfucka, I'm telling you like I told Voss. I don't have nothing to do with that kind of bullshit anymore. Yes, I saw him when he showed up out of the blue, and how he found me, who the hell knows. But I have no idea where he is or what he's up to, and I'm keeping it that way. You want to talk to him about a job, you ask Voss." She'd been keeping her voice low but forceful. "Uh-huh," she said after listening to whoever was on the other end. "See, I know why he put you on me, 'cause he was mad after he figured out it was me that sent that son of a bitch his way. But it's not like I had a choice. But I'm done, and please forget you called me."

As it happened, Vickers exited her stall at the same time as the other woman, a chunky, pretty individual with an iguana tattoo along her neck. She was smoothing out her skirt. Vickers recognized her as part of the small group from the sports merchandising firm.

"That wasn't very ladylike of me," she joked as both women looked in the mirror behind the sinks as they washed their hands.

"I'm hardly one to talk. I swear worse than my teenage son."

"I hear you." She began to dry her hands on a paper towel.

"So besides water bottles, what other kinds of sports stuff do you guys do?"

"Oh, all kinds of goofy things that these crazy fans buy. Like this baseball that opens up and it's an MP3 player, a desk pen set with your team's logo. A lot." She chuckled. "I'm Lilly," she said.

Vickers introduced herself. "Not putting you on the spot, but I used to be in sales. You have any need for new reps?"

Lilly Nash shrugged. "I can't say offhand, but then I just got my own promotion. It's a young company, always looking for talent." She produced a card from her stylish clutch bag. "Send me an e-mail, and we can talk about it."

"Cool. Thanks."

"I'm not just blowing you off, Marci. Drop me a line." Vickers shook the card. "I will."

"Okay." Nash smiled. She knew this wasn't a come-on from the other woman, whom she had sized up as straight. But no harm in being accommodating. They both left the restroom and nodded a good-bye.

Getting back to the assembly line, Reyes said, "What were you two doing in there? Both coming out grinning ear to ear?"

"Get your mind out of the gutter, Nina."

"Okay, sure. But aren't you the one that used to watch that lesbian show?"

"Please," Vickers said, heading to her position at the label stamper. "Haven't men given me enough trouble? I need to double up?"

Reyes replied, "Maybe trying something new will be good for you."

"As long as I tell you all the delicious details."

"Yes," her friend drawled. "Anything to take my mind off our drudgery."

Vickers made a knowing face and got to work.

Due to budget cuts, forty-something Jackie Reyes, Nina Reyes's older sister, had to work late irregular Thursdays at her city job as a clerk in the Bureau of Sanitation, part of L.A.'s Department of Public Works. Today wasn't such a day, but she was glad to have the overtime pay. There had been a rough patch she'd gone through, what with the city's ongoing deficit problems and various department heads imposing furloughs and layoffs.

She was never much of an active member in her union beforehand, but the cuts had motivated her to get more involved. Her local union that included clerks like her was part of the larger, nationwide AFSCME, the American Federation of State, County and Municipal Employees.

Self-interest had her using her vacation time to join with fellow members and allied unions to crowd the fixed wood benches in City Hall chambers when there were hearings about specific cutbacks on the docket. Talking and telling war stories about their time working for the city, dealing with the irate public, capricious supervisors, and weird coworkers, brought her closer to her fellow members. After the latest round of hearings, a massive rally the unions had in front of City Hall, and the subsequent negotiation phase, Jackie Reyes had become more involved in her local. She'd even gotten her coworker and friend Gabrielle "Gabby" Cortez, enraptured as she was with the younger man she was dating, to actually get the sparkle out of her eyes long enough to make phone calls on behalf of their union-backed candidate running for a state congressional seat.

Reyes was heading west on 6th Street as evening came on, nearing the building where her union was housed. She was heading there to attend her monthly meeting. She was driving in the right lane, and to her left were two Swift Trans delivery vans, one behind the other. Three cars ahead of them was a third van. She knew from a guy she'd dated once, a driver for the company, that on any given day several vans would leave their downtown facility and travel to their hub in Mar Vista. In this way they'd have freight ready for delivery in the area and on into the South Bay, San Pedro, and Long Beach. She assumed that was where these vans were heading now on the streets, as taking the freeway this time of day was like trying to move through quicksand.

Suddenly a sputtering Toyota pickup loaded with lawn-trimming gear and bags of fertilizer in front of Reyes veered into the left lane, causing brakes and tires to squeal. The driver of the pickup truck seemed to be trying to make a left, but the truck's motor abruptly quit, the vehicle stopping in the street before it reached the left turnout lane. The Swift Trans van just ahead of Reyes in the left lane swerved to avoid rear-ending the stalled pickup. The delivery van's right front fender collided with the left front fender of Reyes's Ford Contour. A Prius slammed into the rear of the van, popping the cargo doors open. Various cardboard boxes spilled out of the van.

"Shit," she swore as the impact shuddered through the car's frame and into her hands and forearms. She determined the car was drivable, since it kept rolling, so she guided it around the first corner ahead and off of 6th. There had been more screeching of brakes and front ends dipping when the accident happened, but no further mishaps. A shop located on the corner where Reyes turned was called Scorchy's Pizza and Hot, Hot Wings.

The van with the new dent in its fender was stopping, too, at an angle behind her, the front part of the vehicle a target for another hit should a car come zooming around the corner. The Swift Trans driver slid back his side door and came out quickly in his baggy shorts and sweat-stained shirt.

"Aw, fuck," the driver said. He was in his twenties and had a close-shaved head. The arms sticking out of his short-sleeved shirt were veined and had definition—a product of working out with freestanding weights. His wraparound sunglasses dangled from a cord around his neck as he dashed back onto 6th to pick up the boxes that had tumbled out of his truck.

Even in the fading daylight, Reyes noted the faint outlines of the tattoos he was having removed with laser treatments.

"I've got it. Thanks." The driver moved frantically as he picked up a rectangular box. He said this to a pedestrian in a polo shirt who'd stopped to help with the load. His buddy driving one of the other vans had stopped and was out of his truck, talking to the pickup truck driver, a gardener who smelled of beer and fertilizer. Cars slowly maneuvered around the scene.

"Fuck," muttered the driver retrieving his boxes.

"Hold on a second and I'll help you, Manny," said the Swift Trans driver who was talking to the gardener. He turned back to the gardener, a wiry man in a straw hat. Dusk had bloomed, and the timers of the overhead streetlights brought them on. The lights were among the 140,000 streetlights the city planned to retrofit with new LED bulbs. The bulbs used less electricity, yet the soft bluish tinge to their light allowed greater visibility.

"It's okay. It's okay," Manny shot back.

"This is not my fault," the gardener insisted again. "Didn't you see the chica in the Volkswagen? She cut me off."

"The only Volkswagen is the one you imagined. So, yeah, it is your fault," the other deliveryman argued. "And what about that insurance information, man?"

The gardener grunted in his throat.

"What I figured. No insurance," his questioner huffed.

Manny Ramos retrieved a box marked for delivery to a Fix & Go auto body shop in Gardena. He bent to pick it up and had it aloft, heading toward his truck. Reyes had her license and registration out and went toward Ramos as he marched to the rear of his van with his box. Simultaneously, a motorcycle cop did a U-turn and pulled up to the accident.

The gardener cursed and grabbed at his hat, crushing the brim in his calloused fingers. Momentarily distracted by all this, particularly the arrival of the officer, Ramos didn't get the box stacked inside his van's cargo area as he'd intended. Rather it struck part of the frame of the doorway. He pushed on the box, and the accordion effect burst a seam on the lower end of the box. Two plastic Baggies of meth crystals dropped out.

Reyes glared at the drugs, their little chunks twinkling distinctly and clearly under the LED lighting.

"Fuck me twice," Ramos blared as he reached for the product. The Fix & Go box was precariously balanced in the doorway and fell over into the street, further bursting open. Hundreds of good-sized plastic bags of crystal meth spilled splayed across the asphalt like a tide breaking on a shoreline.

Everybody was looking at the Baggies.

The motorcycle cop unholstered his Beretta, demanding, "Let me see some hands," at Manny Ramos and his fellow driver.

His friend complied immediately, while Ramos played the percentages, hoping they were in his favor. Pedestrians had stopped to watch what was happening. This was Los Angeles, and some assumed the confrontation was a variation on those staged incidents testing people ethically to see if they'd do the right thing, such as when a man yelled at and slapped his girlfriend in a public park. Or maybe it was a TV show shoot, and they'd have to sign a release, as their face would be in the background when the show aired.

Several cars had slowed, and Ramos took his chance.

He dove and slid across the hood of a new Camaro, his butt denting it in the process. The car's driver screamed profanities at Ramos, who ripped through the knot of gawkers on the sidewalk. The cop gave chase as he barked his location over his Rover radio unit clipped to his upper torso. Ramos was good at rebounds on the b-ball court and used that speed as he ran north along Virgil.

The motorcycle cop was twelve years older than the suspect and liked his double cheeseburgers with bacon for lunch twice a week. But he did avail himself of the treadmill during his workouts, so he did his best in his pursuit. At least he could clearly see Ramos fleeing down the street. Those new lights were great, the officer admired, running past a set of ugly apartment buildings, sidearm out.

At 3:18 the following morning, Gwen Gardner got a phone call. On the fifth ring she reached across a mumbling O'Conner and removed the handset from its cradle. She propped herself on O'Conner's back, and clearing her throat, eyes closed, she answered sleepily.

"Yes," she said.

"Mrs. Gardner?" said a man's heavy voice.

"This is her," she said.

"Sorry to wake you. I'm Detective Roberts of the Rampart Division."

She got less groggy. "Yes? What's happened?" She prayed this wasn't about her daughter.

"Do you know a Manuel Ramos?" the detective asked her.

She considered he might be an employee in one of her shops, but she played it safe and said, "No."

"Do you regularly use Swift Trans for deliveries?"

"What is this regarding, Detective Roberts?" she asked sharply.

"Could you come down to the station house?"

"I might if you told me why."

"Manuel Ramos is being held for questioning regarding the transportation of a controlled substance. There were five boxes in his delivery truck that were packed with smaller boxes of crystal meth."

"And what does this have to do with me?"

"Two of those boxes were addressed to a Fix & Go auto body shop."

Now O'Conner was awake and looking at her as Gardner moved off him, gripping the handset firmly. "You charging me with something, Detective?"

"We just want to clear this up, Mrs. Gardner," Roberts said evenly.

"Tell you what. You clear it up with my lawyer, Don Spottiswood."

"It doesn't have to be like that."

"Oh yes, it does. Hold on a second while I find his number."

"Okay," he drawled.

She had picked up her smartphone on the nightstand and, activating its screen, scrolled through her address book, the handset nestled against her shoulder as she pressed it to the side of her face. She retrieved Spottiswood's office number and recited it to the detective. He said he'd be in touch and hung up.

"What was that about?" O'Conner said.

She told him, concluding, "Clearly I'm going to have to go out to my shop in Gardena." Her face clouded, and she got out of bed, putting on her kimono-style robe.

"No, that's not what you should do. That's a move a

guilty person would do, and the cops would love it if you did. Put you in the same place as where the drugs were headed." He also got out of bed and put on a robe over his boxers and athletic tee. She'd bought him the robe. It was silk, black, with a pattern of a small white fer-de-lance repeated on the material.

"You know a lot about how cops operate, do you, Connie?"

"I suspect I know more about them than you do, Gwen," he replied. "I know you should have your lawyer, and that dude with the beard who is always going on about the pH balance in his pool is a criminal attorney?"

She sighed and looked off into space, then back at him. "Don handles mostly civil matters but has been to court on a few DUIs, even some burglaries done by the kids around here. He's done some contractual work for me in the past."

He wondered if the B&Eers included the Brill boy but said, "Well, for now you should have him go to the shop, ask his questions, and then report back to you."

"Then what?"

"We assess."

"Then what, Connie?"

He was sitting on the edge of the bed, and she stood apart, arms folded, eyes narrow on him. He spread his hands. "Whatever you want me to do, Gwen. However you want the problem solved, that's what I'll do."

"Because you care for me, Connie? Or because you need to do something . . . violent? Need to bounce a few heads off a wall to show them fools who's the head moth-erfucker around here?"

"That's rather harsh language, dear."

"This is not a joke, Connie."

"I know. But the cops are fishing. They called you

because they couldn't reach the manager of your Gardena location. Maybe he's the connect for the Swift Trans driver they arrested, and he found out and is in the wind already." He imagined the police called the manager and he heard the message on his answering machine, or more likely their call was on his cell phone. He might well have been asleep, so wouldn't know what was up until later today, or it could be he, too, was unaware of what was going on.

"Who else might open boxes mailed to your shops?" he asked, then continued his musing. "Big parts, like bumpers and what have you, are usually delivered by the parts house. Somebody else in the office, right? Like the scheduler?"

"Yes," Gardner said. "There's a person who processes the orders and keeps the flow of what jobs came in when, and when they're due." Gardner was looking at her smartphone again. "Should I tell Don to talk to Melodi? She's the traffic controller at the Gardena shop."

"Is this chick Latina?"

"How stereotyping of you, darling. She's Asian, local girl, Japanese American, in fact."

"Still, money makes friends across all sorts of barriers."

"Now you're Bernanke by way of Meyer Lansky," she cracked.

"What an interesting turn of phrase, dear."

"I'm getting a drink," Gardner declared and walked out. O'Conner followed her into the study. There she got out a bottle of Jameson from the wet bar and poured two, neat. She handed a tumbler to O'Conner.

"It's going to work out, Gwen." They clinked glasses and sat on the couch. "The best move is to not offer the cops any information. Everything goes through the pool man."

"You're a riot," she deadpanned. "This has to be the Mas Trece," she continued. "Right under my nose, like I'm just any other sucker." She took a gulp. "Fuckin' Chanchin." She didn't want to contemplate how much or how little her daughter might know about this.

"You're probably not the only mark. They've got to be distributing their product all over the place," O'Conner offered. "Obviously, too, they have some kind of hookup with Swift Trans." This he'd concluded from his stakeout of their house turned lab in the housing complex.

Gardner stretched out her frame on the couch so that her upper body lay across O'Conner's lap. He touched her face, and she murmured, eyes closed, "How come you said it's a Swift Trans truck? That detective only said it was a delivery van."

O'Conner didn't miss a beat. "I've seen several of them coming and going in the Ridge. More than the other outfits. It has to be them."

She smiled and made a pleasant sound. Gardner adjusted herself into a semi-fetal position, still partly on O'Conner, her head resting on his upper thigh. She began to go to sleep.

He looked at her as she slumbered, inwardly chastising himself for letting himself slip like he did. He took that as a warning he better be as sharp as a skeeter's tweeter come the job, as the old heads used to say. After a while he eased her head off of him, replacing his body with a decorative throw pillow she kept on the couch. He got a blanket from the bedroom and covered her. She snored lightly. He patted the side of her butt and returned to the bedroom.

But now O'Conner wasn't tired. He was trying out

variables in his head, and for the first time it occurred to him, with the expected money he'd make from the score, he'd have enough to bolt from the Ridge. He stood momentarily frozen in the bedroom, taking it in, yet also considering what lay beyond it. When the hell did he become Mr. Middle-Class Suburbanite? If the robbery went well, nobody would know who they were. Indeed, their task included framing another. He wouldn't have to leave; he could well just sit on the money, his nest egg. But what was holding him here? Why did he feel like it was the most natural thing for him to be here?

O'Conner suddenly looked over his shoulder, as if his past was sneaking up on him. Back in the study Gardner still slept, and he took the Jameson and his glass. In the bedroom he turned on the TV and, clicking about with the remote, found a Stef Agar actioner that had just started. In this one, the youthful-looking, in-shape forty-something was an enigmatic prisoner in a max security prison on the moon. Some deadly convicts escaped after a bloody shoot-out, and only Agar, his comic-relief buddy, and a guard were left standing to hunt these rapscallions down across the desolate landscape. Hunter and pursuer soon stumbled on an alien presence and had to form an uneasy alliance to defeat the common enemy. It was called *Moon Zero,* and O'Conner watched it while he sipped judiciously on the Irish whiskey.

While he gained little insight on his predicament, O'Conner did fall asleep sometime before the big showdown in the end. He dreamed he was one of the prisoners, a hand on the bar of his cell, playing a wailful blues number on his harmonica. Then some kind of creature with tentacles and sharp teeth grabbed at him from the dark of his cell.

* * *

In the crash apartment Chanchin Saladago was also awakened early in the morning. He'd long since gotten used to Harley Lynn Demara's snoring, apparently a condition she shared with her mother, she'd told him. This was another trait of hers he found endearing. His ringtone sounded, and he answered his phone and, after a greeting, listened. It was Zacca Alvarez calling to tell him that one of their drivers, Manny Ramos, was in custody and that their shipment had been compromised.

"What do you want to do about Manny?" his sergeant asked. They weren't worried about the boxes being traced back to them. It was Ramos who was the link. If caught, would he be a soldier and accept his sentence? Or should they take steps to bring him in and silence him?

Saladago considered this, then said, "What do you think, Zacca? This is what it means if you want to be a captain. You have to give me good advice. What's good for the organization, comprendes mendes? And I don't mean, like, from out of a ballena you be suckin' on like a ta-ta." Ballena meant "whale" in Spanish, but was also a slang term for a 40-ounce bottle of malt liquor.

"Shit, Chan."

"Shit, Chan, nothing. This is a decision you must make," Saladago asserted. "Do we green-light Manny?"

"Can I think about it? Me and his cousin was crime partners from back in Frogtown."

"This ain't Frogtown, now is it?"

"No, that's for sure."

"One hour," Saladago declared, "you'll hear from me." He severed the call. Alvarez also liked to smoke that crystal, and Saladago had warned him more than once that shit short-circuited clear thinking. Well, he reflected, he'd see if homeboy had taken his advice.

He removed the memory chip from the phone and flushed it down the toilet. He was putting in a clean chip when Demara walked into the front room, in the lounging pants she'd worn to bed. She was topless. She picked at sleep in the corner of an eye.

"Zup?" she said.

"Nothing really," he said. Saladago wasn't inclined to tell her this aspect of the business or that he had a connect in one of her mother's shops. Best to compartmentalize information on who knew what. Even if he did feel that for a heina, she was reliable. He was also impressed she didn't go overboard on the tweaking—getting hollow eyes and sunken cheeks, like some of those bitches got.

He got up and went to the refrigerator and opened the freezer. The compartment lit up from within. Saladago liked this model for that reason. He often got up in the middle of the night for this or that and appreciated the thoughtful engineering that went into providing each part of the fridge with its own light source. He took out a bottle of vodka and poured a taste for himself and for her.

"Little early for this, isn't it?" Demara said, accepting her drink.

"It's late, and there's shit that's gotta get settled." He clinked against her glass. "L'chaim, baby girl."

"What's gotta get done, Chan?"

He had a hard swallow and said, "It's weight."

"Serious Mas Trece business."

"That's right."

"But not for an outsider to know."

"Depends."

"Now I'm feeling like my mom and O'Conner." She had a sip, grimacing.

"Maybe you should get the rest of your sleep. Knowing or not knowing what's going down, you still might need to be moving fast when the sun is up."

"And the shadows are longer." She couldn't remember if that was a line in a script. Suddenly loopy, she considered another sample of her drink but decided not to. Demara put the glass on the kitchen counter and, after giving Saladago a peck, returned to the bedroom. She put on a T-shirt and inserted the DVD Culhane had sent her in her laptop. The disk was *Lunar Riot,* a cable rip-off of the big-budget film *Moon Zero.* Under the covers, the computer on her chest, she began watching the story.

Saladago stood at the counter, a hand flat on it. You didn't tell your squeeze about icing a fool unless she was a soldier. He knew some jefes who used a female now and then to do killings, but you best not get in the panties of those chicks. That got everything twisted up, because the way Saladago understood it, once a woman put a liability down, if they didn't freak and get weepy, that was a dangerous combination. Sex and death was a motherfucker.

In the bedroom Harley Lynn Demara had gotten bored watching *Lunar Riot* from the beginning. She skipped ahead to the scene where Culhane had suggested O'Conner could be found. She looked at the man in question, who did have one line, "Radio says a rocket of cops is on the way." She replayed the scene more than once, frowning. The actor's face and upper body were partially obscured by others, and though he sounded something like O'Conner, she wasn't sure. She yawned and fell back to sleep, the futuristic prison drama playing out as she snored lightly.

In the other room Saladago refilled his glass and had more vodka. Trying not to speculate one way or another on what Zacca Alvarez was going to decide, he let his mind go blank.

Chapter Eighteen

From a printout of Inga Brody's phone records he got from Arceneaux, O'Conner was pretty certain he knew why she was willing to double-cross her biker club. There were two calls to and three calls from a women's clinic in West Hollywood that, among other services, provided abortions. This was conjecture on his part, but he didn't think she was hobnobbing with the Mas Trece just because a Viking had given her an STD. Recalling what Mae Karlson had told him at the recycling facility, he assumed that Brody's condition might have something to do with the one they called H, Holbrook. What if, O'Conner surmised, it wasn't a pregnancy, but Holbrook had infected her with HIV, or vice versa?

His problem was how best to confront her about her consorting with the enemy without getting her so riled, she sicced either the bikers or the vatos locos on him. How much could he tip his hand without her feeling trapped and forced to resort to a violent backlash? Really, all he wanted to know was when her thing was going down—needing to confirm or disprove Ben Reynolds's guess that it was going to be during the Vikings toy run.

But why the hell would she tell him anything if he did confront her?

O'Conner considered his next moves as he finished brushing his teeth after his morning shave. He spit out and rinsed as Gwen Gardner stepped into the bathroom. They were at his place, and she put a hand on his shoulder, squeezing.

"Move, sweetie."

"Pushy broad."

She kissed him on the cheek. "You like it."

He got out of her way as she centered herself before the sink and the mirror over it. She partially swept her hair back to insert an earring.

"Anything new from Spottiswood?" he asked.

"No. Last I heard, the cops are still trying to get something out of this Ramos character."

It had been more than twenty-four hours since she'd received the early morning call about the Fix & Go shop in Gardena being the drop for the Mas Trece meth shipment. Later that same day O'Conner had done a stakeout of their lab and had noted there was little activity there, with no Swift Trans van or any other transport trucks stopping by. Could be they were going to move the lab, O'Conner had concluded. It was what he would do in Saladago's position.

Gardner finished dressing, and O'Conner took a hold of her, pulling her close. "You smell good."

She had on lipstick and opened her mouth so as not to smear her handiwork. They tongued, and then she pulled back, her eyes fixed on him. "I might stay down there tonight, at Anne's house, okay?"

"Bagging an unsuspecting young stud in some cougar-trap bar?"

"Exactly." Gardner sat on several philanthropic boards.

She was driving out to Newport Beach to attend the board meeting of an arts nonprofit. Thereafter she'd spend time with some of her friends there in Orange County. He had a suspicion copious amounts of fine wine drinking and juicy gossip would be involved.

She asked, "What are you going to do to keep yourself busy with me gone?"

"Plotting my takeover of the Ridge."

"Right." She started to leave, resigned she'd get no more out of him.

"You know a Barbara Giffords?"

She stopped, looking at him, calling up the memory. He described the woman.

Gardner said, "I've run into her at a couple of functions in the OC. How do you know her?"

"I don't really, but a friend of mine is dating her personal assistant." O'Conner wasn't going to say more but suddenly added, "Really, this guy is . . . Well, a father figure is going too far, but he was around when I was younger and foolish. He used to go out with my mom."

Now her mouth was open slightly.

"I'd like you to meet him. Maybe have his old ass over here for dinner. Mind you, the chick Ben's going around with ain't much older than you. He's, ah, an interesting cat."

"Okay, fine," Gardner replied, blinking at this unexpected, voluntarily given information about his past. "I'll call you later, Connie."

"Have a good day, baby."

She had an odd smile on her face as she walked out to her Cadillac.

O'Conner went into the bedroom and put on a boxy short-sleeved shirt over his athletic tee. It had been a surprise to him that he'd told Gardner about Ben Reynolds.

He could tell from her body language when he'd made his flippant remark that she was annoyed. It wasn't that long ago he couldn't have cared less that any particular woman was tired of him and his bullshit. He'd move on. O'Conner finished buttoning up and grunted.

Had he now concluded that what he was doing was bullshit? Was he that worried about losing the lifestyle he'd slipped into in Willow Ridge? But wasn't it just a facade, anyway? Here he was, the second gun on a job Reynolds was pulling, and he and Mattie Dodd were up to . . . Well, he wasn't quite sure what it was, now was he?

It wasn't like he was going to confide in Gardner about the takedown, was he? Would she be appalled and cut all ties to him? Worse, call the law? No, she wouldn't turn him in. Maybe he was getting to the point where he should push, test her, as Reynolds had challenged him. She knew enough to know he was no weekend backyard griller, worried about cleaning out the gutters and getting the best crap for the pool, like Spottiswood went on about. The phone rang, saving him from the indecisiveness that seemed to be overtaking him.

"Hey, how busy are you today?" Stan Yamashira asked cheerily after O'Conner had answered.

"Not much. What's going on?"

"You up for breakfast?"

"Yeah . . . yeah. Why the hell not?"

"Good. I'll be there in a minute."

"Bet."

After Yamashira picked him up, the two headed to a local eatery in Hemet. Yamashira chose the place, driving his cared-for, decade-old Grand Am there. He made small talk in the car about the prospects the Dodgers had, and O'Conner pretended to be mildly interested. At the café they sat opposite one another in a booth.

"The spinach and mushroom omelets they have here are quite good," Yamashira said as they perused the menu. "I forget what kind of cheese they use in them, but whatever it is, it makes all the difference."

"I'm kind of hungry," O'Conner said. "Ever had the hotcakes here? I mean, are they like they do them in the chains, on the small side, or big, like a hubcap off a Rambler?"

"They're substantial," Yamashira assured him solemnly, his head down, scanning a menu, O'Conner figured, he must know backward and forward. Whatever it was, he'd get around to it, O'Conner reasoned.

The waitress came over, and they ordered coffee and gave her their food choices. She went away, and Yamashira idly moved his knife by nudging its handle with his blunt fingers.

"I ran into Gwen in the store the other day, and she told me about the warning you gave her."

"Uh-huh," O'Conner said.

Yamashira began, "On paper Blanche's idea makes sense. Buy up foreclosed and distressed properties for a song, since the banks are happy to get these clunkers off their hands. We hold on to them until the market comes up, and, poof, we're sitting pretty." He made an anemic gesture of spreading both hands apart as they lay on the tabletop. "I'm not trying to get rich at my age, Connie. But I'd like to leave a little something more than my baseball card collection for my kids. And then that market tanked. Jeez."

"How much you into her?" Their coffee came, and each man eyed the waitress until she went away again.

"Twenty-eight thousand. I sort of played it off with Gwen. That may not be a lot to other people, but it's damn important to me."

"So you asked her for your money back? But you probably signed a contract, agreement, that sort of thing?" That didn't make it any less a hustle, as far as O'Conner was concerned. You always made the marks feel secure in their wise investment.

"I did. But let me explain. I checked out a few items about that Didi, like you'd told Gwen, and holy smoke, Connie." His eyes went wide behind his lenses.

O'Conner was holding his coffee cup and tipped it toward Yamashira, indicating he should continue. He did.

"Okay, so I got nervous and called Blanche. I wasn't really trying to get my money back so much as I wanted to hear from her how everything was okay."

"I'm sure she told you that."

Yamashira looked off into space, then back at O'Conner. "She did. But that Didi came around to my place after that. A day after that, to be precise." Irritably, he dug at wax in his ear with his index finger. "She got, as the youngsters say, all up in my grill."

O'Conner laughed. "Whoa, slow down, Kanye, 'fore you go off and got to regulate."

"Connie, please." The old man spread his hands again; this time they remained on the edge of the table. "That Didi practically threatened to punch me out if I dared bring up her *mistake,* as she said. Said this had nothing to do with Blanche, and that everything was on the up and up and so forth and so on."

Their food arrived, and O'Conner methodically spread a thin layer of butter on his pancakes, like a grouter at work. "Let me ask you again, Stan. You want me to get your money back?"

"I don't like being bullied."

"Few do." Now he applied syrup to the top of each of his three pancakes. They did indeed fill the plate nicely.

"I guess I want vindication," the old man said. "I want Blanche and her girlfriend to know that if they try and cheat me, that, well, there'll be consequences."

O'Conner chewed and swallowed. There was something extra in the pancake batter. Cinnamon? Nutmeg? Interesting touch. He caught himself. How domesticated was he becoming? All hyped on the ingredients in his food. Amazing. "What stops them from lighting out of town with your and the other investors' dough?"

"It doesn't seem to me that Blanche could stand that kind of lifestyle, being on the run, not getting her waxing done, nails, and what have you." Yamashira had some of his omelet. It was a Denver one, not spinach and mushrooms.

"I doubt they'd be living in a one-room apartment in Barstow, Stan. They'd live large."

"Easily caught."

O'Conner made a small hunch of his shoulder. "There's plenty of cities and towns where, due to deficits in the budget, the police force has been cut. This kind of white-collar fraud isn't a high priority with law enforcement, I hate to tell you. Grifters like them get caught because they keep repeating themselves."

"Didi was caught."

"True." O'Conner had some of his side order of scrambled eggs. "But you willingly gave them your money. All they have to show is some cooked-up math to prove the money's tied up in properties from here to Timbuktu to throw off suspicion."

Yamashira looked pained. "So there's nothing you can do?"

"Not saying that. What I'm really getting at is, are you prepared for the consequences?"

"How do you mean?"

O'Conner cut more of his pancakes using the edge of his fork. Mildly, he said, "What you want me to do is put the scare into Didi. Make it clear that if they do try to screw you, I'll hunt them down and extract payment."

Yamashira worried his lip. "I guess maybe I hadn't figured this out fully."

"You and I are friends, aren't we?"

"Yes, we are," Yamashira agreed, brightening.

"So why wouldn't I go after them? For a cut."

"A cut?"

Now O'Conner spread his hands. "There's expenses involved in this kind of undertaking, Stan. People along the way . . . I might have to grease their palm for information. Hotel rooms. Cut rate, of course, but there's quarters involved in keeping those vibrating beds going, man."

"You pulling my leg, Connie?"

The other man smiled. "Only a little, Stan. But I'm not joking about finding them, if that's what you want." He shook his fork at Yamashira. "But if the cops should come knocking on your door, you gotta be cool, understand? You don't know nothing."

Yamashira ate slowly, deliberately. "I see."

O'Conner reached across and tapped the old man's forearm. "Cheer up. I'll let your little playmate know I'm . . . What do we call this? I have an interest in their activities. How would that be?"

"Like I said, maybe I should have considered this more before talking to you."

O'Conner had a mirthful look on his face. "I seriously doubt the cops are going to give you grief, Stan. You might be surprised to hear this, but I know how to be subtle when I need to be."

"Connie, I don't want you really hurting anyone."

"I'm pretty sure I'm not a psycho."

"No, but . . . ," Yamashira began but was reluctant to continue.

"But?" O'Conner poured more syrup.

"For you, getting to point D from A is a straight line."

O'Conner sat back. "Isn't that what you want?"

"Yes, but no getting carried away."

"Nothing bad will come to your doorstep, Stan. But how do you think you get results with people like Blanche and Didi? Harsh criticism?"

"You sound like that asshole Dick Cheney rationalizing—what did he call it?—enhanced interrogation techniques."

"You can't have it both ways, Stan. You want the firm hand, but you don't want to know what it strikes. Besides, when it's all said and done, we'll be greeted as liberators."

Yamashira snorted. "And other great lies of our time."

They finished their breakfast, and driving back to the subdivision, Yamashira said, "I have no idea what your plans are, of course, or your intentions regarding Gwen."

"Intentions? What century are you from?"

"You're a scream. Anyway, my point is I have the impression you've been on the move for a lot of your life, Connie. Now, of course, I'm the model minority, the 'go to school, get good grades, get a good job, raise your kids, and retire, counting your liver spots,' poster boy. I know that."

"Fascinating, the things you say."

Yamashira shook his head. "What I'm getting to is I envy you in a lot of ways, young man. You've clearly not been a guy who worried about arranging his cubicle space. A man who made his own way in the world."

O'Conner was looking out the side window. The

storefronts and gas stations rushing by in a blur, not registering on him. "But you can only do that for so long."

"There you go," the old man said.

Back at the Ridge, there was an envelope taped to O'Conner's door. The gist of the letter inside it was a warning from the bank that they were initiating proceedings to remove him from their property, which he was occupying illegally. Sitting on a stool in the kitchen, initially O'Conner was going to tear up the notice to show his contempt. What did he care about some goddamn bank and their proceedings? But then he refolded the letter and put it in a drawer.

O'Conner refocused but still had no clever way to get at Inga Brody and get from her what she and the Mas Trece were planning. Trying to bluff his way with her would backfire for sure. She was hardly the delicate type and wouldn't fold. *Screw it*, he concluded. He'd use the direct approach. So he waited for her in his station wagon in the parking lot of the Acorn continuation school and confronted her once the ending bell rang.

"It doesn't particularly surprise me to see you, O'Conner," Brody said. The wind blew her hair, with its white streak, about her squinting eyes.

"I'm not going to bullshit you that I know exactly what you and ole Basketball Shorts are up to." He spoke close to her, hands in his pockets. "But I have a notion or two. Now, normally I wouldn't give a shit, only as it happens, I've got my own action rolling out and want to make sure our wires don't get crossed. I don't want to be trying to dig into this any more than what I've so far stumbled into so as not to fuck it up for either of us."

She got on her Harley, keying the ignition. "Follow me to my place, O'Conner. Let's talk." She kick-started the bike and put her helmet on. She didn't look back at him.

"Right behind you."

O'Conner jogged to his car and followed her to a faded fourplex done in an architectural style of a long-gone era. She killed the motor on her bike and, straddling it, walked it down a narrow passageway alongside the building. O'Conner parked and, getting out, wondered whether he should walk down that passageway. Could be he'd get his head caved in, but it was a little late to be chickening out now. Brody came back around, and they went through a wood and glass door leading to a hallway and stairs going up. They ascended the staircase and entered her place.

"Beer?" she asked, tossing her helmet onto a low-slung, padded chair.

"Sure," he said, remaining standing.

Brody chuckled, her head ducked inside the refrigerator. "Relax, O'Conner. I'm not going to shoot you."

"Okeydokey." Maybe she'd stab him. He sat, anyway, when she handed him a bottle of beer.

She took off her leather jacket, chucking it atop her helmet. She sat on a corner of a small coffee table, eyeing her visitor. "This where we get all cagey with each other?"

"I know you got a reason to get back at Holbrook."

"Yeah?"

He said the name of the women's clinic in West Hollywood.

Her expression didn't change as she took a swig of her beer. "Then you know I'm going to see this through."

"Since we're horse-trading, as Granny used to say, I also know Chanchin and his crew aren't long for the

Ridge. Their meth lab, I mean." He told her about the arrest of the Swift Trans driver. "Even assuming they green-light this fool," he continued, "they're going to have to move it for safety's sake." Maybe he was saying too much. Maybe she'd tell Saladago and they'd come after him. So be it.

"You've been busy."

"Your turn."

"How do I know you're not here scouting for the Vikings? You seem to know the players."

"They broaden their membership rules, did they?" he quipped.

"Who knows what can be accomplished if there are common interests?"

"Profound, Inga. That gets us back to you and your boy Chanchin."

"You angling for a cut, O'Conner?"

"Aren't you worried your new partners might try and take you out of the equation? I mean, it is just you solo on this score, along with some heavily armed vatos, isn't it?"

Again, her face remained placid, but O'Conner knew she was calculating the odds. It wouldn't be the first time she'd considered this, only now he was the wild card. "Like I said, what do you want, O'Conner?"

"How about me in as backup?"

"In what, smart guy? What do you think I'm up to?"

She'd put it to him, and he better come across. "Taking down the club during the Kruisin' for Kids rally or there-abouts."

She sat back some, studying him. "You might be too sharp for your own good, O'Conner."

"I'm just trying to impress you."

"It's working." They both got silent. Then she said,

"You figured you'd brace me, thinking I don't trust Chanchin?"

"Do you?"

"Enough."

He mused, "Like you said, Inga, alliances and whatnot. I know it's in both of our interests to misdirect the cops, some of whom will be participating in the rally. Which, of course, is the brilliant thing about your plan. Hitting the Vikings when they least expect it. But it couldn't be during the parade." He let that linger.

She smiled thinly. "What is it you got going, home slice?"

"A takedown of a cash drop," he said truthfully.

She raised an eyebrow appreciatively. "How you gonna do that and back me up . . . hypothetically speaking?"

"Let's say for sake of argument, my thing goes down a day before. That frees me up for later."

"Assuming you're not on the run or shot up or both."

"Assuming."

"Maybe you need me on your job, sport."

"I have higher trust value on my end," he said.

"Good to know."

"So it's not Chanchin you're worried about, is it?"

"I don't know if you want to rip me off, O'Conner. Playing the big brother and the shoulder to cry on."

O'Conner spread his arms and cocked his head. "Where's the love, huh?"

She got up and paced some, her hands in her back pockets. "Chan's got two right-hand men, Jimmy Puppet and Zacca."

"The one with the Z-shaped scar," O'Conner noted.

"Yeah. Puppet is content to be a soldier, but Zacca's ambitious, wants to move up to be a captain. Only Chan is understandably uncertain and tests him, you know?"

"Which means?" he said.

"One of the reasons Chan puts it to Zacca is he samples the product. Early on when I reached out to them, we met in L.A., at a crash pad they have there, working out the details. Chan made little sketches of the route. Anyway, he goes into the other room when he gets a call from his squeeze. 'Cause you know how us girls like our men to talk lovey-dovey."

"Oh, yes," he said, straight-faced.

"That's the opportunity Zacca takes to push up on me about us double-crossing Chan and riding into the sunset together."

"He whispered that with Saladago in the next room? That's pretty damn bold."

"Texting, old-timer," she smirked. "Back and forth on our cells."

O'Conner frowned. "You'd previously made a booty call to him? That's how you two had each other's numbers?"

"Please," she said. "He must have got my number from one of Chan's burners." She crossed her arms. "He'd made his booty call to me the week before. Ugh. Anyway, I did my best to dissuade him of such a childish notion."

"Only tweakers' dreams are like Mitt Romney's words, Inga. They only fool themselves."

She grinned at him. "Aren't you the poet? But if there's any problem from the Mas Trece, I'm betting it'll be from him."

"Meaning once he sobered up, he got to remembering what he said and wonders if you told your boy."

"I didn't. It would only mess shit up for the job."

"But he's not sure. Could be a bullet to the back of his head waiting for him, for all he knows, after it goes down." He considered this and added, "On the other hand, he knows you're needed to pull off the job, and he's not about to screw up a payday, either."

"Until it goes down," she pointed out, sitting again, this time on the arm of her couch.

"But he's not going to make a move on you with the others around."

She shook her head in the affirmative, crossing her arms. "Okay, O'Conner. What's your price? And don't tell me it's because you want to get in my pants."

"Fifteen percent of your end."

She pointed a finger at him. "Fine. I'll tell you what's going down, but you better not fuck me on this."

"I take a job, I do the job, Inga."

She gave him a lopsided look and told him about the plan to rub the Vandal Vikings' money run.

Elsewhere, Zacca Alvarez was in a bad mood. Not only wasn't he able to fulfill the contract on Manny Ramos, who he'd given the thumbs-down to, but he was in a funk over that biker broad, Inga Brody. He'd sure love to see her down on her knees, slobbering on his knob, that white streak in her hair slowly going back and forth. Moanin' and shit. *Man.* Why the fuck had he texted her that message? Well, he damn sure knew why. But a dude can't let pussy hypnotize him. He just can't. Makes for bad decisions.

He had more of his malt liquor and placed the open container beside him where he was cocooned on his leather couch. Alvarez was bathed in the pixel glow of the video game he played. The distinct imagery of mechanized warriors going about their mass-slaughter duties reeled about on his flat-screen TV. But he couldn't keep his mind on the mayhem.

There wasn't the usual thrill he got when as first-person shooter Rip Torrent in *Mortal Death II,* he'd mow down the alien brain-fluid suckers. Their squishy bodies exploding goo on the inside of the screen also made him giggle. Most times. But not today. He put the control aside and finished the can. This was his second one, and Alvarez left the empty with the previous one on the couch.

He couldn't even get a decent buzz on, because of his current situation. Yeah, that was a good word for it. Situationed up was what he was. Manny Ramos, the Swift Trans driver, was now in lockup in the Twin Towers jail in downtown Los Angeles. If he was in the general population, then it wouldn't be too tough to have him shivved or have a thin rolled towel stuffed down his throat. But currently he was untouchable.

It wasn't like Ramos could give up a lot, he was a link in the chain that Chanchin Saladago had been careful to put together. In his case there were two Mas Treces he could name, as he received his packages of meth from them. In fact, one was a friend from the neighborhood and had recruited Ramos. While Ramos didn't come out of the Ridge directly, he did know secondhand about other Swift Trans drivers being used to freight the product. He didn't know their names, but it was enough to set off an investigation inside the company for sure.

That would take time, but the mileage on the trucks' odometers would be checked against logged miles for routes and so on. Times and distances were also registered on Swift Trans main computer. Mostly this was done to prevent a driver from making stops at the bar or his honey's place for a quickie when he should be delivering. Routinely the drivers had to punch in on their keypads where they were at given times of the day. It was understood that a driver might encounter a traffic snarl or some other type of delay, and this was factored into the system.

The drivers had to account for broad times of day, and not down to the exact minutes, so this allowed the two specific drivers who serviced the meth lab to come a couple of times each day. Their routes crisscrossed the Hemet area, or so Saladago had told his men. That way there shouldn't be a red flag raised with the company, he'd said.

There was, though, the problem of eyewitnesses, and there wasn't anything they could do about that, the Mas Trece members had glumly acknowledged. That was why the pressure was on Alvarez to put the squelch on Ramos. In case those two drivers were singled out, they and anybody else in the loop at Swift Trans had better understand any talking meant death. That was why, then, it was important Ramos get done and gone.

Tempted to have a third brew, Zacca Alvarez got off the couch, stretching and scratching at his lean stomach. He stood motionless for several moments, the muffled sounds of cars going by outside seeping through his walls. He had something better for getting a buzz on, and didn't he get his best ideas with Tina? The crooked teeth of his smile were like those of a pumpkin carved by someone with the palsy shakes. He went into the bedroom and, underneath a small pile of discarded shirts and pants, retrieved his glass pipe. He got his Baggie of crystal meth from his hiding place, in a box of Brillo scrub pads below the kitchen sink.

Returning to the front room, he clicked the wide screen back on to TV mode and sank into his couch again. Thumbing through channels on his remote, he settled on a Stef Agar movie from the mid-nineties. He was briefly fascinated to note how young and buffed the action hero looked then. In this one he was a long-haul trucker who discovered he'd been duped into delivering a dinosaur egg, found frozen in the Arctic, ready to hatch. He was chased by an evil scientist's bad guys in souped-up Corvettes. Of course, the prehistoric creature hatched, and soon there were machine guns blazing, grenades exploding, dudes getting plastered on the front of Agar's truck, and a velociraptor chomping heads off. It was great.

Eyes glazed and tweaking as the Agar movie played, Alvarez beamed as he imagined Inga Brody roaring up to his place on her big bad Harley. He giggled. Harley, Harley Lynn. Funny. Did Chan's squeeze's parents name her that on purpose? Anyway, Inga got off the bike, wearing a black bikini and a leather vest. He could see an edge of her curlies above the top of her bikini bottom. She was tanned, with a sheen of sweat decorating the area where her wondrous breasts touched one another. What about her shoes? She couldn't wear heels commanding no bike, but what the hell? This was his fantasy, and so heels it was.

She came upstairs slowly and entered his apartment. He was sitting in a chair, in his black jeans and wife beater. As she crossed the room toward him, Alvarez got an erection, and she eyed it and him hungrily. He undid his zipper, and gripping his member, she knelt before him. His burner chimed a Kinky tune, and reluctantly he answered the call, loath to dismiss his session with Inga Brody.

"We're moving the lab at midnight. But get over here now, 'cause we got shit to do for preparation, entiendes?

It's *Dirty Dozen* time, home," Chanchin Saladago said and clicked off, not waiting for an answer.

Still aroused, Alvarez masturbated into a towel, then doused his face with cold water and took two antihistamine tablets to cut his high. He didn't need Saladago getting on him yet again about his use of the product. He left the apartment.

Chapter Nineteen

Tug Hintton had a fear of heights. Once, when going up a set of outdoor stairs overlooking a beach on Oahu, he casually looked over the railing and was overcome by the nauseating grip of vertigo. He held fast to the railing, sagging and vomiting, feeling like his body was falling away, spinning, as he went. He had to be helped up and made a lame excuse about a sudden attack of some bug or another. Back in his hotel room, it was only a few hits of meth that restored his sense of well-being.

Piloting his leased chopper over the Sunset Strip that traversed the tiny City of West Hollywood, he had no unease. But put him on a ladder to trim the bougainvillea, and his legs would do the rubber dance. He was aware, too, he was a white knuckler when it came to being a passenger. On plane trips he could not sit by the window and steadfastly refused to look out when taking off or landing. Looking out at a cloud bank was okay, as there was an ethereal quality to being up in the air. It was a control matter with him, he concluded as he banked and came in for a landing on the helipad of the Mandrake

Hotel, atop the Strip. Now, this was exhilarating, like sucking on the glass dick of the pipe, he reflected.

The hotel was at the border of the city where Los Angeles began again, with Sunset heading west and cutting a swath through Beverly Hills before returning yet again to L.A. city limits. The West Hollywood residents who lived in the tightly packed area around the hotel had complained about the noise several choppers caused when approaching and landing on the hotel, particularly when it was discovered these weren't sheriff's patrol choppers, as some had initially surmised.

But since West Hollywood was a small municipality, fee generation in its many forms was a necessity. There had been a town hall hearing, and the compromise was tighter scheduling, with restrictions on who could fly in when, coupled with an increase in costs to the civilian pilots and helicopter services. Hintton would have paid triple the upped fees to have the freedom his flights gave him. From up here, anything was possible. He put his skis just off center in the landing circle and powered down the craft, removing his headset.

Then he descended the interior stairwell and went through the door leading to the penthouse suite, where his German financier was waiting for him. There he encountered, as expected, two of the man's bodyguards on duty in the foyer. One held up a smartphone with Hintton's image on it next to his face. While this was done, the other bruiser patted him down, not for a weapon, but for what the financier truly feared, a microphone connected to a recording device.

Cleared, Hintton was buzzed in, and over a late lunch of Chilean sea bass and white wine, the two agreed to a three-picture deal, based upon various goals to be met per picture. Their business concluded, Hintton left, and back in his helicopter, he headed toward another hotel, this one the Argon in downtown Los Angeles. There he landed and, getting down to the street, walked the three blocks to the Staples Center and his skybox.

"Hey," Harley Lynn Demara greeted him as he entered the skybox. She had a glass of something amber in her hand.

"Hey, yourself," he replied, giving her a kiss on the cheek.

Tomika came over and gave him a peck on the lips. "Baby," she said leisurely and drifted away.

There were several others in the suite, drinking and sampling food from the buffet line laid out on one side of the room. Reo Culhane was among those gathered, and he was chatting up a tall, busty woman with blond hair streaked electric blue who went by the handle of Grinquist. Hintton knew she was a performance artist turned singer. The skyboxes were designed such that they were partly an open-air, carpeted suite that led to bleacher-style seating. Down on the hardwood, the Comets warmed up, as did their opponents for the evening, the Fresno Terrapins.

"You taking any bets, Tug?" Culhane asked.

"Coach tells me like he said on the radio this morning. Casey's out of his slump," the partial owner of the team replied. He was referring to Warren Casey, the Comets' star forward, who'd had two less than stellar games in a row.

"Plus, you have to figure Duddly and Keiffer will step up," Tomika added.

Demara and Culhane exchanged a look. Neither would have figured the seemingly vapid wannabe was interested in anything but her current nail polish color, let alone that she'd be into b-ball.

"So I'm happy to take anybody's money on tonight's contest," Hintton challenged in a friendly manner, sipping from a cognac he'd poured.

There were no takers. The Comets won handily, 102 to 89. Casey was in low double digits on the scoreboard, but he made key assists and a timely three-pointer in the fourth quarter. Tomika had pumped her fist as the ball swooshed through the net.

Afterward, Hintton said good night to his guests, and Demara, Tomika and Culhane lingered. The four, as if they'd shared an unspoken, telepathically communicated message, were silent and departed as one group, two abreast. Their immediate destination didn't entail exiting the arena. They went downstairs, and in a hallway leading to the locker rooms, Hintton was recognized by Comets staffers, given he owned a piece of the team. He and his companions were let into the locker area. He chatted up several players, made introductions, and for a few moments conferred with the team's general manager.

Warren Casey spoke to Harley Lynn Demara off to one side in the spacious trainer's room. His freshly scrubbed smell from his shower contrasted with the aroma of used towels and liniments permeating the room. The athlete wore a charcoal-gray suit with an open collar. His six-six frame towered over her, and he had to dip his head toward her face to hear her.

"Tug says you're the girl with the party supplies."

"He wasn't bullshitting."

His smile was engaging.

Not long afterward the five were in one of the VIP rooms at the Trident Lounge on Flower Street, not far from the Staples arena. The door to the room was locked. They shared the lit pipe of crystal meth. As they did so, Tomika quizzed a bemused Casey about what sort of defense he planned against his counterpart on the Newark Stallions, who they played in three days.

"Let the man enjoy his buzz," Hintton said.

She flipped him the finger, eyes smoldering with mock indignation.

"Okay, Tug, I'm down to do your muff tease show," Demara told Hintton, referring to the reality show he'd spoken to her about a few days ago—throwing gay and straight women together, with a lot of commingling encouraged.

"That's great, Harley Lynn," he said. Hintton was still drinking cognac, mixing it with his meth. "We'll make you queen bee of the nest. You're gonna be fabulous."

"Aren't we all supposed to be fabulous in la-la land?" she joked.

"Hell, yes," he replied.

In the main section of the Trident Lounge Marci Vickers and Lilly Nash stood at one of these elevated round tables, having cocktails. Vickers had e-mailed Nash, and Nash had suggested they take in the Comets game, given her company routinely received comp tickets. Vickers wasn't much into sports but liked the excuse to have a night out in L.A. and accepted the offer. She had to use some vacation time to take off early enough from work to make the two-hour drive and avoid most of the rush-hour traffic. They'd headed to the bar a few minutes before the game ended.

"I don't know, Marci," Nash was saying. "Before I got this job, I was kind of, you know, bouncing around out there, and let me tell you, that can wear out your nerves." Vickers had been talking about how boring her job at Pearson Plastics was, and Nash was remarking about stability not being such a bad thing.

Intrigued, her companion asked, "Bouncing around how?"

Vickers looked at her over the rim of her martini glass. "I don't want to scare you."

"Try me."

Nash inclined her head slightly. "I used to—how do I say this?—I used to be what certain individuals call a broker."

"You mean like stocks and bonds?"

She bent in closer. "I mean like stealing stocks and bonds."

Vickers frowned.

Nash held her hands apart. "I was the one who'd put a crew together with the financier or the inside person. Not surprisingly, a lot of the serious takedowns you see on the news involve somebody with intimate knowledge of the target. It's the first angle the cops will naturally take, so part of what I did was help erase that trail, as well."

Vickers stared, transfixed, at her.

"See, told you it would scare you."

"It's not that. I was just trying to imagine how you got in that line of work."

"Aw, well, the usual story about a broken home, teenage runaway, the whole bit. But when I was, like, seventeen, I hooked up with this older guy, Brad. This was up in Seattle. He was twenty-five, all studly and streetwise, so I fell for him hard."

Vickers wanted to hear more.

"Brad was on this other plane of hustler. He didn't try and hook me on drugs to turn me out. None of that shit. He'd been in the service, was honorably discharged, so he had some sense of discipline and organization. Turns out his mom was kind of a noted professor of physics at Stanford."

"No shit?" Vickers said.

"No shit. So he would plan these robberies of dough-nut shops, grocery stores with other street kids, but real cool. Nobody got hurt. In, flash the guns, grab the cash, exits covered, out, no fucking around."

"You part of these . . . takedowns?"

"Yep." She shook her head. "But the more I helped him, it was clear I was the person who could spot the talent, so to speak. Case the scores, that sort of thing."

"Wow," Vickers said, impressed. "You're the first outlaw I've ever met."

Nash held up her glass, as did Vickers, and they clinked them together. "Here's to aberrant behavior," Nash joked.

"What happened to you and Brad?" Vickers asked.

"We went on for a few years, a few times getting close to being busted but managing to stay free. We were young, and it was all very hip and edgy."

"But . . . ," the other woman said.

"But we took down a weed house one time . . . some college boys, so we figured there'd be no reprisals even if they did find out it was us. Only the goddamn place was under surveillance since a few of the daughters and sons of the city's finest were known to frequent this establishment. This house was near the University of Washington, so the administration had pressured the cops, and, well, there you have it."

"Brad got arrested," Vickers stated.

"Him and two others. I was there on the side street, behind the wheel in our getaway car, well, old-school Volkswagen hippie van with a rebuilt engine in it. Great camouflage. But I'm parked in such a way I look up and can see the cops rush in from out of nowhere. No time to warn anybody. I get out of the car and pretend to be among the college kids looking at the three thieves being marched out in cuffs. Brad looks right at me and winks. He was that kind of guy."

She made a dismissive wave with her hand. "Anyway, I leave town and more or less keep doing what I was doing until this one job about five years ago in the Bay Area." Nash seemed like she was going to continue but didn't.

"It didn't turn out good?" Vickers asked.

The woman with the iguana tattoo offered a wan smile. "Let's just say I was lucky to come out with a whole skin and knew better than to keep pressing my luck." She chuckled mirthlessly. "Though, yet again a crazy motherfucker figured in the equation."

"A boyfriend?"

"Oh, hell no. This dude was not only the one who put the job together but also the one who supplied the seed funding. Even though he handpicked his crew, one of them double-crossed the rest. But this guy, he's fuckin' ruthless. He got back at the bastard who betrayed him, and it came down to me either being with him or against him. And I wasn't about to get on his bad side." She finished her drink and signaled for the waitress.

"You have a boyfriend now?" Vickers asked.

Nash leaned in again. "I've been off dick for a while, girl." She looked into the eyes of the other woman, who didn't blink.

* * *

Past eleven the circle of participants broke apart. Tomika departed with Warren Casey in his Jaguar XK after she kissed Hintton good night.

"Huh," Reo Culhane said to the producer as the other two drove away.

"Chick's more my little sister, man," Hintton explained. "We're cool. Say, you two want to come on out to the house? I got the chopper." He waved a hand in the direction of where the helicopter was parked, atop the hotel rising in the background.

"Naw, that's okay, Tug. I've got a breakfast meeting in town in the morning," Culhane said, yawning despite being wired.

"I need to stick around, too," Demara said. She knew Saladago was moving the lab tonight, and he'd asked her to be by the phone just in case he needed her for communication purposes. As she spoke, she checked her phone for messages. There weren't any.

Culhane and Demara gave Hintton a ride back to the hotel.

"Hey, Tug," Demara began as they pulled up, "why don't you get yourself a room for tonight? Get some rest."

"Yeah," the producer agreed, rubbing a hand across his face. "That's probably a good idea." To underscore her point, as he tried to extricate himself from the front seat, he stumbled and went down on a knee on the paved rotunda in front of the hotel. A doorman came over and, together with Culhane, got Hintton checked in and upstairs.

"You're the best, Reo," the high producer said, lying in his clothes, shoes off, atop a bed.

"Then I got a pitch for you. A modern *Canterbury Tales* set in East Los Angeles."

Hintton stuck a thumb up. "We'll do it, baby. Let's talk about it tomorrow, okay?"

"Righteous. Good night, Tug."

"Good night, Gracie."

Culhane left the nightstand's lamp on when he departed.

In Willow Ridge there was also a low light on, a Tensor lamp on a nightstand, as O'Conner and Gwen Gardner made love in her bed. Outside, O'Conner was also aware of the rumble of the engines of two trucks in low gear going by. He surmised the vehicles had been rented by the Mas Trece, who must have dismantled their lab and were moving the equipment. Gardner hastily breathed words of encouragement in his ear, and he returned his full attention to her, quickening his pace.

At several minutes past eight in the morning, Tug Hintton showered and shaved, feeling refreshed and ready for the day. He had a couple of scripts to read, some calls to return, but other than that, he had no particular tasks to fulfill on his schedule. He had a Denver omelet and coffee in his room and checked out. Hintton warmed up his craft's engines, and after a quick check-in with the LAPD's Air Support Command to make sure they weren't circling downtown in their choppers searching for felons, took off.

Uncharacteristically, the air was smog free over the L.A. basin as he gained altitude. He was swinging toward the ocean when suddenly a shortness of breath was upon him and a fierce rigidity seized his upper chest and left arm. Reflexively, he pulled back on the controls and over his headphone speaker assembly shouted, "Mayday, Mayday, helicopter seven-nine-four-six-twenty in trouble. Need medical assistance. Repeat, need medical—"

But Tug Hintton didn't finish his distress call. He blacked out, and his chopper veered and swooped out of control. Pedestrians on the ground at first assumed this was a flying stunt for a TV show or a film being shot. The helicopter zoomed northward. It went up, almost doing a loop, then down again and slammed into the Hollywood sign in the Hollywood Hills. It didn't burst into flames or explode like in some action-adventure spectacle, but it did tear out half the alloy letters of the sign before it crashed into the mountainside beyond, killing Tug Hintton instantly.

Naturally, the helicopter crash was covered on network and cable news outlets. Amazingly, there was no phone or other amateur video of the chopper going down and smashing into the sign. There was a brief round of speculation among the authorities that the incident had a terrorist dimension. But once it was learned that it was a member of the so-called industry who'd gone down, the notion lost steam. Drugs were then assumed to be the reason for the fatal accident.

When it became known it was a filmmaker who'd perished, the scramble began in earnest to get footage of the scene, preferably before the wreckage fully cooled. A video paparazzi stringer for the likes of celeb outlets like TMZ, who had several scanner apps he monitored constantly on his phone, got the jump given he was in the area. He made it partway up the rise of Mount Lee in his hundred-thousand-mile-plus Toyota pickup truck and the rest of the way on foot.

Where the Hollywood sign resided was cut off to civilian traffic by cyclone fences and patrolling park rangers.

But the rangers had converged on the crash site, so there was less scrutiny on the perimeter, at least initially. The stringer had prior experience getting to the sign and, aided by some bolt cutters to create openings in the fences, got to a position where he was able to zoom in on the stretcher as emergency personnel extricated the mangled body of Tugwell Barthany Hintton. Yet he was ready for his close-up. The stringer captured a head shot just as the paramedic was closing the zipper on the body bag. Hintton's face was surprisingly serene and unmarked. His Chinese character good luck piece was still around his neck.

Sitting in the Kosmik Koffee Shop near her great-aunt's facility, Mattie Dodd watched the coverage about the chopper crash on her laptop. She was still at a dead end on how to pay back Vi Moon for the shit she'd tried to pull on her. Inspired, if that was the right word, by the helicopter crash on her computer, she briefly considered ramming a truck through that riot gate of hers and snatching up boxes of the knockoffs. The drawbacks to that sort of action were many, including the narrowness of the alleyway into Vi Moon's place, which prohibited maneuvering and aiming a truck at the gate. And what the hell would she flee in if she wrecked the truck?

She slowly sipped her latte. She was good at moving the fake designer wear and would soon need to fill her inventory. That meant going back to Moon and maybe having her try to chump her again. Dodd had concluded that Vi Moon hadn't sicced the supposed robbers on her to merely get her goods back and keep the money. Moon wanted to show her she was boss. If she'd been successful in ripping Dodd off, she had no doubt the old crow would have forced her to take an even shittier cut, because she'd argue that Dodd had cost her some valuable inventory.

The thing was, Moon had the best product, and Dodd's clientele might know the stuff was bootleg, but that didn't mean they didn't want quality. Her shit was getting tweeted about, and that meant increased interest and sales, and that also meant Dodd had to come crawling back to her highness.

She smiled wanly, having another sip of her coffee. She could fuck O'Conner's brains out and get him to regulate Moon and her tatted boyfriend. But to what end? If he did that, and she knew realistically he'd do the deed only if it served his own interests, that didn't mean Moon's contacts would do business with her. After all was said and done, Dodd didn't doubt that Moon probably had direct connections to the Chinese government hierarchy, the secret police, or some such entity, and she surely didn't need to bring that kind of grief down on her head if she were to physically have Moon assaulted.

Dodd sat back from the small table she was at. There was good old Bradford. O'Conner wouldn't come panting if she whistled, but Bradford would. She figured she still had him by the short and curly. He was a venal, self-absorbed man-boy who had no sense of loyalty or any of that when it came to Moon. Sure, he was pissed at her about O'Conner, but that gave him motivation to get back in solid with her, Dodd reflected.

If ripping off Vi Moon wasn't the answer, then what was? Driving back from their downtown excursion, O'Conner had remarked about studying crabs one time, how they came at what they wanted sideways. He'd been hung over, but she got it now. There were times when you could use force, be blunt, but your experiences should give you the understanding when subtlety was called for in a situation. Turning your enemy's strength against them, like in martial arts, she analogized.

Vi Moon, unlike a lot of knockoff scammers, did care about one thing, Dodd knew. She cared that her customers spoke well of her goods, since this made for repeat business and increased sales via word of mouth. What if some of the underground fashionistas started bad-mouthing her shit? What would she do then? But Dodd knew she had to be careful. Her singer friend, Grinquist, was looking to be the next big thing in entertainment, and she didn't want to mess that relationship up. If she played it right, she'd be known as Grinquist's fashion consultant, and that was worth a truckload of Vi Moons. She wouldn't try to have Grinquist bad-mouth Moon's knockoffs or have anyone else do it directly. But a whispering campaign on the Internet could be devastating to that sandbagger. She supposed O'Conner was right about her being a schemer.

She got out her smartphone and was surprised to see a text message from O'Conner on the screen. She didn't think he knew how to do that. He told her about a Kim Schmitz, who used to work at Heyden Glenn. He also told her Schmitz would be down to talking about matters, as he called it, since she'd been out of work for months. She was hurting. He sent Dodd Schmitz's e-mail.

She nodded her head, saving the e-mail. Dodd then texted a message to Cody Bradford. In a few minutes he responded, like she knew he would. They set up a time to meet. Satisfied that one part of her plan was in motion, she returned her attention to her laptop and sent out e-mails to a few key contacts. She had some work to do.

Chapter Twenty

O'Conner entered the compact Allen Real Estate office in the Willow Heights Shopping Center. Blanche Allen was sitting behind the only desk in the shotgun space, talking on a landline phone. She looked at O'Conner, then continued talking. He came up to the desk and grabbed the phone out of her hand.

"Hey," she yelled. "What the hell is wrong with you?"

O'Conner pulled the handset free from the body of the phone and, dropping it in on the floor, stomped on it, destroying the casing. He leaned into her widemouthed face, pointing.

"If you and your girlfriend are running a scam, I'm going to come after both of you." She started to speak, and he said, "Shut up and listen. Stan Yamashira has invested money with you two in this property-buying pool of yours. Fine and dandy. Now, we know housing goes up and it goes down. It's been down for a long time, so he understands he's not going to see a return right away.

"But don't even think about skipping out. You just be working your leads and making the motherfuckin' magic happen, got me? Because if you don't, I'll fuckin' find you, Blanche. Your carpet munch buddy might like life on the edge, but I know you won't, girlfriend. I'll hunt you down. I'll make your life miserable before I get Stan's money back. And I can assure you if it takes three weeks or three years, I'll do it."

He turned and headed toward the door, then stopped and turned back again. "Please make sure you tell Didi I stopped by, okay? 'Cause later, if she's feelin' frosty about my visit, she can come by my place and we can chop it up, like the kids say. Oh, and she better not get in Stan's face again, or I won't be so goddamn amiable if I have to repeat myself."

O'Conner walked out. Blanche Allen closed her fists tightly, trying to stop herself from shaking.

Across the way from her office was the storefront with ANSON SERVICES in small letters in one corner of its window. The reflective material behind the window and glass door allowed whoever was behind them to see out, but passersby couldn't see in. Allen and O'Conner would have been surprised to know that at that moment, as O'Conner backed his Sable station wagon out of its parking slot, Inga Brody was inside the mirrored storefront.

She and a scruffy-looking man sat at a bank of closed-circuit monitors displaying various settings. She had seen O'Conner arrive on one of the monitors and had zoomed in to watch him go inside Blanche Allen's office.

"What's he up to?" the scruffy-looking man asked her offhandedly.

"Who knows? But you can bet whatever he told her, he wasn't bullshitting. We better look into what Ms. Allen is up to."

The other one nodded and opened a program on one of the computers.

* * *

In his sparse backyard, sitting before his empty pool, O'Conner had made a decision. Impulsively, he'd decided to go into Blanche Allen's office. At the breakfast with Stan Yamashira he'd had a good time goading the old-timer. What did he care if Allen and Crawford were up to no good? So was he. O'Conner was on the verge of a sweet score that would line his pockets, and he'd be in the wind. The motorcycle was ready, and so was he— time to move on to the next opportunity. He had the perfect excuse, what with the bank sooner or later sending the sheriff knocking.

Sure, he had feelings for Gwen Gardner, but it was not like they'd talked about making their thing permanent. She was tough; she'd be all right. There was her daughter, Harley Lynn, who, he was pretty sure, wasn't just banging Chan Saladago for the thrill of it alone. He was certain she must be slangin' to the Hollywood crowd, as that was the kind of opportunity O'Conner would exploit if he were in her or Saladago's position. Gardner had asked him to look out for her, but what could he do? Scare her straight, like with Allen? Hardly. O'Conner had always avoided the drug trade, aside from ripping off drug monies a time or two in the past. But being in that game was a sucker's bet. Half of the ones involved were untrustworthy, and the other half were hooked—bad combinations all around as far as he was concerned.

At some point the odds indicated the daughter was bound to get burned, but she was an adult. Nobody was twisting her arm to do what she was doing. Still, if she got busted or harmed, Gardner would be heartbroken. But what could he do? He was hardly a father figure. It wasn't like he was a prize, anyway, he reminded himself. He'd been walking the razor blades for a long damn time, and it didn't seem like he'd be abandoning his precarious undertakings now. It wasn't like he was looking to do the nine-to-five bit—if such were to be had by the likes of him.

Enough of this bothersome introspection, he concluded with a grunt of irritation. There was work to do prior to the Felcor heist less than three days from now. He stood, momentarily gazing at the empty pool, imagining a swimsuit-clad Gwen Gardner lazing the afternoon away as she floated on an inflatable raft on its imaginary water. Himself standing at the outdoor barbecue, grilling steaks and burgers, his char marks just so as he sipped a lemonade. He shook loose from this bucolic notion and got back to it.

Later at the nameless strip mall located on Chapman in the city of Orange in Orange County, he and Reynolds for the second time examined the exterior of the Felcor facility. There was an Old Towne area with antique shops and the like that was designed to encourage walking and browsing. But this part of the city, located a few blocks off the 55 freeway, was meant for the ubiquitous Southern California solitary driver. You could enter this utilitarian mall, park, fetch your dry cleaning and maybe a soda at the 7-Eleven, and get back in your car and go.

The land around the facility was flat, and behind the strip mall was a grassy strip of land bordered by concrete risers. Beyond the mall itself were perpendicular streets leading into the residential section. Giffords's pet supply store, Pet Zoo, was two doors down from the ATM supplier, and as was usual for this type of design, they shared a common roof and duct system. Due to fire safety precautions, there were thin metal walls separating the ducts at each business, as there were plenty of examples of fires spreading rapidly in these kinds of shopping centers without such fire breaks.

But cooled air and heat had to get through to each store, so each metal break had vents in it, and that was the key to how their robbery would go down. Felcor, given that the company had large sums of money on hand twice a month before distributing the cash, was constructed like a box within a box. Inside its Sheetrock walls was a steel inner shell. O'Conner and Reynolds had no intention of cutting into that or attempting to commandeer the armored car crew due to make a drop early in the morning.

Barbara Giffords had snaked a lipstick camera through her duct, past the sandwich and soup eatery between her shop and Felcor, and had been spying on the interior of Felcor. This didn't afford a view of everything going on in there, but it was enough to know that the money collected from various machines came in via a metal rear door. This door was in addition to a roll-up cargo door, which was raised when it came time for free-standing ATM machines to go out or come back in for repair, but this wasn't too often. Once the accounting was done and the proper splits and fees were calculated, the money went back out via armored car again. The procedure had been explained by Giffords to Reynolds, who relayed the same to O'Conner.

"Got the clone from Arcie," O'Conner said, referring to the retired engineer and current gentleman farmer in Compton.

"Good," Reynolds said. "I've got the rig working right and secured our firepower." He dribbled hot sauce from a packet on a taco and added, "Just so you know, Darla's pretty handy with a piece."

"Yeah? She take a shot at you already? Don't tell me the wheels are coming off the blissful relationship wagon so soon."

Reynolds didn't miss a beat. "She grew up in one of those households where her mom and dad were gun"—he paused to look over at O'Conner as he bit down—"enthusiasts."

He and Reynolds were parked across the street from the strip mall, at a Taco Bell. They crunched away on their hard-shell tacos, sitting in a new model Mustang that didn't belong to either of them. The unmarked front of the Felcor operation was in their line of sight. There were two closed-circuit cameras at either end of the facility's flat roofline, mounted on ball joints. Periodically, the cameras would swivel about, affording the viewer a panoramic of the mall's parking lot and the wide boulevard beyond.

The two had driven around the strip mall earlier. Most of it was one story, but on one end was a two-story building containing such entities as a Weight Watchers and an immigration attorney's office.

O'Conner wiped his mouth with a paper napkin. "You couldn't talk Barbara out of being in on the grab, huh?"

"Nope. Can't say I pushed it much," the older man admitted.

"How Zen of you."

Chewing, Reynolds looked over at him again but didn't say anything.

After they finished their late lunch, O'Conner started the Mustang and they took a drive through several of the residential streets leading to the strip mall, familiarizing themselves with the geography. Afterward, they returned to the freeway in the car supplied by Giffords to finalize details of the robbery.

* * *

In Los Angeles plans were under way for the funeral and industry testimonial for the late Tug Hintton. Reo Culhane was pressed to serve on the committee for this as, his manager assured him, not only would it be seen as a magnanimous gesture, but it would be good for networking, too. But at the moment he was commiserating with Tomika as they rode the bump in Hintton's Malibu mansion. The house was keyless, employing an electronic combination lock. Tomika knew the code and was currently encamped there until she got kicked out.

"I think there's a teenage son somewhere," she said, rubbing her nose with the back of her crooked finger.

Culhane asked, "You know who the mother is?" Drowsy, he sat back, enjoying his elevated state. The two sat side by side on the couch in the conversation pit.

"No, I don't. But I assume we'll hear from her or her lawyer, right?"

"Right. They're looking for a will, but I doubt Tug left one."

"Huh," she said. She held the glass pipe, but they'd exhausted its contents. She put it aside. "You think it would be worth it to get my own lawyer, Reo?"

"You were with him, like, what?"

"Almost four months."

"That's an eternity in this town."

They both giggled. Tomika put a long leg over his, and they remained that way for some time, comfortable with one another.

"You're more quiet than usual," Gwen Gardner remarked to O'Conner. They were holding hands as they walked in a part of San Jacinto offering trendy shops and the like.

"Enjoying your company, my dear." They'd had dinner at an Italian restaurant and now were on their way to a movie at the cineplex.

"Oh, Mr. Sly Fox."

"I'm an open book, baby." Why the hell was he so tongue-tied about telling her he planned on leaving Willow Ridge? And why was he twisted up about telling her at all? Once the job was done, he would get on his bike, and over the next hill he'd go, no looking back. He let go of her hand and put his arm around her shoulders.

She leaned into him and gave him a quick kiss. Gardner didn't pull back and regarded him as they stood still, other people moving around them.

"What?" O'Conner said. "You trying to put the hoodoo on me?"

"I imagine it's been tried. Let's get a move on," she replied. "I'm going to indulge myself and have some butter goo on my popcorn. Plus, I don't want to miss the coming attractions. You can learn a lot from the previews."

They started walking again. "Is that right?"

"Unlike in life, we can stand back and see what's going on in a movie."

"You can still sometimes get surprised even in the movies, Gwen."

"Yeah, I hate that," Gardner said.

In the movie they shared a tub of buttered popcorn. She had a diet Pepsi, and he stole sips of her drink. She'd picked the film, which wasn't the chick flick he'd figured she'd choose. Rather, it was a story of psychological tension, wherein a married woman awoke one morning in a hotel room with a man who was not her husband. This fellow wasn't a stranger but a man she knew more than ten years ago in college. He was a man who was supposed to have died a few years ago in a car accident. She had been to his open-casket funeral.

Afterward, O'Conner noted as they walked out, "That bad boy had a few twists and turns in it, you know."

"I liked it."

"Aren't you the one who said you didn't dig that kind of flick?"

"Hmm, yes, well, I did, didn't I?"

They went along. Then O'Conner said, "That supposed to be some deep, Zen woman, mysterious thing?"

"Maybe so." She took in a breath. "Or could be I'm confused about what I like and what I don't like." She looked off into the distance, touching a finger to the corner of her eye.

Driving back to the housing division, they passed Department of Transportation workers in their Day-Glo vests putting out plastic sawhorses along the route. There were already temporary tow-away signs posted from a few days before. Bleachers had been erected at various intervals, as well. They were preparing a large stretch of Esplanade Avenue for the Kruisin' for Kids toy run and parade on Saturday, less than twenty-four hours away.

Gardner remarked, "We're coming to the parade, aren't we?"

"I'll be there for the start but gonna get busy a little later."

"That right?"

"Promised someone I know I'd help them out on a matter."

She was quiet for a while, then said, "You expect me to be your alibi?"

"No, of course not."

"Why not?"

That surprised him. "Because you're a solid citizen, Gwen, and my life is not your life."

"This the big blow off, Connie?"

"It's not like that."

"What is it like?"

"The less you know, the better it is. That way if you get jammed up, and that's unlikely, you can be totally honest with the cops if it comes to that. What with the Swift Trans business, it's not like you're not on their radar."

"You haven't been totally honest with me all along."

"You know damn well I haven't been what you'd call suburb material."

"I know how I feel about you."

Now he was quiet as they went along. Eventually, he pulled into Willow Ridge's unmanned gate. "I don't want you hurt. This is not a life for you, honey."

"I'm a grown woman. I can make my own damn choices."

He blinked hard. "You want the burden of knowing, Gwen? 'Cause if you do, if you want a peek inside that room, you can't just back out again."

"What about you? You don't have a choice?"

"Not before."

"And now?"

"I think I'm too old to change."

"Huh," she said, an odd look on her face. "It's more like you don't want to."

His station wagon pulled in front of her house, and O'Conner put the car in neutral. "What do you think I can do, Gwen? Be one of your managers? Maybe get a job as the handyman around here?"

"You're smart and clever, Connie. You've just never put your mind to normal activities."

"Would you have been attracted to me if I was a strait-laced dude?"

"And you were just attracted to me 'cause I was an easy lay? The lonely middle-aged broad you could dazzle with your aura of danger?"

"You know I care for you." He reached for her, but she slapped his hand away.

"Fuck off." She got out of the car and walked quickly to her door. She went inside, the door closing with a quiet click. He stared at the door for a few moments, then putting the car in gear, drove to his place on Larkspur. He went inside and had two belts of hard liquor and went to bed, sleep eluding him.

Less than a day later, after taking care of last-minute details, O'Conner rose at 2:07 a.m., stretched, brushed his teeth and shaved in his boxers, and splashed on some aftershave. In case the job went south, no sense not looking presentable laid out on the slab, he dourly reflected. He got dressed in dark clothes and steel-toed shoes. As he'd previously loaded an athletic-type equipment bag with specific items, he retrieved that from the side of his bed. The bag was padded so it did not clink as he walked.

He left the house, and three freeways and an hour and twenty-five minutes later, keeping to the speed limit, he arrived ahead of time at the shopping mall in Orange. Rather, he parked a block away and walked over to where the other three were already waiting, in the Pet Zoo pet food and pet supplies store. Coffee in paper cups and croissants were laid out on the counter. O'Conner, slipping on overalls, a mask, and gloves like the ones the others were wearing, gave a questioning look to Reynolds. A turtle in its aquarium eyed both of them lugubriously.

Reynolds said, regarding the food, "Barbara figured we could use the energy."

O'Conner bent down and zipped open his bag.

Darla Ballard was at the window, peering out through the small gap she'd opened with her fingers in the blinds. "Figuring the other time frames we've clocked, the armored truck should be arriving in about fifteen minutes."

The air and heating vent cover was already off, and an assembled length of copper tubing, a quarter inch diameter, had already been pushed through the wall's interior as well. Strapped to the tubing was an articulating fiberoptic scope similar to what law enforcement used. The scope fed a picture to a laptop that was open atop a stack of organic dog food. The image on the monitor showed a similar grate-type vent cover looking into the Felcor facility. The copper tubing was designed with an L shape at the threaded end pushed toward their target.

O'Conner removed two Remington 870 MCS semi-auto pistol-grip shotguns from the bag.

"Oh my," Barbara Giffords said. She stood with her arms folded, body rigid.

"Mostly for show," O'Conner assured her as he watched Reynolds attach the female end of the tubing to the male fitting of a pressure valve screwed into a metal cylinder, like a half-scale-size helium tank. This he rested on the paint-can platform that was part of a five-foot plastic ladder. It was next to the open square of the vent system.

They waited, staring into space, but not each other. Then the sound of a heavy-duty engine brought all four of them alert and ready. Sure enough, it was seventeen minutes after Darla said the truck would arrive in about fifteen minutes. On the laptop they could see the skeletal crew of the Felcor four going into action. One went off camera toward the rear metal door and let in the guards with his delivery in a nylon sack on a dolly. Another guard stood nearby, hand on the butt of his holstered gun. Their truck idled quietly.

Reynolds removed two smallish firecrackers from his pocket and handed them to Giffords. They had considered using a cherry bomb but had dismissed the idea as the noise it made going off might be too loud. Ballard had one of the shotguns next to her on the counter. She munched on a croissant, mumbling a prayer.

Crooks were something else, O'Conner thought as he watched her pray. He returned his attention to the laptop. Soon he saw the three men and one woman back inside, chatting about ordinary concerns, as they heard the truck drive off.

"Now," he said quietly.

Ballard and Reynolds exchanged a quick smack on the lips for luck. Giffords and Reynolds stepped to the door of the pet shop and, opening it a crack, lit their respective firecrackers and tossed them out onto the empty macadam of the lot. They shut and locked the door as the two firecrackers exploded, one right after the other, with decided pops.

As expected, this drew the attention of the crew inside the money house. O'Conner opened the pressure valve, instantly sending liquid chlordane spilling into the wall and onto the floor of the Felcor space. The stuff was clear like water and odorless.

He quickly extracted the tube, and Ballard screwed a small clamp with a pipe thread base onto the end of the L shape. Reynolds had lit five wooden matches and secured them in the fingers of the clamp. The Felcor employees were returning after looking out, with one even poking his head out but, of course, not seeing anything.

O'Conner fed the tubing with the matches back through the interior of the wall. He had to hurry, but not so much that it would blow out the fire. Two of the matches went out, but the other three got to their destination. He was able to manipulate the clamp, given the L shape of the tube at his end, and drop one of the matches through the vent cover grating. The liquid chlordane that had been splashed on the wall and floor caught fire. One of the Felcor employees retrieved a fire extinguisher, and another opened the rear door just in case. This was what the robbers were banking on happening. Ballard and Reynolds were already in position, ski masks covering their faces.

When the rear door came open, Reynolds stepped from where he was flat against the wall opposite. He cracked the man holding the door on the head with the barrel of the Remington. The struck employee was stunned and fell back inside. Reynolds and Ballard rushed inside.

"Put down the fire extinguisher," Reynolds said.

"You nuts?" the one handling the thing said.

Reynolds put a round in the ceiling. "You hear me now?"

The device clattered to the floor.

"I better see all four of you right now, or it's gonna be a problem," Ballard said evenly. Three of the employees were visible as they came in. The fourth had to be hiding in the row of ATM machines off to one side. He couldn't be in the restroom, as the door to it was to the left of the thieves.

"I'm here," said a man with sandy hair and glasses,

standing up from behind the machines. He held one hand down, and Reynolds aimed his shotgun.

"That better be empty, or you're losing your head."

The man's other hand came up with a cell phone in it. Reynolds ran to him and snatched the phone away.

"Sir? Where are you, sir? How many robbers are there?" the 911 operator said. "I couldn't hear you clearly."

Reynolds stepped on the phone. He didn't think the operator had gotten a fix on the phone just yet. He jerked the muzzle of his weapon for the caller, who had both his hands up now, to join the others. O'Conner was inside now, too, squirting accelerant about to obfuscate their point of origin. They didn't want to leave a telltale trail to the pet shop.

Possibly, the employees were hoping the silent alarm one of them must have activated was being answered. Giffords had obtained a copy of the work order when it had been installed in the shopping mall by the alarm company. O'Conner had Arceneaux reroute the connection on their first visit so it would still read positive on the other end but the signal would actually go right back into the Felcor offices.

Fire and smoke filled the area. The four employees were hustled out back and tied and gagged with nylon-lined packing tape. They were made to lie facedown on the dewy grassy strip, but their legs weren't bound so they could run away in case the fire got out of hand. The money had been wheeled out, as there hadn't been time to disperse it yet.

"Keep your fuckin' heads down," Reynolds warned the employees as the loot was carried into the rear of the pet shop and put in a cabinet, which Giffords locked. If the fire trucks hadn't been approaching, they would have alerted the fire department, as they didn't want other stores going up in flames. Couldn't have the fire spreading—though by now they could hear the approach of sirens.

The four had stripped off their overalls, masks, and gloves and had thrown the clothing into the growing fire. The Felcor offices were engulfed in fire, and the flames were threatening to spread. By the back door Giffords threw a cell phone inside, purposely letting it break apart. It was a burner, a disposable cell, but several numbers on it were linked to Paul Stevenson. They then walked briskly to where their cars were parked on the residential streets, having left the dolly in the open at the strip mall. The first of two blaring fire trucks rumbled onto the parking lot behind them. Three of the thieves went down one street, and O'Conner a parallel one.

"What's going on?" asked an older woman in a housecoat and curlers, standing just outside her open doorway. A cat curled around her ankles. Dawn was still several minutes away.

"Some kind of fire at the shopping center," O'Conner answered as he put the equipment bag in the station wagon's cargo space. He was parked in front of the woman's house. "But the fire trucks are there now."

"Oh, that's good," she said, uncertainty in her voice. She could tell he wasn't a neighbor. She took a step back inside her house but watched as O'Conner drove away. His luck the old girl probably did crossword puzzles, so memorizing his license plate wouldn't be tough. His plate would come up with a different address than the Willow Ridge house he was squatting in, anyway. As for his description, she could supply something of a general nature, but he'd chosen her house because it wasn't under a streetlight. So he didn't think she'd seen much of his face. He'd made sure not to look at her when he answered her question.

Back on the freeway, the sun was coming up and there was traffic, but nothing like the morning rush heading into Orange and L.A. counties. He got back to Hemet and had to maneuver around to get to the housing subdivision due to closed streets for the parade. But there were alternate routes outlined for the locals online, and he'd made a note of this beforehand. He parked at his house and got out, still keyed up from the job but also knowing his duties weren't over yet for the day.

Inside O'Conner brewed coffee, as he hadn't had any at the pet shop. Giffords would return later to clean up and retrieve the money, the fire an excuse to give her employees the day off. She would have to allow the store to bleed her for another month or so, but then she would close it up for good.

O'Conner had his coffee and, despite still being charged, dozed in an easy chair. He awoke at fifteen minutes past nine. He hadn't planned to attend the parade until toward the culmination at the amphitheater. But loath to admit it, he wished to see Gwen Gardner, if only for the last time, so he had another cup of coffee and walked over to another shopping center, the Willow Heights one across from the Ridge. There he waited with the other squares for the shuttle that would take them to the parade. Steve Brill and his wife were among those gathered.

"Hello," Jane Grainger-Brill called as O'Conner waved to them as he walked up.

"How're you guys doing?"

"Oh, fine. Where's Gwen?" Grainger-Brill asked.

"We had a spat," he said.

"Sorry to hear that," she said. "I'm sure you two can make up."

"We'll see."

An uncomfortable lag in their conversation wore on but was interrupted by the arrival of the shuttle. They and the others who were waiting got on and were driven to their destination. It was still early enough that onlookers were still gathering for the Kruisin' for Kids parade. As with the Rose Bowl Parade held annually in Pasadena, some loyal fans had camped out in parkas and on blankets and lounge chairs to ensure a prime spot to view the festivities. The crowd, O'Conner estimated, was a mixture of local residents, bikers, and judging from the several RVs he spied coming in, out of towners, too.

Gardner had told him that a lot of these folks were not only into the parade but were also fond of the early California play that topped off the event and was held at the amphitheater. From what he recalled of her recap, *La Tajuata* was the classic story of forbidden love. In this case it was between a Mexican general and a Cahuilla maid. This against the backdrop of gold prospecting, land grabs, and the machinations of duplicitous bankers and a saloon keeper. There were several big production numbers involving singing and dancing. It turned out as a teen, Gardner had been a singer in the play.

"Son of a bitch," O'Conner had kidded her then. She'd shown him several Polaroids taken by her folks from that time. "You sure had big teeth," he'd mentioned, earning a slap on his arm.

"Connie, good to see you," Stan Yamashira was saying, bringing O'Conner back to the present. "I didn't think this would be your kind of thing."

"Always up for new experiences, Stan."

"Say, I don't know exactly what you did, but I want to

thank you. Heard from Blanche, and she's getting the investors together for a meeting," Yamashira told him, beaming.

"Good," O'Conner said and was surprised he meant it. This place must be getting to him. "I'm going to take a look around," he said.

"Sure. See you later," Yamashira answered, clapping O'Conner on the shoulder.

He walked on past vendor carts selling the usual, such as hot dogs and syrup-flavored ices, as well as trendy ones offering such fare as Korean barbecue tacos and seaweed-wrapped sushi. The mixed aromas made him suddenly hungry, but he stuck to a traditional food to satisfy his craving, a charred hot link with extra onions. He didn't see Gwen Gardner about, but he did see that kid from the copier shop who dealt meth for the Mas Trece.

"Mr. O'Conner," the young man greeted. "How it bees?"

"Aw, you know, just trying to make it from one day to the next, youngster."

"I heard that."

O'Conner wondered where the Mas Trece had relocated their lab, but that wouldn't be polite conversation in this crowd. He nodded to him and went on. Soon the parade started up. A Flying V of Vandal Vikings roared by on their hogs to applause and whoops. He saw H among them. He turned his head to glare at O'Conner, his eyes behind mirrored shades.

O'Conner figured that would be the high point of the day, as he expected the parade to be an assortment of threadbare floats, but damned if the procession didn't lead off with a restored horse-drawn coach. The conveyance was done up like something from a fable, with red and gold and silver flourishes as twelve large white horses drew the thing along the avenue.

There was a sort of princess atop it, standing and waving to the crowd. She wasn't dressed in a gown but had on a mixture of goth and steampunk attire, complete with a leather skirt, torn fishnets, and black gloves of the kind where the fingers were exposed. Her derby had a good-sized chain connected to it, leading to a ring attached to her broad belt. She was a hit.

Looking across to the other side of the street, O'Conner saw Inga Brody momentarily. Funny. Why wasn't she riding with her crew to have an alibi? Then she was gone. As he stood on the sidewalk, a floating apparition of a cartoon character came by, tethered via lines held by pretty women in skimpy pirate girl outfits. The giant balloon character seemed to be part creature and part metal, as it had an anthropomorphic body but its legs and arms ended with tires, as if it were a biological motorcycle. It wasn't as big as one of those Macy's Thanksgiving Day balloons, but it was substantial enough.

"Enjoying yourself, pops?" Mattie Dodd said behind him. She pinched his butt.

O'Conner turned to glare at her balefully. She grinned and walked on, absorbed in her texting. He turned back around.

Also passing behind O'Conner was Cody Bradford. He didn't announce himself. Bradford was calling Ian Childes on his phone, seeking to find out where his friend was among the parade watchers. He saw the older man and was tempted to come at him, but he was sober, so he knew better than to let his anger control his actions when it came to that cocksucker. He'd fix him, but he'd do it right. He reached Childes and walked over to where he was in front of the hardware store. They found each other and bumped fists.

"Where's Doug?" Bradford said.

"Figured he was with you," Childes said.

Bradford shrugged as he looked at his iPhone. It was another tweet he was following from Mattie Dodd. He showed it to Childes. "That sideways bitch thinks she's all that. She's been trying to hook me into a new scheme of hers, going up against Vi. Says she's working on a new hookup on gear."

Childes read the tweet. "She's clowning her knockoff gear?"

"Yeah. But fuckin' with her money can get you hurt. Vi don't play, man."

"What's Mattie want you to do?" On the street a float drove past them, outfitted over a flatbed truck. It was a diorama of astronauts in their silver suits battling space zombies. There was a tricked-out rocket ship with massive chrome pipes in the center of their alienscape.

Bradford said, "Mattie's gonna keep talking shit about Vi's stuff but also send people to her new shit. Give it a couple of weeks, and Vi should see a dip in her profits. Then she's all mad, of course, and I broker a peace treaty sit-down."

"Will that work?"

"It might. Mattie's got her girl Grinquist doing some tweets, and she's got a following among those music types Vi desperately wants to be in with. But Vi is unpredictable, man. She might just try and get me to work Mattie over."

Childes regarded him. He knew Doug Brill was pretty sure she was banging O'Conner. But he only said, "Would you?"

"Fuck, I don't know," Bradford replied listlessly.

A block and a half away from those two, Harley Lynn Demara was also reading a text. It was from Chanchin Saladago and was about them hooking up at a specific time later that day. This was a lie, she knew, but it was done to help establish an alibi should the Sheriff's Department deem him a likely suspect. She was startled when her mother came up to her.

"Thought you were back in L.A.," she said after giving her a brief hug.

"How could I miss this?" her daughter replied. She squinted. "Where's big daddy?"

"Oh, we had a fight."

"Yeah?"

"Yeah. I don't know. I guess I'm not sure where we're going, and neither is he."

"Mom, I'm pretty sure he can't be domesticated."

She smiled at her but resisted saying, "You should know." "I realize that. Only, well, I guess I was getting pretty comfortable with him."

"You sayin' it's over? He didn't hit you or anything?"

"No. Connie wouldn't do that."

"To *you,*" her daughter stressed. "So?"

"So I don't know."

"But you hope it's not."

Her mother didn't answer as she looked out at the parade. The high school marching band came by, belting out a rollicking version of Lady Gaga's "Poker Face" on their tubas and xylophones. This was followed by the parade's grand master, action star Stef Agar. He looked good in a sharkskin suit, starched French cuffs, and a starched white pocket square. He rode like grand masters did, sitting atop the rear section of a classic Lincoln Continental convertible with suicide doors. A petite redhead sat next to him, and she had on a silver-gray gown of spangled material that dutifully shimmered in the sun. Her hair was teased and puffed out, a throwback to '80s big hairstyles.

A series of loudspeakers had been attached to buildings along the route, and there were two announcers perched in a portable guard tower sort of structure positioned midway down. The male announcer was a local fixture who hosted a jazz program on the weekends on local radio. His companion was a much younger woman who was a dog whisperer and counted among her clients one of the Kardashians.

Charred hot dogs were eaten, fresh lemonade was drunk, and kids watched in wonder as a man on stilts dressed as an Uncle Sam cowboy marched along in the procession. He wore a loose black leather fringe vest, a Stars and Stripes vest buttoned inside of that, a shirt with the short sleeves rolled up, suspenders, and a big white Stetson, which he waved about.

O'Conner saw this as he faded back from the festivities and, checking his watch, left the main route of the parade. He'd seen Gwen Gardner and her daughter together but hadn't approached them. They hadn't seen him. Not all the floats would wind their way to the amphitheater, but several had been preselected to arrive there by the afternoon. This would allow some time for people to get up there and maybe have a picnic or just hang out. Both a Catholic priest and a shaman would be on hand as the featured floats were put on display. They would each do a blessing of the play, emphasizing that it stood for cultural unity.

O'Conner figured the time to pull off the robbery had to be as the floats arrived, but before it got too crowded for them to effectively make their escape. There'd be a lag in the time it took the deputies to get there, as they'd want to make sure no drunks were loitering on Esplanade. When Inga Brody told him about the plan, he'd done a reconnoiter of the amphitheater and guessed Saladago and his crew would make their getaway down the slope that dropped off behind the open-air venue. It was gradual and let out on the roadway separating the hillside from the Willow Heights Shopping Center. For sure they'd park below. He also guessed they'd have to hit the Vandal Vikings hard and fast with the knockout gas, and he'd sized up where they'd do that, too.

Back on the parade route, one of the featured floats was making its way along the avenue to applause and grins. This was the Vandal Vikings masterpiece of achievement. It was a bright and cheery display on a large rectangular disguised trailer adorned with a massive construct of a Harley chopper spitting flame, ridden by a Thor-like being, with his big-breasted Valkyrie holding on to him from behind on the motorcycle's seat. All this was made from wood, flowers, sequins, sparklers, and nontraditional materials, like suede and metal sheeting. Ringing the twenty-two-foot-tall chopper and its Paul Bunyan–sized riders were real biker chicks in bikini tops and shorts, some with vests and chaps. One year a few had gone topless, much to the delight of thirteen-year-old boys and their fathers. But this was a family event, after all, so they had remained covered up since then.

The giant motorcycle was being towed by a tricked-out tractor with huge tires, and bristling with supersize exhaust pipes. The vehicle was like what could be found churning earth and belching flames at a monster truck rally. Occasionally, the tractor would pop a wheelie, the front rearing up as it went forward on its rear wheels. The crowd whooped and applauded.

Doug Brill hooked up with Childes and Bradford. Through Brill's high school friend Nicolette Parsons, Nickel Bag Nicolette, the threesome and some others had a second-story view of the tractor doing its thing. Parsons's mother and father owned a trendy cupcake and coffee shop called Breathless. They had actually not seen much of a downturn in their business since the Great Recession hit, and they attributed this to the fact that even in challenging times, people needed their sugar fix.

Recently the couple had been approached by a chain, as their location and customer base were seen as advantageous. The money was too good to pass up, so they sold their business. The shop, which was on the ground floor, was being redesigned prior to the transition. Where Brill and the others had stationed themselves was in the storage area, which some of the businesses on the second floor also used. The large room had a bank of windows looking out onto the main thoroughfare. Parsons's parents were out of town, so she'd said, "Why not watch the parade in style?" Empty cans of beer and grease-bottomed pizza boxes were about, and two joints were being passed around.

"That motherfucker," Cody Bradford muttered, feet on a windowsill.

Childes, standing and looking down, shook his head as he inhaled deeply. "You better let that shit slide, brah."

Bradford eyed him sideways, a sneer pulling back his lips. He partook of the chronic and had more of his beer, too. He gazed off into the sky, then took a Baggie from his shirt pocket. He shook it and said to Childes, "Let's really enjoy the show."

Childes held up a hand. "I'll pass on the chicken scratch."

Bradford beamed. "More for me, then."

"You better do that Nazi nose candy somewhere else, Cody," Parsons said, pointing at him.

"The fuck, Nickel?"

"Somewhere else." If her parents found out about her party, she knew they would only scold her about the beer and marijuana, given that they still toked up now and then. But hard drugs would be inexcusable. She did some subcontracting dealing through Childes, but that was business.

"You heard her," Parsons's boyfriend echoed. He was a good-sized individual and was heading to Cal on a partial football scholarship. He'd had a good year as a linebacker for the team.

"You all can suck my dick," Bradford said, getting up and walking out, giving those gathered the finger to put a period on it.

"What a major asshole," Parsons said.

"Yeah," Brill agreed, and Childes nodded.

The bobbing and grinning head of the jack-in-the-box dangled on the end of its short spring as the flatbed it was on crested the small rise. This jack-in-the-box was not a somewhat sinister clown's face but a rendering of down-right sinister Karl Rove. He put forth a demonic glare and had a mini-bowler tipped to one side atop his round head. When people saw him going by, they had a vague sense they knew that face, but couldn't place it—and this feeling then gave way to unease.

Several Vandal Vikings on their Harleys also crested the rise. Their float with the giant motorcycle was coming up behind the Rove one. Except for a small crew for the amphitheater, no other staff was around or rather was supposed to be around. In the base of their float were the collected monies from their endeavors, including drug and unlicensed weapons profits. On the blacktop of the parking area were several ten-foot-long bobtail trucks, like what would be used for moving furniture. Their roll-down doors were open, the drivers were off at a lunch tent. There were already toys, bats, soccer balls, and the like in the vehicles' cargo areas, with more items to be added as the play's viewers gathered. The illicit funds would be off-loaded from the float, then placed into a few specific trucks.

The Vikings were practiced in this handoff, and in less than twenty minutes they'd have the work down. But before they could begin, the Mas Trece struck with precision. Jimmy Puppet popped up and shot out the tires of a float coming over the rise, thus blocking the roadway. Simultaneously the gas canisters Chanchin Saladago had bought from Ben Reynolds were tossed at the feet of the bunched Vikings, releasing their noxious contents.

"Tear gas," one of the bikers erroneously yelled. He reached for a small gun tucked into the leg of his boot but suddenly got woozy in the head and vomited on his footwear as he doubled over, then fell down.

The Mas Trece crew, in gas masks and overalls, Kevlar vests cop style over their upper bodies, tore into the Vikings like locusts on wheat. Saladago had drilled into his men to keep their words to a minimum, lest they be ID'd by their phrasings. He knew well how his homeys sounded, and he knew, too, that their East Los sound would be readily picked up on by the Vandal Vikings. They used hand signals and grunts mostly as they head butted and gut checked their targets.

Two of the Vandal Vikings got on their motorcycles. One of them rode into the crush of falling bodies, and shotguns swung like tire irons. He ran over a Mas Trece member, breaking his thigh bone. But another of the gang put out an arm and clotheslined the rider, who landed hard on the asphalt. As he was stomped, the other one attempted to ride off. He was cut down by a spray from an assault rifle. His head was severed from his neck. For a few moments the rest of his body rode along on his chopper. Then the motorcycle crashed into the entrance gate to the amphitheater.

"We fuckin' did it, carnal," Zacca Alvarez said proudly to Saladago, who'd just banged the head of a Viking into the side of a bobtail. The truck was idling, as the ignition had been hot-wired using a rectangular device with a pointed end jammed into the ignition. This device, devised by Arceneaux, overrode the vehicle's electronic control unit.

Saladago grinned under his mask as he ordered, "Let's hit it."

As one the attackers moved quickly to depart. The drone of a helicopter swooping in low overhead had them looking up and swearing.

"Don't even think about it, Saladago," a voice roared, but not from the helicopter.

Jimmy Puppet turned, ripping off his gas mask with one hand, while in the other he blazed away on an Ingram. "Pinche bastards, suck my dick," he blared.

Saladago heard himself holler, "No."

An ATF sharpshooter fired into Jimmy Puppet, in the gap between his armored vest and his collarbone. Jaime "Jimmy Puppet" Prado staggered back and fell down on his knees, as if struck by a sledgehammer, the assault weapon clattering from his now lax fingers. A Vandal Viking and a Mas Trece soldier were swearing at each other as they grappled like wrestlers on the ground, the biker doing his best to bury his large knife in the other's side.

The Viking ceased this activity as the stock end of a Colt M4 carbine collided with his skull with force. The command "Be still or be shot," accompanied the action. Several other similarly armed and armored ATF agents swarmed the area, coming out of hiding, guns aimed on the dual sets of gang members.

On his knees, fingers laced behind his head, Zacca Alvarez was sad as an ATF agent shoved a foot into his back, knocking him over. The barrel of the agent's assault rifle pressed against his neck. The side of his face ground into the dirt, Alvarez wondered how long it would be before he could be with a woman again. His Inga Brody fantasies would have to sustain him. He almost cried.

Chanchin Saladago had managed to back up to a concrete wall where it was at its lowest, given this section was built into the side of a hill. This did not go unnoticed by two ATF agents, who swung their muzzles in his direction.

"On your face, asshole," one of them blared as Saladago tossed his gun to the ground. He'd done this as a distraction, as he'd placed a flash-bang grenade in his shirt, and pretending to surrender, he got the grenade free and threw it between himself and his would-be captors. The thing went off as it was designed to do, with a percussive boom and a white flare of light.

"Motherfuck," yelled the other agent, a woman with a ponytail, as she let loose blindly with a spray from her weapon.

Saladago was already in motion and dove over the wall. He tumbled and slid down the hill, tearing his clothes and taking skin off his arms and face. The season had been dry in this part of the Southland, so there was little resistance in the form of moist ground to his rapid descent. Ice plants and what have you were ripped away as his body was partially obscured in brief clouds of kicked-up dirt.

He came to a stop against the base of the cyclone fence at the bottom of the hill. There was shouting from above, and several rounds sank into the earth near him. But he crawled behind a low mound of shrubbery and out through the opening in the fence his crew had previously made to facilitate their anticipated escape.

From somewhere up above he heard the whoosh of the helicopter as he got to his feet, fear of prison stronger in him than the adrenaline coursing through his veins. Bleeding, he ran across the highway, cars swerving and screeching as drivers stomped on their brakes. He headed for the Willow Heights Shopping Center. An image of running back turned actor Jim Brown was steadfast in his mind. Big Jim as Jefferson running and throwing the grenades down the air shafts of the chateau to trigger the bombs to blow up the trapped sieg heilers in the basement in *The Dirty Dozen* powered him. He prayed though he didn't wind up like Jefferson at the end of that scene, cut down by machine gun fire. He ran and ran.

O'Conner drove his station wagon to keep his appointment with Inga Brody. She was supposed to meet with Saladago to get her payoff. She'd told him this was to go down at a Sonic burger stand in Hemet, and she'd given him the address to it. His role was to be her backup, and he would scout the location to make sure Saladago wasn't planning a double cross. He had the Remington with him.

* * *

Cody Bradford was sufficiently hyped on the meth he'd snorted as he drove his Corolla. He'd parked several blocks away from the parade, which was by then winding down. He knew some of the floats would then be driven up to the amphitheater for the blessing and the play. He chortled. He'd been dragged to that corny play when he was a kid, and even then he didn't like the damn thing.

"Shit," he sneered, imagining the squares half blitzed on wine and sun, sitting on the hard-ass cement of the amphitheater or on a cushion, having shelled out for its rental, watching *La Tajuata*. Getting all excited as the Indians and whites came together for the big finale, the wedding in the end.

Stomach gurgling, he suddenly realized he was hungry. He was near the Sonic and figured he'd have himself a double cheeseburger and some chili fries. He sure liked his chili fries. He'd have onions and cheese on them, too. Knowing well where the burger joint was, Bradford closed in on the place using a side street that took him to its parking lot.

"Fuck me," he mumbled as he spotted O'Conner coming along the same street from the opposite direction. He grinned and howled. "Got you now, bitch. Got your sorry sack in my hands, Coltrane, and gonna squeeze extra hard." He pushed the accelerator down, the car gunning forward rapidly, as he reached into the glove box for the old-school .38 snub-nosed revolver he'd bought from the weed head Franzen after O'Conner kicked his ass.

At that same moment, Marci Vickers was exiting the

Sonic drive-through with Lilly Nash in the car. The woman with the iguana tattoo had her hand between Vickers's legs, and being sufficiently hot and bothered, Vickers turned to kiss her new lover as they came out the driveway.

"Oh, shit," Nash hollered as she peripherally caught a glimpse of Bradford's speeding Corolla. He T-boned their car, instantly breaking Nash's arm. Bradford wasn't wearing a seat belt, and his head collided with his windshield, cracking it. He kicked his door open and tumbled out, gun in hand.

On the other side of the accident O'Conner had screeched to a stop. He was out of his car, glaring incredulously at Nash, who was being comforted inside Vickers's car. Nash momentarily looked over at him through the windshield, equally stunned to see him, as well.

"Die, shithead," Bradford screamed and shot O'Conner. The older man dropped to the ground, and a triumphant Bradford rushed around the rear end of Vickers's car to empty his gun into his enemy. From the ground, O'Conner put a bullet from the Glock he'd brought with him in Bradford's face, through the nose, heading upward, killing him instantly as the bullet entered his brain.

His blood on the macadam, O'Conner stood, and his first inclination was to flee. He figured he could make it to Reynolds's place and the old man would see to getting him patched up. Then, with his share of the haul, he'd get in the wind and be done with goddamn Hemet. Time slowed for him, and he looked back at the faces at the window of the hamburger stand.

He put the Glock on the hood of his car and said aloud for the first time in his life, "Somebody call the police." Vickers and Nash were also out of their car. Nash's mouth gaped when O'Conner spoke. He laughed roughly, holding his bleeding side.

Tomika threw a shindig at the late Tug Hintton's home. She had heard from some lawyer and was supposed to be out of the place by the end of the week. Well, before she left, she'd have a time of it, she'd concluded. Reo Culhane was there, and so was Harley Lynn Demara. As Grinquist sang on the tented-over helipad, backed by a five-piece band, Culhane danced with two Comets cheerleaders, and Demara was downstairs in the sunken garage. She was saying good-bye to Chanchin Saladago. They stopped kissing.

"I ain't gonna send for you. I can't."

"I know," she said. Tomika had let Demara pick which set of keys she wanted to one of Hintton's cars. The Porsche Boxster was one sweet sled, but it was too ostentatious for where Saladago was heading, Demara had reasoned. She settled on the Range Rover for him.

Tenderly he touched her face. "Remember, don't do drugs."

"Nitwit." She smiled and hugged him tight until both were tearing up.

The rumor went around Willow Ridge that Inga Brody had been a snitch or an undercover ATF agent, and due to her parents' background, it had been easy for her to infiltrate the Vandal Vikings to bust up their drug-running activities. When the opportunity presented itself to rope the Mas Trece into a trap, she'd made that happen. This was speculation, as her apartment was empty, Brody long gone. Ben Reynolds had driven out to the supposed women's clinic address in West Hollywood, only to find a post office box drop.

"I told the cops you had the gun on you because I was afraid after hearing about the Mas Trece using one of my shops for a drop." Gwen Gardner had on white jeans, sandals, and a colorful top. She had a casserole dish in her hands, and O'Conner stepped aside to let her in. He walked stiffly, his side aching from where the doctor at the ER had dug out the bullet and had sewn him up.

"Gwen, I . . . ," he began.

"Shut up," she said, going into the kitchen. He followed her. As she was getting plates down, he opened the drawer and handed her the letter from the bank. She read it, then said, "What are you going to do?"

He'd been thinking about his answer, should he see her again. "I'm going to use the money I made from a robbery to make a down payment." A day ago Lourdes MacShane had dropped by with his cut in an equipment bag. "Figured your boy Don could help me with clearing up the paperwork and whatnot." He sat heavily on a stool, regarding her.

Gardner was spooning out portions of the chicken parmigiana and penne pasta she'd made. She brought the food over to the counter and handed him a plate. She sat next to him at the counter and, a fork to her mouth, turned to look at him.

"Guess that makes you a Hemetian, then."

"It would seem so."

"Sucker."

"I am for you, baby."

She laughed, and they ate.

A READING GROUP GUIDE

THE WARLORD OF WILLOW RIDGE

GARY PHILLIPS

The following questions are designed to facilitate
discussion in and among reader groups.

DISCUSSION QUESTIONS

1. Is *The Warlord of Willow Ridge* a commentary on suburban mores?

2. It's clear that O'Conner has a criminal background. Can an antihero be portrayed in a sympathetic way?

3. Does O'Conner take on the mantle of hero, in contrast to the characters around him?

4. Why is Gwen Gardner attracted to O'Conner?

5. The book has multiple subplots and shifts points of view. How does this enhance the story?

6. Are there clues as to the true identity of Inga Brody?

7. How is dialogue used to advance the plot?

8. Is *The Warlord of Willow Ridge* a crime novel or a novel where crime is involved?

9. Has O'Conner really gone legitimate in the end? Will he trade in his ill-gotten station wagon and guns for a Prius and weekend barbecue tips from Stan Yamashira?

Chapter One

Friday, 8:00 a.m.
Greyhound bus terminal, Atlanta, Georgia

Just as I was about to cuff Misty Wetherington for ditching DUI court for the fifth time so she could hit the slots at Harrah's casino with her book club buddies, my phone buzzed. I looked down. It was my calendar app, reminding me that I had to be at Bella's school in ninety minutes.

"Crap, I forgot." I sighed.

My daughter, Bella, had asked me if I could join her at Sugar Hill Elementary School today for Doughnuts for Dads. It was a PTA event to celebrate fathers, but more like a backdoor way to get men into the classroom without them feeling awkward. However, Bella's best friend Lacy's mom came to the last one, and according to my friends at the Sugar Hill Church Ladies' Brunch, no one seemed to mind.

And . . . today was Bella's seventh birthday. I had to be there.

However, I was a little under an hour's drive from the

school. If I could punch it without getting a speeding ticket, I would make it in time. The only problem was I didn't know what to do with Misty.

With the exhaustively long lines at the City of Atlanta's traffic court, who knew how long it would take to process her? I wondered as I looked down at her bleached, moppy hair.

She was still on the parking lot ground, face to the gritty, piss-stained pavement while I straddled her back. My handcuffs dangled in my hands.

"Misty, you have been caught on a particularly good day for you. . . ."

I placed the cuffs on the ground near her face so she could see them. I waited until she turned her head in the cuffs' direction before I continued.

"Look. It's my daughter's birthday, and I need to be with her. We both know that what I'll make for hauling your butt to jail is about the cost of two tickets to the Atlanta aquarium, the Coke museum, and one night's stay in the Georgian Terrace. So here's my proposition. Today I let you go. I'll have Big Tiger finesse the city into giving you another FTA hearing, but on one condition. You fork over the money you were about to spend at the casino. I can surprise my girl with a kid-cation in Atlanta. What do you say?"

Big Tiger was the bail bondsman who kept me under contract. He introduced me to bail recovery and taught me the tools of the trade.

"And if I don't?" she grunted.

"How confident are you that the City of Atlanta will grant you a new FTA hearing after five no-shows without some help from Big Tiger? How confident are you that some other bail recovery agent isn't lurking behind any of these cars out here, waiting for the chance to take you from me? And, uh . . . where are your gambling buddies when you need them?"

Her eyes searched the parking lot. "Did they leave?"

"Darling, they are the ones who turned you in. Now, those are friends to keep. I can be your friend, too. Just say the magic words."

She sighed. "The money's in my front pocket, Angel."

"Bingo." I hopped off her and flipped her over.

She reluctantly pulled the money out. I stretched out my palm until she placed the money into my hand. Misty was carrying five hundred dollars.

I placed the money in my back pocket and smiled. "Happy Birthday to Bella."

Friday, 10:10 a.m.
Sugar Hill Elementary School, Sugar Hill, Georgia

Sugar Hill Elementary School was unusually packed when I pulled into the parking lot. "I can't believe this many men are here to eat doughnuts," I said to myself as I sped up the boardwalk to the school's entrance.

When I walked into the foyer, Dale Baker, the president of our home owners' association, waved me down and mouthed, "Good morning." I waved back and continued toward the front office. Inside, I spotted the parents' sign-in sheet, pulled a pen out of the flowerpot penholder, and signed my name.

The front office manager, whose name I could never remember, because the constant scowl on her face reminded me of the taste of bitter honeysuckle, pulled her glasses down her nose and shook her head at me. I called her Mrs. Bitter behind her back.

She pointed to the sign-in sheet. Her aged fingers

seemed swollen, even for someone her age. "Uh . . . Miss Crawford, you don't sign in here. This is for Doughnuts for Dads."

"I know that," I said with a don't-start-with-me smile.

"Honey, I know you're rough and tumble. I see you on the news, busting down doors and pushing men around. But here at Sugar Hill we don't need that kind of confusion for Isabella."

"No offense, but I know what I'm doing." I brushed her off.

This wasn't the first time an older Southern woman had tried to tell me how to parent. It didn't offend me, but today I didn't have the time to extend her more kindness than the fake smile I'd already offered. Doughnuts for Dads lasted thirty minutes. Ten minutes had already passed, and Bella was still waiting in her homeroom class to be called.

"Can you please call Isabella Crawford up to the front before it's too late?" I checked my watch and turned away from her.

She huffed. "I'm sure you think you know what you're doing, but have you thought of how *what* you do affects Isabella?"

And she didn't shut up. While I watched her mouth moving, my fingers curled into a ball. This was the first time since I became a single mom that I felt inadequate. It angered me. Thus, my resolve to be good faded the more she preached. Mrs. Bitter was about five seconds from getting her feelings hurt. I counted to ten real slow and hoped for some miracle to stop me from knocking the taste out of her big, meddling mouth.

"Mrs. Montgomery, I'm afraid this young lady has

plans for Ms. Crawford." Justus Morgan's voice made me tremble.

I turned around. He stood in the front office threshold and looked down. Bella was in front of him. Her smile was as wide as the summer days were long. The shame I'd just felt faded away with every second of her presence in the room.

"Surprise, sweetie!" I knelt down and hugged Bella.

She broke free and grabbed my hand. "Come on, Mommy. Mr. Baker has saved us the biggest sprinkled cupcakes in the entire world because it's my birthday."

I mouthed "Thank you" to Justus as Bella whisked me away from Mrs. Bitter. When I glanced back, I noticed her head had dropped. Justus was saying something to her that made her cower.

After Doughnuts for Dads, I thanked Dale and the rest of the PTA Room Moms' Committee for putting this together and walked toward Justus. He had just completed a conversation with Principal Boyd.

He must have seen me coming, because his face lit up bright. It made me blush.

Justus was my pastor and once my secret crush. Now I avoided him when I could, because apparently he had a thing for me, too, which was even scarier than pining for him from afar. The last man I loved died in my arms and left me his daughter to parent on my own. I was still gun-shy of good love and terrified of Justus "Too Hot to Be Holy" Morgan.

"Thank you," I spat out before I lost the nerve.

"For what?" He grinned. His deep right dimple humbled me even more.

"For coming to my rescue with Mrs. Bi . . . Mrs. Montgomery."

He looked down and chuckled. "I finally get to be the hero."

"Look around this place, Justus. You're always the hero."

He didn't respond, just looked at me in that way that made me feverish around my lips.

"What are you doing here? Trish's boys needed a stand-in?"

Justus's sister, Trish, was a military wife. Her husband, Mike, was deployed overseas more than he stayed stateside. Yet they managed to have three children despite his long stays away. They had a teenage drama queen daughter named Kelly and twin sons who were about Bella's age. But the rumor around Sugar Hill Community Church was that Trish had a new bun in the oven.

"No, actually, Mike was here. He couldn't stay long. You probably missed him when you were chatting with Mrs. Montgomery."

"Good news for them." I smiled.

He stopped smiling. "He's being called to Afghanistan."

"Wow."

"Wow indeed." He nodded. "I'm here because I came to invite the dads to the North Georgia Bike and Car Show."

"Bike and car show?" I stepped back in surprise. "You bike?"

"Among other things. Since you keep giving me rain checks on our date, you miss out on these cool things about me."

Our date? I folded my arms over my chest. *Are we still on that subject?*

The last time Justus and I were together was at my brother-in-law Devon's home-going celebration. I had admitted that I had considered a relationship with him, but the reality was that our situations didn't seem like they would ever mesh. He was a minister and I was . . . Well, I needed a lot of prayer. He had brushed off my excuse as if I'd never said it, while I'd dodged him every chance I'd gotten since then.

Today, after what he'd done for me, I owed him at least a straight answer.

"Justus—"

"Wait, before you come up with another weak excuse why you can't date me. Let me stop you by telling you that I'm letting you off the hook. You don't owe me anything," he said.

"Good, because I don't want to date you . . ."

The fire in his cheeks had gone out. "I understand."

I walked closer to him and stood short of his boots. "I want to know if we could have a future together."

His eyes blazed. His smile outdid Bella's. "What if I already know the answer is yes?"

"Then I'm giving you the chance to prove it."

"No time like the present," he said. "Tonight we begin."

"You make that sound really, really, really hot, but I don't have a baby-sitter for tonight. It's Bella's birthday. Besides, Whitney has plans. Her bestie is getting married, and the bridal team is getting together to powwow about the wedding plans. Ava is taking the kids to spend time with Devon's family, and Momma . . . Hopefully, she's on her honeymoon with my quiet-is-as-kept new stepdaddy."

"You want to know if I can fit into your world. That

world includes Bella and her perfect birthday. Let's do her up big. Let's take her to the circus. They're in town."

"Last-minute tickets for something like that is a killer," I said while those five hundred dollars burned holes in my pocket.

"My treat," he said.

"That's sweet, but a night at the circus with a kinder-gartner doesn't sound like hot date material."

"Who says I want a hot date?" He touched my hand. "I want you. That's all. Any time with you is blue hot in my book."

There was something about his hand squeeze, the sin-cere look in his eyes, and his way with words that made me wish very hard that was true.

"Okay, then. Tonight we begin," I said, but it didn't sound as cute as when Justus had said it.

Chapter Two

Friday, 11:30 a.m.
Gwinnett County Detention Center (GCDC),
Lawrenceville, Georgia

My flexible work schedule was the main reason I became a bail recovery agent. My former job at the *Atlanta Sentinel* had so much structure, so many rules, and that feeling of an invisible thumb on your back that it was driving me batty. But now I set my own hours. Now I was the boss. I slept in and hit the clubs at night. I could bop into Bella's school for Doughnuts for Dads, hop over to Big Tiger's to skim through his current jackets, and then take a quick run to the Decatur Hotel, the nickname for the DeKalb County jail.

Today, because it was my designated day to run Bella's car pool, I was on my way to GCDC. That jail was twenty minutes from Sugar Hill Elementary. So I had a solid ninety minutes to get in, get what I needed, and get out of there with time to spare.

I needed to check through the inmate list to see if one of my skips was already inside. Although both the national warrant and the prison system intranet service did decent jobs connecting charges, sometimes they missed a few. Especially if the prison was a private institution or the inmate had a common name, like Miguel Lopez, Kim Li, Mike Jones, or my current skip's name, Cesar Cruz.

Cesar had an FTA jacket that was ten skips deep. At the bottom of the habitual bail jumper's barrel was Big Tiger's twenty-five-thousand-dollar Fulton County newly forfeited bail bond. If I found Mr. Cruz in less than 150 days, then I would take home five thousand dollars. That was my mortgage payment for almost six months.

Since Gwinnett County had a large immigrant population, this was the best place to start. I also had a snitch on the inside, Rosary DiChristina. Her ex-husband was related to Cesar. She needed a few dollars on her commissary. If she gave me a good lead, I would take care of her toiletries for a few months.

After I checked in as an inmate visitor, I took a seat in the lobby, waited for my last name to be called, and scanned the place for the familiars and the newbies. I could spot a newbie within seconds of them entering the jail: the dropped jaw, the turned-up nostrils from the part urine/part bleach/part stank stench, and the realization in their eyes that this nightmare actually existed. For the rest of us, the ones who'd grown accustomed to the fluorescent lighting, beige cement walls, exposed-pipe ceiling, and air so cold and stale your nose and fingers grew numb on impact, we knew to wear our worst jeans and a bomber jacket.

I had spotted at least four newbies when my name was called.

"Hey, Angel." One of the women correctional officers on call today waved at me. She had a tiny crush on Tiger.

"Hey, girl. You got time after I come down? I need to check on some folk."

"It depends. I'm off the clock in forty."

I nodded as I passed by. "I'll see you before then."

"Who you come to see?" She reached for the sign-in clipboard. "Aw, lawd, not her."

I stopped short of the elevators leading to Rosary's living pod but didn't turn around. "What's wrong with Rosary?"

"Your girl has gotten into some more trouble. I can get her out of it, but she's not cooperating. Maybe you can talk some sense into her before it's too late."

I pursed my lips. I was confused. Rosary didn't seem like the bad-girl type. There must be more to this than she was telling me.

I pushed the elevator button. "She's a good girl. Don't worry. She'll listen to me."

"She better, or she's going to catch a new case," the officer scoffed.

"A new case?" I spun around and sighed. "What do you want me to do exactly?"

If you'd been in one county jail's inmates' quarters, you'd been in them all. They were quartered off in polygons, with the officers' station planted smack-dab in the middle. This way, they could keep their eyes on the prisoners, whose rooms resembled glassed-off pet rat cages. My best definition for *county jail* at GCDC was a cross between a science lab and a day care, except the baby rats wore blue jumpers.

Rosary entered the visitation chamber about two minutes after I arrived. We were separated by a scratched glass partition. Both our cubes had a phone nailed to the wall, a steel table attached to the glass, and a beige Piper stack chair. The "I don't know what it is, but it burns my nose" smell was the only odor in the room.

She sat down. Before she lifted her phone to her head, I knew what Trina meant. Rosary appeared groggy and listless. I crossed my arms over my chest and didn't pick up the phone receiver. What was the point, since my informant was drunk off buck?

Buck is the term for moonshine made from fermented fruit. Most prison inmates used bread, orange peels, and orange slices to concoct their brew. They would put that nasty mess in a plastic bag and let it sit for days, until the bag popped. The pop indicated the alcohol was ready.

Therefore, fruit peels were forbidden inside, so Rosary was in trouble. If I didn't get her straight and find out who brought her the orange peels, she would have another charge tacked onto her current DWI charge.

I huffed. I didn't come here for this.

She tapped the window to get me to pick up my receiver so we could talk.

I snatched the phone off the wall and didn't put the receiver on my ear. You would be surprised what some of these visitors did to that thing.

I spoke into the receiver. "Looks like you began the party without me."

"No, just sleepy." Rosary lisped. Her tongue was heavy from drinking hooch. "They keep it so cold in here."

"Rosie, don't play. You're drunk, and you just wasted my time today."

"It's cold in here. I need something to keep me warm."

"I would have put enough money on your account for you to buy some long johns, but now . . ." I shook my head. "I'm not wasting my money."

She sat up straighter. "*Qué estás diciendo?* You're not putting any money on my commissary?"

"Why should I? And your Spanish is getting rusty."

"Not fair, and my Spanish is just fine." She pouted.

"Not fair? Let me tell you what's not fair. I came straight from my daughter's school to see you, and you're drunk. You knew I was coming, yet you insult me."

She giggled. "This stuff doesn't get you drunk. I'm just a little buzzed."

"Honey, even through these thick walls I can smell orange hooch on you. Let me tell you something. . . . The staff is onto you, too. If you don't tell me who brought you the orange rinds, then they're going to stack another case on. More than likely, you won't get out of here until after Christmas if they do. That's not going to look good to your boss, who's been nice enough to hold your job for you. Plus . . . how do you think little Lucia is going to feel about having an alkie for a mom?"

"I don't want that. I promised her she wouldn't go through what I went through." She began to tear up. "Help me, Angel. I'll tell you who's supplying us. It's Day Day, one of the servers in the cafeteria. He gave it to me in exchange for cases of Pop's cigarettes."

I gasped. "Pop's cigarettes?"

Rosary's dad, Pop Calhoun, had made a name for himself with the alphabet agencies—ATF, IRS, and GBI—and with the prison world because of his creation, sale, and distribution of both illegal cigarettes and apple pie–flavored moonshine.

"When you called me and told me you were in here, and that you didn't want to be bailed out so you could get cleaned up, I thought you had learned your lesson about your father. I thought you had finally got it in your head that he doesn't care about you."

"Well, he sent Day Day the cigarettes, so he must care a little." Her eyes were so dilated, I shook my head in disgust and disappointment. "Don't look at me like that."

I sat back and placed the phone on the steel table. This conversation had gotten darker by the minute. I checked my watch. I needed to line up for Bella's car pool within the hour. I picked the phone back up.

"I'm sorry, Angel. I won't do it again," she whispered. "What else do you need from me to get my commissary back?"

"Nothing. Right now I can't trust anything that comes out your mouth."

"Come on, Angel. It's hard in here. You know how it is. . . ."

"No, I don't know how it is. I'm on the other side of the law, the right side."

"Okay. I'm about to be on the good side soon."

"You could've fooled me," I said.

"For real. I'll prove it. Who are you searching for right now? Who do you need me to help you find? I got connections."

"Your cousin Cesar Cruz." I pulled out a picture of him from my back pocket. "He's changed his hair, but that's still him."

She observed the picture and nodded. "I saw him at Big Tiger's a while back."

"Yeah, you did. Is that all you got?"

"Cesar's new girlfriend is Tara Tina Ramirez. They live in Doraville, off Peachtree Industrial. She works as a hostess at Grits Draft House in Johns Creek. Want the number?"

"No, and I don't need anyone tipping her off, either."

She threw her hands up. "I won't tell."

"All right, I'll check this out."

"You gon' hook me up now, *manita?*"

"If you agree to more rehab, then yeah, I got you."

"I don't need to do more rehab."

"Then you can kiss your job good-bye, because they'll take your bartending license for good if you don't go, and you definitely won't get my money. Matter of fact, maybe you shouldn't be working in a bar. Have you ever thought of that?"

"I have. I got a plan for something better," she said.

"Good." I stood up and got out of there before the stench made me pass out.

More of the Hottest
African-American Fiction from
Dafina Books

Come With Me J.S. Hawley	0-7582-1935-0	$6.99/$9.99
Golden Night Candice Poarch	0-7582-1977-6	$6.99/$9.99
No More Lies Rachel Skerritt	0-7582-1601-7	$6.99/$9.99
Perfect For You Sylvia Lett	0-7582-1979-2	$6.99/$9.99
Risk Ann Christopher	0-7582-1434-0	$6.99/$9.99

Available Wherever Books Are Sold!

Visit our website at **www.kensingtonbooks.com**.